HITMAN™

ENEMY WITHIN

By William C. Dietz
Published by Ballantine Books

HALO: THE FLOOD
HITMAN: ENEMY WITHIN

Books published by The Random House Publishing Group
are available at quantity discounts on bulk purchases for
premium, educational, fund-raising, and special sales use.
For details, please call 1-800-733-3000.

HITMAN™

ENEMY WITHIN

William C. Dietz

BALLANTINE BOOKS • NEW YORK

Hitman: Enemy Within is a work of fiction. Names, places, and incidents either are products of the author's imagination or are used fictitiously.

A Del Rey Books Mass Market Original

Copyright © 2007 by Eidos Interactive Ltd. & ® or ™ where indicated.
All rights reserved. Used under authorization.

Eidos Interactive Ltd., the Eidos logo, Hitman and the Hitman logo are trademarks of the Eidos group of companies. IO Interactive A/S and the IO Interactive logo are trademarks of IO Interactive A/S. All rights reserved.

Published in the United States by Del Rey Books, an imprint of The Random House Publishing Group, a division of Random House, Inc., New York.

DEL REY is a registered trademark and the Del Rey colophon is a trademark of Random House, Inc.

ISBN 978-0-345-47132-1

Printed in the United States of America

www.delreybooks.com

OPM 9 8 7 6 5 4 3 2 1

Marjorie, thank you for the dance,
and everything to come.

ACKNOWLEDGMENTS

Many thanks to Thomas Howalt, Jesper Donnis, Peter Fleckenstein, Keith Clayton, Tim Mak, and Steve Saffel for their help and guidance in putting this book together. It would have been impossible without you!

ONE

It was a beautiful summer day as Aristotle Thorakis walked out of the castle's gloomy great room onto the sun splashed terrace, and looked down into the Rhine River valley. The air smelled sweet and sunlight glittered like gold on the water as heavily laden boats churned past, headed in both directions. Many of the river craft were owned by families who lived on board, evidence of which could be seen in the playpens that occupied what little deck space there was and the gaily colored laundry that fluttered from lines rigged for that purpose.

It was an idyllic scene, and for one brief moment the international shipping magnate wished he were down there, standing behind the wheel of a heavily loaded freighter headed for Basel or Amsterdam. Such a life would be simpler, and in some ways more enjoyable, than the one he was living. His was a high-profile existence in which he was forever doomed to walk the slippery slopes of international finance while trying to

William C. Dietz

protect both his lifestyle and the business empire founded by his grandfather.

But sweet though the river life might appear from a hundred feet above, Thorakis knew how hard such an existence could be, and had no desire to give up the luxuries to which he and his family were accustomed.

"A penny for your thoughts," Pierre Douay said as he appeared at the Greek's elbow. The approach had been silent, notably so, and Thorakis gave an involuntary start.

"It's a beautiful day," the shipping magnate replied neutrally.

Douay nodded. The castle was the Frenchman's, and though Thorakis had inherited his wealth, he knew that Douay was a self-made man. Wealthy though the Greek was, it was *he* who had come begging, and Douay who would decide the shipping magnate's fate.

"What do you think of it?" Douay inquired, as the other man took his first sip of the chilled Riesling.

"It's dry," Thorakis observed, "and crisp. Which is to say perfect for a day such as this." The fifty-two-year-old business tycoon had black hair streaked with gray, and a tight, "sculptured" face. Though he had been something of an amateur athlete in his younger days, the Greek had put on some extra pounds over the last few years—weight that a baggy black shirt was unable to conceal. Khaki pants and a pair of Gucci loafers, sans socks, completed the look.

Douay, by contrast, was ten years younger, rapier thin, and in excellent shape. With the exception of a thin black leather belt and the black sandals on his feet, the Frenchman was dressed entirely in white.

"I'm glad you like it," he replied. "It comes from the

Moselle valley, rather than the Rhine. It's the slaty soil that makes the difference."

Thorakis had no idea what that meant, nor did he care, but didn't say so as he sought a way to open the conversation that both men knew was coming.

"Some years are better than others," the Greek observed thoughtfully. "For wine *and* for shipping."

"Yes," Douay agreed soberly. "Who could have predicted that one of your tankers would run aground off Portugal, that a cruise liner would be lost to pirates, *and* that your CFO would be arrested? All in less than a year? It defies imagination! Come. Lunch is ready and we will have plenty of opportunity to talk about wine, women, and shipping."

A linen-covered table had been set in the shade provided by a large canopy made out of blue and white striped canvas. The canopy rustled gently as a breeze blew down the Rhine and caressed the castle's stone walls.

Thorakis studied the table carefully. Though frequently given to excess where food was concerned, he had a severe allergy, and was therefore particular about what he ate. That was why a personal chef prepared most of the Greek's meals when he was home, accompanied the shipping magnate wherever he went, and stood guard in the kitchen when Thorakis ate in restaurants. Having noted that the sleek-looking chef was there, standing a discreet distance away, the businessman knew the food would be safe as he took the chair opposite Douay.

"To a long and profitable relationship," the Frenchman said as he raised his glass. Yet rather than the bonhomie he might have expected to see in Douay's eyes,

Thorakis saw something else instead. Something hard and calculating.

"Yes," the Greek agreed, raising his own glass of Riesling. "Here's to a long and profitable relationship."

The glasses made a gentle clinking sound as they met, and there was a brief flurry of activity as Douay's servants hurried to serve the food. The first course consisted of chilled shrimp served on a bed of leafy greens and accompanied by a basket of crusty bread.

Rather than toying with Thorakis, Douay went right to the point. "So," the Frenchman began, as he buttered a piece of bread. "I hope you won't be offended by my directness . . . but how much money would be required to take care of your present difficulties?"

Though surprised by the other man's bluntness, Thorakis was pleased, since he had been unsure of how to open the negotiations. He swallowed a bite of shrimp, chased it with a sip of wine, and dabbed his lips with a napkin.

"About 500 million euros would see us through. A secured loan mind you, with a five-year term."

"That's a lot of money," Douay observed mildly. "But not *too* much, so long as the collateral is sufficient." He paused, and looked directly at his guest as he added, "And if you're willing to provide me with certain kinds of information."

The first requirement was to be expected, but the second was unusual, and caused Thorakis to frown. "Information? I don't understand."

"It's really quite simple," the Frenchman replied, as he speared a shrimp. "You sit on the board of directors for an organization known as The Agency. I have a similar relationship with a group you know as the *Puis-*

sance Treize—or the Power Thirteen. As you are probably aware, the *Puissance Treize* has begun to challenge The Agency both in terms of market share and gross revenues. Nevertheless, a gap remains, at least for the moment.

"But with certain key information, supplied by you, it might be possible for our brand to dominate the market within months, rather than years."

Suddenly the freshly baked bread seemed excessively dry, and Thorakis needed a mouthful of wine to wash it down.

His affiliation with The Agency centered around problems related to transport and logistics, and was supposed to be a secret. Yet Douay knew.

Blood pounded in his temples and he felt the sudden need to urinate.

"That's absurd," the Greek said weakly. "I have no idea what you're talking about."

"Oh, but I think you do," Douay insisted, as he placed a folder of photographs on the table. "Here, look at these . . . pictures of you meeting with other members of The Agency's board in Rio, going aboard one of the organization's yachts in Cape Town, and exiting their private plane in Dallas."

Thorakis took the time to compose himself as he removed two of the photos, examined them, and produced a shrug as he tossed them back onto the table.

"I know all sorts of people. If they happen to be associated with this organization of which you speak—this . . . 'Agency'—I know nothing about it."

"Please," Douay said sadly. "Don't embarrass yourself. The record is clear. When the cruise ships owned by Señor José Alvarez began to take business away from you, he somehow drowned in his own swimming pool. That, in spite of the fact that he had been a member of Mexico's Olympic swim team some fifteen years earlier!

"Then, after a journalist named Harry Meyers wrote a story about the way your tankers dump toxic materials into the Atlantic Ocean, he inexplicably committed suicide. Just two days prior to his wedding!

"Oh, and let's not forget Countess Maria Sarkov, who had the terrible misfortune to be hit by a truck as she crossed 42nd Street one week after referring to your wife as 'an ugly pig' in a New York society column. No, my friend, you not only work for The Agency," Douay added grimly, "but they pay you in blood.

"Yet even The Agency can't do anything about the fact that you and your company have been turned away by bankers in Zurich, London, and New York. Your stock is down thirty percent, the litigation from the oil spill will drag on for ten years, and your cruise ships are sailing half-full. Still, you know best, so we'll speak of more enjoyable things. . . .

"How are your children? Well, I hope."

Thorakis felt a rising sense of despair, and desperately tried to keep it from showing. The thing he feared most was that *he* would be the one to lose the Thorakis family fortune, and not only bring shame onto himself, but rob his children of their birthright.

Finally, after an uncomfortable silence, the Greek looked up from his plate.

"Perhaps I was too hasty in my response," he said hesitantly. "What sort of information would you be seeking? Who knows . . . there may be some way for me to accommodate you."

"There, you see," Douay replied genially. "I knew we could do business! In answer to your question I want to know everything you know. Especially whatever you can tell me about the man called Agent 47."

TWO

The plume of dust was quickly followed by a blur as the man who was about to die topped a distant rise.

Both the rider and his motorcycle were soon lost from sight as the gravel road took him down into one of the many gullies that separated Agent 47 from his target. The oncoming biker was still too far away for a positive identification, so the assassin lowered his binoculars and allowed a sun-warmed rock to accept his weight. It was a hot day and the road seemed to shimmer as the man called the Grim Reaper rematerialized in the distance. His real name was Mel Johnson, and his main claims to fame were a long criminal record and a willingness to kill anyone who got in his way. He wore wraparound shades, a black leather vest similar to the one 47 had on, and a pair of faded Levis. The sort of outfit real bikers wear, and wannabe weekend riders emulate, hoping to look tough.

Not Johnson, though. He was the real deal, and his meaty arms hung straight down from ape-hanger handlebars as the chopper barreled up the road toward a meeting with the rest of the "Big Six." A fun-loving consortium of motorcycle gangs led by a swell guy known as the "Big Kahuna," the "Big K," or just BK for short.

The Big K ran the joint enterprise for the benefit of all its members. A business strategy calculated to ward off incursions by vertically integrated competitors, like the Colombian drug cartels.

That's how it was supposed to work, although there were rumors that some of the gangs weren't all that happy with the Kahuna's self-serving management style. Which explained why chieftains like Johnson had been ordered to come alone. The Big Kahuna didn't want to be outgunned.

It was a rather sensible policy, from 47's point of view.

Satisfied now that he was about to kill the right man, 47 lowered his binoculars and checked his Audemars Piguet, Royal Oak Offshore wristwatch. Johnson was running late, which meant 47 was running late, but it couldn't be helped.

Agent 47 felt the familiar hollow sensation in the pit of his stomach as he stood and forced himself to take a long, slow look around. The assassin knew from hard-won experience how many things can change during the brief amount of time it takes to sip a mouthful of coffee, piss against a wall, or check a safety. A witness can appear out of nowhere, the wind can strengthen unexpectedly, or any of a thousand other variables can interfere with the machinery of death.

But there were no witnesses here, other than the hawk that circled high above, and the wind direction didn't matter as 47 made his way out onto the bridge that spanned a mostly dry watercourse. The wire had been there for hours by now, laid crosswise across the dusty road as cars, trucks, and motorcycles rumbled over it. With the steel thread already fastened to the railing on the opposite side of the bridge, it was a simple matter to lift the wire and secure it to the framework. Then, having concealed himself in the deep shadow the harsh sun cast next to the two-lane bridge, all the assassin had to do was wait for Mel Johnson to come along and execute himself.

Harleys make a very distinctive sound, and it wasn't long before he heard a throaty growl as Johnson approached. At the last moment, 47 gauged the size of his prey and realized that he had set the wire a little too high. The technique, which had been utilized by both the Germans and the French underground during World War II, was extremely effective against motorcyclists and people riding in open vehicles.

There was no way to know if the gang leader saw the wire at the very last second, and had time to process what was about to occur, but it didn't seem likely. Rather than make contact with his throat, as it was supposed to, the steel wire caught Johnson across his partially opened mouth. The gang leader was traveling at a good fifty-five miles per hour at that point, so the wire sliced the top of his head off and left the lower part of his jaw attached to his neck.

A mixture of blood and brains flew back over the roadway as the top of Johnson's helmet-clad skull bounced off the wooden planks, even as the Harley carried the rest of his body north. But only for a short distance, before Johnson's hands fell away from the handlebars, the engine lost power, and the front tire hit a pothole. The result was a horrible grinding sound as the $25,000 motorcycle toppled over and slid along the gravel road, taking the blood-spurting corpse with it, before finally coming to a stop.

After a quick check to make sure the hit had gone unobserved, Agent 47 began to run. The binoculars bounced off his chest, and it was necessary to reach up and grab them as he ran toward a small, isolated structure.

There was no way to know what the wooden building's original purpose had been, and the assassin didn't care. The only thing that mattered was the fact that the structure was large enough to accommodate the four-wheel-drive Dodge pickup truck that was parked within. It was a few degrees cooler inside the shed, but 47 didn't have time to enjoy the difference as he jumped into the cab and brought the big V-8 back to life.

Dirt sprayed the back wall as the assassin gunned the vehicle out into bright sunlight, turned onto the dirt road, and traveled for about twenty feet before he was forced to apply the brakes or hit the body that was partially trapped by the Harley. Then it was time to put the binoculars aside, exit the 4×4, and round the front end of the truck. After checking the contents of Johnson's saddlebags, the next task was to work them free.

Once the leather bags were stowed in the cab, he hooked the pickup's winch cable to the chopper, and dragged the nine-hundred-pound bike behind the shed. The trip was kind of hard on what remained of Johnson, but the dead biker didn't seem to mind, even though his body flopped free halfway through the process.

As soon as the wreckage was safely out of sight, 47 freed the winch cable, and took the time necessary to back the truck into the shed before returning to the bridge. He had been assigned to work in the asylum's slaughterhouse at the age of ten, so the assassin was used to looking at dead bodies, and felt nothing beyond a sense of annoyance as he scanned the roadway for the top of Johnson's head. Fortunately the chunk of skull and upper jawbone were still tucked inside the minimal half-helmet that so many bikers preferred. The bloody mess lay next to the road where it had come to rest and it was a simple matter to kick dust over the bloodstains and drop the brain bucket into the watercourse below.

With that chore out of the way, it was time to remove the now-sagging wire and coil it up as he made his way back to the point where the badly mauled corpse lay. Having stowed the wire in his back pocket, the assassin got a good grip on the back of Johnson's vest and began to drag the body toward the shed. He was only half-way to his destination when a large cloud of dust appeared to the south. It seemed that something big—and potentially nasty—was on the way.

The assassin weighed 187 pounds, and even without the top portion of his head Johnson topped 225, so it wasn't easy to haul the dead biker across the intervening space. Agent 47 tripped and fell over backward, as the sound of the diesel grew louder. Genuinely concerned now, he scrambled to his feet, sought a new grip, and put everything he had into towing the body to the shed. As darkness wrapped itself around 47 a huge motor coach topped the nearest rise and thundered onto the bridge.

There were plenty of holes in the side of the ancient shed and the assassin peered through one of them as the maroon bus rolled over the very spot where Johnson had been killed fifteen minutes earlier. He saw the rig bounce slightly as it came off the bridge deck and heard gravel rattle as it flew back over the bridge. An expensive mural had been painted along the side of the coach. It featured a biker on a chopper, a coyote howling at the moon, and jagged mountains in the background.

All of which goes to prove that crime pays, 47 mused. *Especially drug trafficking.*

Satisfied that his actions had gone undetected, 47 began to go through Johnson's pockets. The search turned up a wad of pocket lint, a wicked-looking flick knife, and an outdated Binion's $500 casino chip complete with a horseshoe-shaped design. It was a rare item, and one that 47 was going to need in order to crash the Big Kahuna's party.

His next step was to retrieve the saddlebags from the truck's cab. One of the hand-tooled leather bags contained a gun rig, complete with a pair of Johnson's signature Colt Pythons. The other held two bags of heroin. The assassin emptied both packages onto the ground prior to replacing them with two kilos of street-smack that The Agency had given him. Both were laced with fentanyl, which was 50 to 100 times more powerful than morphine. The problem was that while the mixture produced a higher high, it had been known to kill unsuspecting addicts by causing their respiratory systems to shut down.

Which was exactly what 47 had in mind.

But before he could put the Big Kahuna out of commission, permanently, and thereby fulfill The Agency's contract, the assassin would have to penetrate the annual meeting of the Big Six.

He checked to ensure that both .357 Magnums were loaded before buckling the western fast-draw holsters around his waist and securing the tie-downs to his legs. It felt good to have a couple of weapons, even though he preferred semiautomatics. But, given the fact that Johnson was known for his six-guns, 47 was stuck with them.

He was covered with sweat by the time he got back behind the wheel. The air conditioner roared as he took a moment to examine himself in the rearview mirror and check the key component of his subterfuge. The face that stared back at him looked more like Johnson's than his own. A blue kerchief concealed most of the assassin's bare scalp—and the fake beard was still in place. Beards could be dangerous appliances, given their tendency to come loose, and 47 had been careful to use plenty of spirit gum, so even the sweat from his exertions hadn't loosened it.

Of equal importance were the small things, those details that made a person like Johnson memorable. Like the swastika-shaped tattoo that the assassin had inked on his left cheek, what appeared to be a scar just above his right eyebrow, and the silver rings that dangled from his ears. His clothing consisted of leather gloves, a matching vest, faded Levis, and a pair of lace-up combat boots.

But would the disguise be sufficient to get him through the meeting? The folks at The Agency thought so, especially since Johnson had been in prison for the past four years, and therefore out of circulation. Which meant most of the people who could ID him were still behind bars. Agent 47 took comfort from the thought as he steered the truck out onto the road, and turned north.

Having been raised in Europe, the assassin had no desire to actually own one of the inefficient, gas-guzzling trucks that Americans loved so much, but could understand the appeal. With a brawny 345-horsepower engine under the hood, and a stance that placed the driver almost eye to eye with long-haul truckers, the four-wheeler conveyed a sense of power. Which offered 47 some comfort as he topped a rise and discovered an ancient road grader parked across the road. It was a precaution intended to keep farmers, telephone repairmen, and lost tourists from crashing the Big Kahuna's party. As the assassin applied the brakes, and the truck began to slow, two heavily armed bikers strolled out to greet him. They positioned themselves on either side of the truck so their M16s could put him in a crossfire.

But Agent 47 wasn't looking for trouble—not yet—and plastered a friendly smile on what was supposed to be Mel Johnson's face as he brought the truck to a halt. The side windows whirred as they went down. A man with the look of a part-time bodybuilder sauntered up to the driver's side. He had bushy eyebrows, a walrus-style mustache, and a pugnacious jaw.

"So," he said conversationally, as the second biker stuck his head in through the passenger side window. "Who the fuck are *you*?"

"I'm the Reaper," 47 replied with what he hoped was a sufficient amount of gravitas.

"Yeah?" the man replied. "I've heard of you. They call me Nix. And that's Joey. They told us you was comin' on a bike."

"That was the plan," the assassin agreed soberly. "But the chopper broke down, so I borrowed this."

There was a burst of static from the other side of the truck, followed by some unintelligible conversation as Joey brought a walkie-talkie up next to his ear. After listening for a moment, he replaced it at his side.

"That was Skinner," the biker proclaimed importantly. "The Big Kahuna wants to start the meeting, but they're waitin' on this guy."

"Sounds like you'd better get a move on," Nix advised. "But nobody gets in without a chip."

Agent 47 nodded, plucked the $500 casino chip out of his vest pocket, and handed it over. Nix produced a disc of his own, compared the two, and returned the first one to "Johnson."

"You're good to go, Reaper," Nix said. "Hold a sec while Joey backs the grader out of the way. You're the last guy on the list, so we might as well escort you in."

There was a pause while Joey fired up the grader's diesel engine, backed the big machine off the road, and waited for the pickup to pass. Then he moved it back into place. Five minutes later Nix and Joey straddled their choppers as they waved the truck forward.

The choppers threw up a cloud of dust, and quickly moved into the lead, so 47 eased his foot off the gas and let the pickup fall back a ways. That allowed him to see better as the threesome blew through a second checkpoint and sped toward the odd collection of structures where the meeting was being held.

A metal silo stood next to a run-down barn that was fronted by a new double-wide mobile home. A variety of small sheds in various states of disrepair were nestled here and there, as a forest of tall weeds did what it could to consume a row of junked cars. The big motor coach that Agent 47 had seen earlier, a red Mercedes, and four brightly painted motorcycles were parked off to the west side of the seedy complex. All of them wore a fine patina of Yakima road dust.

A black-clad biker appeared as Nix and Joey came to showy stops and sprayed the area with loose gravel. The assassin turned the truck into the makeshift car park and positioned it for a quick getaway. The man in black was waiting as 47 opened the door and dropped to the ground. Johnson's saddlebags were draped over his left shoulder, and they bounced as he landed.

"The name's Skinner," the long-faced man announced laconically. "Welcome back to the real world. The brothers are waiting. Follow me."

Agent 47 expected Skinner to object to the six-guns that were strapped around his waist. But judging from the Glock that protruded from the back of the biker's leather britches, personal weaponry wasn't just acceptable, it was expected. The fact struck the assassin as both comforting and worrisome as he followed his guide past the off-white mobile home, up a deeply rutted driveway, and toward the looming barn. Which, judging from the *thump, thump, thump* of music that issued from inside the ancient structure, was where the meeting was about to be held.

As he walked up the path 47 compared the layout to his mental picture of the satellite photos while paying special attention to potential escape routes, structures he could use for cover, and the surveillance cameras that were tucked here and there throughout the property.

Skinner hooked a left where an old refrigerator had

been put out to rust, made his way up a slope, and nod-ded to the tough-looking gang members posted to either side of the huge tractor-sized door. Both thugs were equipped with M16s, pistols, and a lot of tattoos. Agent 47 had one too—aside from the disguise—a bar code that incorporated both his birth date and production number. Largely meaningless, now that his clone broth-ers were dead, but a permanent link to the past.

It was cooler inside the barn, and darker, too, so it took 47's eyes a moment to adjust as the music died and lots of eyeballs swiveled his way. It had been years since farm animals had been quartered in the building, but a faint hint of their musky odor still remained. Dust motes drifted through the shafts of sunlight that slanted down from holes in the roof. There were windows, but they were covered with grime, which meant most of the illumination came from bare bulbs that dangled above. In an effort to give the meeting a festive feel, tavern-style bunting had been draped across the rafters. It con-sisted of Corona beer placards hung from strings of multicolored Christmas lights. The advertisements shiv-ered in the breeze produced by two rotating industrial-strength fans that swept the air across them.

But that attempt at gaiety was blunted by the pres-ence of the corpse that hung from one of the rafters. The victim's hands were tied behind him, a length of cord was knotted around his ankles, and his face was purple. The rope creaked as the fans turned and the ar-tificial breeze hit the corpse, causing it to sway. Agent 47 could feel the full weight of their stares as a dozen men and two or three women waited to see how he would react.

"That's a nice piñata you have there," the assassin said lightly. "Who's the birthday boy?"

There was a moment of silence, followed by the sound of raucous laughter as a man in a well-cut white suit emerged from the gloom. Good clothes were one of the few luxuries a professional assassin could enjoy, so Agent 47 knew an Yves Saint Laurent suit when he saw one. Even if it was a bit grimy.

Based on data provided by The Agency, that suit was the signature "look" the Big Kahuna had chosen for himself. A pair of stylish sunglasses hid the crime boss's eyes, but the rest of his broad, moonlike face was plain to see, as was a body that harkened back to his days as a professional wrestler. He was surprisingly light on his feet, and seemed to float just above the dirt floor as he came forward to embrace the newcomer. The result was a quick man-hug, in which their chests collided briefly before they both took a step back.

BK and the Reaper were acquaintances, according to a file that 47 had been given, but nothing more, which was important to remember if the assassin was going to fool him.

"Haven't seen you in four years—but you're still one *ugly* son of a bitch," the Kahuna growled affectionately. "What happened? I'd swear you were a good thirty pounds heavier the last time we saw each other."

"Prison food sucks," 47 complained. "But I'm starting to bulk up again."

"There you go!" BK agreed approvingly. "What you need is some meat and potatoes! Come on. We've been waiting for you."

"So, who's the party favor?" the assassin inquired, as the former wrestler led him past the body.

"We don't know his real name," the Big Kahuna answered matter-of-factly. "But Marla pegged him as an FBI agent—and she was right."

Agent 47 was just about to ask who Marla was when a woman stepped up beside them.

"Did someone mention my name?" She wore leathers, and made them look good. Two other women were present as well, both of whom had pretty faces and large breasts. But this one was different. Looking into her bright green eyes, it was like looking into a bottomless well. Somehow, without being told, the assassin knew that Marla was the most dangerous person in the room, outside of himself, that is. . . .

But what was this woman's role? Given the fact most of the people present were male—and the other females were clearly here for recreational purposes, she was an enigma.

"Hello, I'm Marla," she said softly, as she extended her hand. "You're the Reaper. I've heard of you." Her grip was strong, and cold.

Careful to stay in character, 47 held on to Marla's ice-cold hand at least three seconds longer than necessary, and ogled her ample cleavage.

"And you must be the answer to my prayers," he replied solemnly, before finally releasing her hand.

But somehow 47 could tell that Marla wasn't buying it, as the Big Kahuna replied on her behalf.

"She's out of your league, Mel," the big man dismissively. "So don't waste your time." The two of them were separated as one of the Big K's flunkies led 47 to brand-new, executive-style leather chairs that must have been purchased for the occasion. The big man took his own position, and opened the meeting with a tiresome review of the brotherhood's successes. The woman named Marla stood over his right shoulder and it seemed to 47 that she spent most of her time staring at him.

She *knew*.

Which would make the task of killing her supersized lover that much more-difficult.

Video blossomed on a 60-inch flat-panel monitor that had been set up off to one side, as the six men seated at the table were treated to a financial presentation similar to what any board of directors might see. But 47 was more interested in the men seated around him than in how many tons of grass the brotherhood had success-fully smuggled in from Canada. Judging from the ciga-rettes half of them had lit, at least some of the profits were going up in smoke.

While most of the gang leaders were fairly attentive, one rather ugly specimen had already nodded off, and was soon facedown on the table. A phone chimed, and its owner stood up and walked some distance away in order to take the call. But the rest were paying attention and interjected questions from time to time—queries that seemed to cast doubt on the veracity of the Big Kahuna's facts and figures. But the Big K's entourage was sizable, and the guests were seriously outgunned, so they had very little choice but to accept the crime boss's answers. For the moment at least.

Later, when they reunited with their gangs, the trash talk would begin.

A full thirty minutes elapsed before the last pie chart disappeared and bottles of cold beer were distributed.

"So," the Big Kahuna said, as he began to summarize, "We have plenty to celebrate . . . but we're facing some problems, as well. Primary among them being competition from the Colombians, who are bringing large quantities of coke into the country in miniature submarines, and undercutting our prices. But by working together, we should be able to counter their efforts. That will take money, however. So, painful though it may be, it's time for everyone to ante up."

That statement was followed by a chorus of groans and a small commotion as the gang leaders placed their quarterly payments on the table. The tributes included two attaché cases filled with tightly packed bills, a leather pouch half-filled with diamonds, a money belt loaded with gold wafers, a sheaf of bonds, and the two kilos of lethal smack that were stored in Johnson's saddlebags. Which, given the crime boss's appetite for the stuff, BK would no doubt sample before the day was done.

Marla chose that moment to speak, and all hell broke loose.

"Excuse me," she said politely, "but before this process goes any further, I think we should run some tests on the dope that the so-called Grim Reaper put on the table. Because the *real* Reaper is dead."

They say the truth hurts, 47 thought. In this case it hurt the man who was seated directly across from him. The setup had been blown, and the only thing the assassin could do was shoot his way out.

From the moment he noticed Marla's stare, he had held one of Mel Johnson's big revolvers under the table. The .357 bucked in 47's hand, there was a muffled *boom,* and the biker sitting across from him never knew what hit him as both of them went over backward. The difference being that while the gang leader was dead, 47 was alive, for the moment at least.

Marla removed a Walther PP from its hiding place under her jacket and began to empty a clip in Agent 47's direction. Fortunately the gang leader seated to the assassin's left chose that moment to stand, and took two 9 mm slugs to the neck and head.

That bit of misfortune led one of the surviving chieftains to believe Marla was acting on the Big Kahuna's behalf, which caused him to produce a Browning BDM and begin to shoot at her. He missed Marla, but put a slug into the Big K's head, which caused the ex-wrestler's sunglasses to fly off. His sheer bulk kept him from being knocked off his feet. The crime boss just stood there for a moment, as if deciding what to do, before he toppled facedown onto the dirt floor.

Marla took offense at that, brought the German semiauto up in a two-handed grip, and dropped the gang leader with two carefully placed shots. One bullet to the chest and one to the forehead, so that body armor wouldn't be enough to protect him.

Agent 47 couldn't target Marla from his position on the ground, as one of the gang leaders jumped onto the loot-laden table and prepared to fire down on him. The assassin brought the wheel gun up and fired twice. The first bullet hit the rat-faced man in the stomach, and the second blew his balls off, which caused him to grab his crotch as he fell toward his killer.

But rather than wait for Rat Face to fall on top of him, 47 rolled to one side, came to his feet, and drew the second Colt just in time to see Marla take cover behind a sturdy post. Splinters flew from wood as a heavy slug nicked the timber.

Then it was Marla's turn as the Walther barked twice. Agent 47 felt something nip his left arm and was forced to spin away. She might have nailed him then and there if it hadn't been for Joey. With plenty of targets available, the M16-toting gang member began to shoot indiscriminately at anything that moved.

As the assault rifle began to rattle and bullets blew divots out of the barn's dirt floor, Marla was forced to duck back, then defend herself. Her bullets missed, but the return fire forced Joey to duck, and that gave the woman time to throw a folding chair through the nearest window. Glass shattered. Casings from Joey's weapon continued to arc through the air as he began spraying the room again. Marla took three running steps and dove through the newly created opening.

Agent 47 swore as the mysterious woman disappeared, and ran a mental check on his ammo supply. One of the Pythons was empty. And while the loops on Johnson's western-style gun rig held twelve hollow points, it was unlikely the bikers would give him the time required to reload.

He had to get back to his truck.

So he holstered one revolver and drew the other as he backed toward the door. One of the gang leaders was busy harvesting the loot from the table when another took exception to that initiative and shot the first biker in the back.

Having missed Marla, Joey swiveled the M16 toward 47, and fell as a bullet removed the top of his head.

Harsh sunlight washed over the assassin as he hit the door, backed outside, and the biker named Nix appeared. The gang member clutched a stubby sawed-off shotgun in his hands and was panting heavily.

"Reaper . . . What the hell's going on?"

"That Marla chick shot the Big Kahuna!" 47 lied. "But I think he's still alive. Go on in. The big guy needs your help!"

Nix nodded gamely, charged through the open door, and staggered as a burst of 9 mm bullets slammed into his unprotected chest.

Agent 47 turned and began to run. An automatic weapon began to chatter from the direction of the mobile home as one of the Big Kahuna's security guards began to chase the assassin with bullets from an AK-47.

Fortunately the biker was short on experience. Rather than lead his target the way he should have, the goon brought his weapon around in an attempt to catch 47 from behind. And since he was firing on full automatic, the assault rifle's banana-style clip quickly ran dry. That gave the assassin the perfect opportunity to stop, drop, and roll under the high-riding truck.

Agent 47 discarded the Python in order to snatch two micro-Uzis that were clamped to the truck's frame. Then, with a machine pistol clutched in each fist, the rearmed assassin rolled out from under the far side of the truck just as the idiot with the AK-47 opened fire again.

Safety glass shattered, and the 4×4 shuddered as a hail of lead struck it. The biker was advancing by then, teeth bared as he fired the automatic weapon from the hip. It appeared as if the guard believed the fugitive was hiding in the cab, as half a dozen 7.62 mm slugs pinged the driver's side door. That was when 47 made his way around the front end of the truck and fired a three-round burst from the left-hand Uzi. Though he was right-handed at "birth," the asylum's staff forced their charges to use both hands equally. A skill for which the agent was thankful.

Mr. AK-47 looked surprised as the bullets hit him, and he fired a final burst of slugs into the clear blue sky as he pitched over backward, and skidded across some loose shell casings before finally coming to a stop.

The assassin might have left at that point, and very much wanted to, but knew he couldn't. Not without retrieving whatever memory device the surveillance system was hooked to. Partially to protect his identity, and to obtain images of Marla, which would help The Agency identify her. That meant he would have to cross open ground, enter the mobile home, and deal with anyone who blocked his way.

But then a final gunshot was fired inside the barn, and an eerie silence settled over the farm.

A jetliner drew a white line across the sky as 47 crossed the open ground, and flies buzzed around the assassin's head as he opened the screen door. An energetic white dog came out to greet him. The animal yapped madly and danced circles around 47 as the agent entered the double-wide's living room, and his eyes adjusted to the gloom.

Empty beer cans sat everywhere, part of a motorcycle engine was resting on the coffee table, and dry dog turds lay scattered about. The lights were off, so what little illumination there was originated from cracks around the shaded windows, and the cartoon show on the flat-panel TV. The audio was turned down, which was why the assassin could hear the sound of a child crying. He followed it through the filthy kitchen and into the hall beyond.

Having passed a bathroom, 47 peered into what was clearly the master bedroom, and saw a half-naked woman stretched out on a messy king-sized bed. Judging from the drug paraphernalia that was scattered about, she was unconscious rather than asleep. A theory that squared with the crying baby, who looked up at the assassin with pleading eyes, and lifted its arms. The Big Kahuna's child perhaps?

Yes, 47 thought. *Not that it makes much difference.*

Leaving the master bedroom the assassin followed the filthy shag carpeting back to a second bedroom that functioned as an office. Rather than take the time required to examine the items on top of the cluttered desk, or rifle through the three-drawer filing cabinet, Agent 47 focused his attention on a video monitor perched on top of a cheap plant stand. The picture showed part of the driveway outside, but quickly dissolved to a shot of the barn's body-strewn interior. Then, having held that view for about five seconds, it switched to another scene. All of which reinforced the assassin's suspicion that images of the barn battle had been stored on a retrieval system of some sort.

There was a beep from behind, and he whirled—guns at the ready—only to discover that the Big K was receiving a fax.

His heart continued to beat like a trip-hammer as he searched for the storage unit—perhaps a computer, or a DVD burner. There was a rat's nest of wiring and dusty black boxes to paw through, but it wasn't very long before the assassin found the digital video recorder, and freed it from the system.

Then, having shoved a mini-Uzi into one of Johnson's empty holsters, Agent 47 tucked the DVR under his left arm and exited the office. He made his way past the wailing child, entered the living room, and was reaching for the door handle when the dog saved his life.

As the animal began to yap at the door, 47 threw himself sideways. He heard the sound of a 12-gauge shotgun a fraction of a second later. The double-aught-buck blew a fist-sized hole through the screen door and the opposite wall, to reveal daylight beyond.

Having dropped the DVR, the assassin fisted the second Uzi as he came to his feet and glanced through one of the kitchen windows. That was when he spotted Skinner. Judging from the congealed blood on the right side of the biker's face, and the kerchief tied around his right thigh, he had been wounded during the melee. He was game, though, and determined to exact some sort of revenge for what had taken place.

"I know you're in there!" Skinner shouted. "There's no place to go. Come out and fight!"

Never one to refuse a polite invitation, 47 threw a greasy frying pan through the window, and as Skinner swung the shotgun in that direction, the assassin had the opportunity he needed. The bullets passed through the screen door and punched half a dozen holes in the biker's chest.

The biker went to his knees as if praying for help, but having received no response, collapsed facedown on the oil-stained dirt.

The dog yapped excitedly and danced about.

Agent 47 holstered both machine pistols, went back for the DVR, and saw that a bag of dry dog food had been left on the kitchen counter. The assassin paused long enough to dump the entire contents onto the ground on his way out. The dog liked that, and began eating greedily, as his benefactor returned to the car park.

The red Mercedes was gone, which probably meant Marla was driving it.

Most of the safety glass was missing from the truck's side windows, so 47 removed the rest, in hopes that people would assume that the windows were rolled down. The bullet holes in the driver's side door weren't so easy to disguise, however. All he could do was get in, place the DVR on the seat beside him, and drive away.

Two bikers lay sprawled in the road next to the first checkpoint, where Marla had dropped them on her way out.

The grader blocked the road farther on, but if Marla had been able to bypass the machinery with her Mercedes, then 47 knew he could do so as well. There was a slight bump as the big off-road tires passed through the ditch that bordered the road, followed by a momentary roar as the agent gunned the engine and steered the rig back onto the gravel road.

Then, with nothing to stop him, 47 hit the gas.

The Big Kahuna was dead, but the operation could hardly be called a success, given how messy the outcome had been. So, rather than take a few days off as he had originally planned, it was time to go back to the motel and lick his wounds. One of which, judging from the persistent pain in his left arm, was quite real.

He arrived at an intersection ten minutes later, paused

to let a sixteen-wheeler pass, and pulled onto the two-lane highway. A barn, silo, and farmhouse were visible in the distance, but that was all that broke up the landscape, other than the green-apple orchards that bordered both sides of the road.

In spite of the fact that he had been to the United States dozens of times, the assassin never failed to be amazed by how large the country was. After eliminating a target in Belgium, he could generally be in Great Britain a few hours later, but not here. Whenever he had an assignment in the States, some sort of base was necessary.

In this particular case, Agent 47 had staged his activities at a second-rate motel on the outskirts of Yakima, Washington. The sort of mom-and-pop enterprise that had been largely replaced by low-cost hotel chains over the last decade, but still existed here and there, and suited him to a tee. There were exceptions, of course, but most of the small motels didn't require ID at check-in, and they rarely had surveillance systems. Not to mention the fact that it was often possible for guests to park directly outside their rooms.

But before 47 could return to the slightly seedy embrace of the Blackbird Inn, there were some things to get rid of. Including the Mel Johnson disguise and the newly ventilated truck. So as he approached civilization, he turned into a sprawling apartment complex and pulled into the most remote slot in the parking lot. Perhaps The Agency would be able to recover the vehicle before the manager had it towed. If not, the cost of the truck would be added to the fee paid by the person or persons who wanted the BK dead.

The Colombians perhaps?

Probably, although 47 didn't really care.

Fingerprints weren't a concern as he prepared to abandon the vehicle, since he had worn gloves throughout the operation. Nor was DNA likely to be an issue, since the agent wasn't about to leave any cigarette butts, pop cans, or used Kleenexes in the cab. So all he had to do was pull the cleanup kit out from under the seat, and use the contents to remove both the beard and the blood that had dried on his wounded arm. Having pulled a plain blue T-shirt down over his head, 47 checked to make sure that his left sleeve was long enough to cover the bullet wound. He dumped everything except the DNA-bearing wipe into a plastic sack, which went into a gym bag next to the machine pistols and the DVR.

As 47 exited the truck and made his way across the parking lot, he looked like an average guy on his way to a workout at the gym. It was a short two-block walk from the apartment complex to the motel, which was good, because Americans rarely walked when they could ride. That made pedestrians something of an oddity, and oddities are memorable, which was the last thing the assassin wanted to be.

The black Volvo S80 was right where he had left it, in front of room 102. Rather than look out of place, as one might expect at a low-rent hostelry like the Blackbird Inn, the sedan wasn't even the most expensive vehicle in the lot. That honor went to a white Escalade parked a few doors down. *Because just about anyone can buy a fancy car in the United States—so long as they don't mind living in a crummy flat.*

The DO NOT DISTURB sign was still dangling from the

doorknob, but that didn't mean much, so 47 checked the nearly invisible thread that had been spit-welded across the doorjamb. It was still there. A good sign. But knowing how dangerous assumptions could be, the assassin took the extra precaution of slipping his right hand into the partially open gym bag that dangled from his right shoulder. Then, with a firm grip on one of the Uzis, he turned the key.

It was cool inside the dimly lit room, and a quick check of the bathroom was sufficient to confirm what Agent 47 had already sensed, that everything was the way he had left it.

Duty demanded that he upload a full report to The Agency, but he'd been looking forward to a shower, so he decided that the management types could wait for a while. It felt good to shuck the dirty clothing and step under the shower. Cognizant of how many people he had killed in bathrooms, he kept a .45 caliber Silverballer within easy reach, knowing the water wouldn't damage the stainless steel weapon.

But no one attacked the agent as the stream of hot water pummeled his lean body, found the partially open gunshot wound, and caused it to sting. He just stood there for a while, thinking about Marla, before turning the water off and stepping out of the tub. The bathmat was too small, but managed to absorb at least some of the water that ran down off his legs, as 47 ran a scratchy towel over his body.

Who was the woman with the Walther? he wondered. *And how did she know about the smack?*

Then it was time to retrieve his first-aid kit and examine the flesh wound in the bathroom mirror before squirting antiseptic ointment onto it. A self-adhesive bandage went on over that. There had been other cuts, abrasions, and puncture wounds over the years, and many of the scars were visible.

With that part of his regimen completed, and clad only in white boxer shorts, 47 went back to work. The Blackbird Inn didn't offer Internet access, but it didn't matter, since all of the agent's interactions with The Agency were handled via scrambled and encrypted satellite uplinks. So it was a simple matter to transfer the surveillance video over to his laptop, connect the computer to his cell phone, and hit a few keys. He heard a series of tones, followed by a momentary burst of static, before Diana's well-modulated voice came over the line.

The assassin had never seen the woman whose voice he heard, but imagined her to be attractive. There had been times—*hard* times—when Diana had been his only link to the possibility of salvation. Like one of the guardian angels that Father Vittorio spoke of, who could reach down from the heavens and pluck a soul to safety. And for that reason he liked the sound of her voice.

"Good evening, 47," Diana said evenly. "How did it go?"

"Poorly," the assassin replied honestly. "The target was terminated, but only after I was fingered, and the entire setup was blown."

"I'm sorry to hear that," Diana said sympathetically. "Are you all right?"

"Couldn't be better," the agent lied. "Stand by for a digital upload. The whole affair was captured on surveillance video, including footage of the woman who blew my cover."

"We're ready," Diana said. "Send us what you have."

So he typed a command into the laptop, waited for the upload to complete itself, and forced himself to sever the link. Doing so always left him feeling cut off, but such was his fate, and it was shared by anyone who practiced his trade.

Time to take out the trash, and he was hungry, so he spent the next few minutes getting ready. Agent 47 began the process by donning a crisp white shirt, a red silk tie, and a pair of pants prior to slipping his arms into a two-gun shoulder-holster rig. A suit jacket went on over that, which, thanks to the efforts of his English tailor, effectively hid the twin Silverballers and a garrote. Black socks and a pair of well-polished shoes completed the ensemble. Once he was dressed, it was a simple matter to lock his possessions into a pair of armored suitcases, set the built-in security systems, and slide them under the bed. Then he exited the room with the half-full garbage bag dangling from one hand.

Having opened the Volvo with the remote, Agent 47 slid inside, placed the garbage bag on the seat beside him, and started the car. Two minutes later he was out on the street trolling for a Dumpster. It wasn't the perfect means of disposal, since whatever one person put into one of the big bins another person could remove, but it was better than leaving the materials in his room.

Dumpsters located behind restaurants were best. Once the contents had begun to rot, the smell was so bad even the homeless wouldn't enter them.

Having disposed of the Johnson disguise behind the Green Jade Palace, but not being in the mood for a sit-down dinner, Agent 47 bought a couple of hamburgers from a local drive-through. It was his opinion that food purchased from small, independently owned burger joints was always better than the stuff the big chains churned out.

Back in his room, 47 flipped through the channels until he located a soccer game. Not because he cared who won, but for some sort of company, as he unwrapped the burgers and ate another meal by himself.

One of what? Hundreds? Thousands?

There was no way to know.

Eventually the game ended, so he stripped down and hung his clothes in the closet. Then 47 prepared to sleep on the floor. He was well aware of the fact that if a counterassassin forced the door open, the first thing they would do would be to put a few slugs into the bed. So, rather than run that risk, he took his place on the floor, where an intruder's first shot would miss him. A hard surface, but no worse than the pallet he'd been required to sleep on as a child.

The Silverballers were comforting—and he was asleep five minutes later.

THREE

As Marla parked her Mercedes in an underground garage and entered a well-appointed elevator, the *Puissance Treize* agent had a feeling she didn't experience often.

She was frightened.

And with good reason. After being promoted to Assistant Sector Chief, and posted to the Pacific Northwest, she had been ordered to rid the Big Kahuna's organization of an undercover FBI agent, and protect the crime boss from an assassin. And she'd been successful up until the moment when she decided to out the assassin. That's when things went horribly wrong, and people began to die, including the man she'd been sent to protect. It wasn't that Marla really cared. In fact, those who had died no doubt deserved their fate. But not on her watch.

Now, Marla was on the way up to meet with her new supervisor, a hard-eyed woman called Mrs. Kaberov, who, in spite of her polished exterior, had once been a member of the dreaded KGB, the Russian State Security Committee, before the *Puissance Treize* had hired her away. Which was why it felt like an ounce of liquid lead was sloshing around the pit of Marla's stomach as she left the elevator, crossed a beautifully decorated lobby, and entered the private club.

The restaurant was called The Pacific Rim, and it boasted a sweeping view of Seattle's Elliott Bay and the snowcapped Olympic Mountains beyond. A prissy maître d' was there to greet her and lead her to what was unarguably the best table in the restaurant. That's where Kaberov sat, gazing out over the sparkling bay, as she spoke on her cell phone. A cruise ship was pulling away from a nearby dock as it departed for Alaska and a green and white ferryboat was about to dock as Marla stopped just short of the table.

Her supervisor's white hair was pulled back into a tight bun and she looked stylish in a simple blue knit dress from St. Johns. Tasteful gold jewelry and the Hermès handbag completed the outfit. Marla, who was dressed in a two-piece gray business suit and wearing a pair of colorful Pikilino shoes felt dowdy by comparison.

Finally, having ignored Marla for at least two minutes, the older woman closed the flip-phone and eyed her guest with glacier-cold blue eyes.

"You may sit down."

It had been awkward, standing there like a child waiting for permission to sit, and it was a relief to take the other chair.

"I was speaking on the phone with Ali bin Ahmed bin

Saleh Al-Fulani," the Russian said, in a voice pitched so low that only Marla could hear her. "In spite of ample evidence to the contrary, he insists that you are normally quite competent, and should be given a second chance. I'm not so sure. . . . Perhaps you will find the means to convince me."

Marla would have answered, but a formally attired waiter chose that moment to intervene, and Kaberov ordered for both of them. Something Marla would have taken exception to, had her hostess been anyone else. But in this case she was willing to tolerate just about any indignity in order to escape what could be a death sentence. Because while the *Puissance Treize* could be generous to its more reliable employees, it had a very low tolerance for failure.

"So," Kaberov began. Her English was quite good, in spite of a slight Russian accent. "I read the report you filed, and was impressed by how objective it was. You made no attempt to conceal your incompetence or evade responsibility for what can only be categorized as a disaster. You had been told who was coming, when he would arrive, and what he planned to do. Yet you managed to take what should have been a routine hit and turn it into a major debacle. Now, having had time to reflect on what took place, tell me where you went wrong."

Marla felt an obstruction block the back of her throat, and struggled to swallow it.

"In retrospect I realize that I should have warned the Big Kahuna, and enlisted his aid *before* The Agency's assassin arrived."

Kaberov nodded her agreement.

"You were grandstanding. Trying to impress everyone with how omnipotent you were. And it cost you. . . .
Worse yet, it cost *us*. Fortunately the witnesses are dead.
With one notable exception. And someone took the surveillance tape. Was that you?"

"Yes," Marla lied smoothly. "I destroyed it."

"Good," Kaberov replied grudgingly. "That, at least,
was the competent thing to do. Although it should have
been included in the report. In any case, based on the
number of bodies that were found, it's clear that Agent
47 escaped. And eliminating him was the true purpose
of sending you there."

There might have been more, except that the waiter
arrived with what turned out to be excellent chicken
salad, hard rolls, and iced tea. And rather than continue the conversation, the Russian launched into an
analysis of fall fashions. A subject Marla knew very
little about, but greatly preferred to a further discussion of the "Yakima Massacre," as CNN now referred
to it.

But talk of clothing came to an end when the dishes
were taken away, and Kaberov removed a small, carefully wrapped gold box from her purse.

"Here," the Sector Chief said, as she offered the object to Marla. "A present for you."

The gesture was entirely unexpected, and Marla
didn't know what to say, as she accepted the gift.

"Go ahead," Kaberov urged. "Open it."

So Marla removed the red ribbon, broke the seals
that held both halves of the box together, and lifted the
lid. There, lying within a perfectly formed velvet-lined
recess, was a single, hand-loaded, 230-grain, .45 caliber

bullet. The round had been polished, and seemed to glow as if lit from within.

The Russian was waiting when Marla looked up.

"It's part of a matched set," the older woman explained sweetly. "And, if you fuck up again, you'll get the second one right between the eyes."

FOUR

Agent 47 awoke with a jerk, eyed his wristwatch, and saw that it was 5:58 a.m.

Waking without an alarm clock was one of the many skills he'd been required to master as a child. And the only way to avoid a blow from one of the "memory sticks" that the asylum's staff members carried was to wake up a couple of seconds early, and clearly signal that fact.

So 47 sat up, placed both Silverballers on the bed beside him, and stood. Early morning light filtered in around the curtains, and a car door slammed in the parking lot. A few steps carried him around the foot of the bed to the far side, where there was barely enough space for him to complete his morning exercises. The carpet was worn and far from clean, but he'd seen worse.

After a hundred push-ups, two-hundred sit-ups, and the rest of his regimen he entered the bathroom, pistol in hand. The automatic went on top of the toilet tank where it would be easy to reach.

Having brushed his teeth and taken a shower, 47 prepared to shave. He removed the DOVO from his kit. The straight razor was made of stainless steel, equipped with a French point, and could also be employed as a weapon should the need arise.

The gel felt cool as 47 smeared it over his cheeks, and the DOVO made a rasping noise as it carved a path through his whiskers. The task was complete five minutes later.

Next he set about the extremely difficult job of removing all of the forensic evidence from the hotel room; if someone was tracking him, he saw no reason to make their task easier. That was why he routinely wiped everything down, double-flushed any items that might carry his DNA, and kept a sharp eye out for stray socks, telltale receipts, and loose cartridges. Once the room was clean he put on a fresh white shirt, his signature red necktie, the two-gun harness, and a black suit with matching shoes.

One was scuffed. A quick buff put it right.

Then, having eyed the parking lot through the window, Agent 47 carried the matching suitcases out to the Volvo and placed them in the trunk. Having paid for his room in advance, he had no need to check out prior to breakfast, which he generally regarded as the most important meal of the day.

In France, that meant coffee, tea, or hot chocolate with a baguette or croissant. A meal that might lack substance, but certainly made more sense than the eggs, sausage, and mushrooms that were sometimes served in Great Britain.

Which was why 47 preferred to eat breakfast in the United States, where he could choose from a wide array of items, including regional specialties like biscuits and gravy or huevos rancheros.

So, having no interest in the fast-food crap put out by the restaurant chains, Agent 47 was eternally on the lookout for the one-of-a-kind restaurants that locals frequented. It was a somewhat risky strategy, since he was more noticeable in such eateries than he would have been at a McDonald's. But that reality had to be weighed against the fact that most fast-food franchises have antitheft surveillance systems.

All of which led 47 to the Copper Kitchen. It was located on a busy street, and the parking lot was nearly full, which he considered a good sign.

As was his habit, Agent 47 backed the Volvo into a slot where it would be positioned for a quick departure, and took a moment to identify the restaurant's rear exit before crossing the parking lot to the front door. A newspaper rack was positioned next to the entrance, so he paused to buy a copy of the *Yakima Herald-Republic,* then followed a man wearing overalls into the restaurant. The farmer took a seat at the well-worn counter, while 47 eyed the booths off to the left, the most distant of which was located next to the kitchen door. That was the sort of spot most diners tried to avoid, but he actually preferred.

"A booth, please," he said, as a woman with gray hair arrived to seat him. "The one in the back looks nice."

The woman nodded mechanically, grabbed a plastic-covered menu from the rack next to the cash register, and led the assassin back to a Formica-covered table that was flanked by two Naugahyde-covered benches. Agent 47 chose the one that put his back to the wall and provided a good view of the front door. The kitchen door, which could be used as an alternate exit, was immediately to his left. True to its name, the eatery was decorated with all manner of copper cooking implements that sat on shelves, dangled from the ceiling, and had been screwed to the walls.

He spent the next few minutes assembling a rather unhealthy breakfast from the long list of à la carte items the Copper Kitchen had to offer. Then, having placed an order for two fried eggs, country-style hash brown potatoes, and a side of crisp bacon, he proceeded to scan the paper. The headline proclaimed BARNYARD SLAUGHTER in big, bold letters. A description that seemed accurate enough, all things considered. Not that society had any reason to mourn the thieves, drug dealers, and murderers who had been killed at the farm.

Agent 47 had just begun to read the accompanying text when the front door opened, and the man who entered the room caught his attention. The man had carefully combed black hair, Eurasian features, and stood about five-ten or -eleven. His clothes weren't all that different from those the assassin wore, except that his suit was dark blue, with gray pinstripes. Though 47 had never seen him before—just as he had never seen Marla prior to the meeting at the barn—he instinctively recognized the newcomer as a player.

He already had one hand inside his coat, and was preparing to exit the booth, when the stranger saw him and . . .

Waved.

At that moment, the assassin could stay, and run the risk that the man in the pinstriped suit had been sent by the Big Kahuna's associates, or he could duck out the back. And run into what? An ambush in the parking lot? There was no way to know.

Finally, as was so often the case, the decision came down to a gut feeling. So 47 remained where he was as the other man slid into the seat across from him. The stranger had yellowish-brown eyes, a straight nose, and extremely white teeth. They gleamed when he smiled.

"Good morning!" the man said heartily. "I notice only one of your hands is visible. Does that mean what I think it means?"

"Of course," 47 replied cautiously. "What did you expect?"

"Nothing less," the other man replied evenly.

Agent 47's waitress appeared at that point, placed his order on the table, and agreed to bring a cup of coffee for the man with the yellowish-brown eyes.

"So," the assassin said as the woman walked away. "Who are you?"

"My name is Nu," the man with the perfect teeth responded. "*Mr.* Nu. We work for the same organization. The difference is that I'm management, and you're labor."

"Really?" 47 inquired skeptically. "And why should I believe you?"

"Because I know how important the number 640509040147 is to you," Nu replied confidently. "Go ahead and eat. Your food is getting cold."

The revelation came as a shock. Only someone from The Agency would be privy to the serial number—the one that had been issued to the assassin on September 5, 1964. But even though Nu appeared to be who he said he was, Agent 47 kept a Silverballer aimed at the other man's stomach. That left one hand with which he could eat his breakfast.

"All right," the assassin allowed, "Let's say you are who you claim to be. What brings you to Yakima?"

"Your most recent report brought me," the other man replied, as the waitress arrived with his coffee. Waiting for her to depart, he continued. "Having reviewed the surveillance footage, the entire management team came to the same conclusion. The woman who calls herself Marla not only knew you were coming, but was aware of the contract on the Big Kahuna, *and* the way you were supposed to take him out."

Agent 47 chased a mouthful of food with some of the Copper Kitchen's lukewarm coffee before putting the cup down.

"Which means?"

"Which means that someone has found a way to penetrate our organization," Nu replied darkly. "The personnel department will look at the most recent hires first, and if that strategy fails, we'll expand the scope of our investigation."

"That makes sense," the assassin allowed cautiously, as he wiped his mouth with a paper napkin. "But what about the larger question? Assuming a mole exists . . . who is behind him?"

"That's what we want you to find out," the executive replied grimly. "We know who the Marla woman works for, so that's where you'll start. Everything we have is on this," Nu finished, as he pushed a USB memory stick across the table's surface.

"All right," Agent 47 replied flatly, as he palmed the device. "I'll take care of it."

"We knew you would," the executive said, as he got

up to leave. "We need to find this person, and find him—or her—fast."

"One last thing," 47 put in. "Where is the GPS tracker located? In my car? Or in my computer?"

"That's for me to know," Nu answered with a grin, "and for you to find out!" With that he was gone.

Agent 47 waited until the executive had exited through the front door before he returned the Silver-baller to its holster and finished the meal. Then it was time to pay the bill, exit the restaurant, and go looking for a woman named Marla.

SEATTLE, WASHINGTON, USA

Thanks to its location on the water and proximity to both the Olympic and Cascade mountain ranges, Seat-tle was a beautiful city. Especially on a warm sunny day, when all manner of small boats were out on the lake, just north of downtown.

It was late in the day by the time Agent 47 arrived and began to stalk his target. Always a challenge, but even more so when the target was armed, and had at least three kills to her credit. A record that—while not all that impressive by 47's standards—still qualified the *Puissance Treize* agent as a worthy adversary.

According to the information on the memory stick, in her role as a control—an agent assigned to direct a field assassin—the woman had been indirectly responsible for more than a dozen hits in the Med. The woman's real name was Cassandra Murphy, and according to the data supplied by Mr. Nu, she'd been born in Belfast. She was thirty-six years old.

Adding to the challenge was the fact that he would have to gain control of the woman in order to communicate with her, which would probably be more difficult than simply shooting her. According to the information he had been given, the target was currently living on a houseboat moored in Lake Union. Years ago, there had been more of the floating domiciles, but a variety of government regulations and economic pressures had reduced the waterborne community to a few hundred water-level homes located on the lake and in neighboring Portage Bay.

It wasn't clear how 47's superiors had been tracking Marla's movements prior to the massacre in Yakima, but there wasn't any doubt as to why, since The Agency routinely kept track of anyone who had ever been employed by one of its competitors. Especially those having links with the *Puissance Treize*.

As he followed a side street down to the waterfront and the small parking lot that served the houseboats, a couple of problems quickly became apparent. The first was the cyclone fence and gate that had been put in place to prevent thieves, sightseers, and other undesirables from making their way out onto the community dock. The second was the fact that the area was so open that there was no place from which the assassin could safely observe his target's comings and goings prior to making a move.

A red Mercedes was parked in the lot, though, and while there hadn't been an opportunity for him to memorize the license plate, the assassin would have sworn that it was the same vehicle he'd seen parked outside the barn in Yakima. A thick patina of dust seemed to confirm that theory, as 47 executed a U-turn and left the area.

It was nearly dark by that time, the streetlights were on, and the orange-red sun was in the process of dropping behind the Olympic Mountains as the assassin searched for a place to stay. There weren't any mom-and-pop-style motels in the downtown area, but Agent 47 happened by a seedy motor inn on the west side of the lake. It met all of his requirements. According to a sign in the lobby, the proprietors were willing to let rooms by the hour, day, week, or month. So he registered as Mr. Metzger, paid for five days in advance, and carried his suitcases up to a second-floor room.

The door opened into a claustrophobic space that was all too reminiscent of other hotel rooms he had stayed in over the years. The relatively early hour, along with the rhythmic *thump, thump, thump* of a bed hitting the wall next door, suggested that his neighbors were taking advantage of the motel's hourly rate.

The energetic couple was still at it when 47 left shortly thereafter to return to the Volvo.

His first task for the evening was to find dinner down by the water. That was easy enough to do, since there were plenty of restaurants along the lake's south shore. It was while he was looking for a place to park that Agent 47 stumbled across a nonprofit organization dedicated to the preservation and use of wooden boats. The organization also offered some boats for rent.

That could come in handy, he mused.

Having made a mental note of what time the center opened, 47 walked east, turned into a waterfront shopping complex, and entered an upscale restaurant. Predictably enough the interior boasted a nautical theme,

the menu emphasized seafood, and the waitstaff wore
blue polo shirts, white slacks, and deck shoes.

The assassin ordered wild salmon and a glass of ice
water, then settled back to wait. It was dark outside the
windows, so there was nothing to do but watch the
people seated around him; individuals whose existences
focused on office politics, leaky roofs, and demanding
children—all of them variables to be circumvented or
exploited. Unpredictable objects that could block a
shot, suddenly morph into a counterassassin, or be used
for cover should it become necessary.

There had been a relationship with another living being once. Not with a human, but with the mouse that
had lived in the wall near his bed and emerged each
night to collect the crumbs the little boy brought him
from the asylum's spartan dining room. Though never
really tame, the rodent would stare up at its benefactor
through beady black eyes as it ate whatever treat it had
been given.

The relationship lasted for about a month, but came
to an abrupt end when 47 returned one evening to find
the dead mouse lying across his pillow. Its head was
matted with dried blood, and its eyes were glassy. That
was when one of his clone brothers erupted into laughter, the rest of them followed suit, and the bond between 47 and his pet ended the way all relationships
must. In death.

"Here's your salmon, sir," a female voice said, and 47
snapped back into the present as his food arrived. The
meal was better than he had expected.

The night in the motel wasn't.

*   *   *

It was raining when the assassin arose the next morning.

Seattle was known for its rain, which often manifested as little more than an intermittent mist, but this was the real thing. The Volvo's wipers made a soft slapping sound as he drove to the local Denny's restaurant, which in the absence of a mom-and-pop option, would have to do. After a "grand-slam" breakfast, it was time to return to the Center for Wooden Boats, park the sedan, and make his way down onto the floating dock.

Classic wooden boats were moored to the right and the left. Many had rainwater sloshing around under the floorboards. A seaplane roared as it passed overhead and made a neat two-point landing on the steel-gray lake beyond, one of a fleet of such planes that ferried people to and from the San Juan Islands, about 80 miles to the north.

A left, a right, and a short walk carried 47 out to a cedar-sheathed structure labeled BOAT HOUSE. The door to the office stood open, and with the exception of a single attendant, the room was empty. A fact that wasn't all that surprising, given the time of day and the nature of the weather.

"Good morning!" the man said cheerfully. The attendant standing next to the counter was sixty or so and was wearing a blue baseball cap with the words USS PONCE LPD 15 stitched across the front. The rest of his outfit consisted of a paint-smeared sweatshirt and a pair of baggy khaki pants. "My name's Hal," he continued genially. "What can I do for you?"

"I'd like to rent a boat," Agent 47 replied.

"Well, there's plenty to pick from," the attendant said. "What's your fancy?"

"Something light," the assassin answered. "Something easy to row."

"Then I have just the thing," Hal replied confidently. "Follow me."

The attendant showed a keen knowledge of the wooden boats, and by the time 47 had been issued a pair of oars and a life jacket, he knew all about the vessel he was about to rent. Twelve-foot-long Whitehalls had originally been designed for use as water taxis in New York harbor, and first put into service about 1840. Because they were faster than the other harbor taxis of their day, Whitehalls were favored by the boarding-house "crimps," or runners, who went out to meet incoming ships and bring seamen ashore.

Hal watched Agent 47 as he rowed away, waved once he was comfortable that his customer was competent, and went back to the office.

Though far from an expert, 47 knew how to row, and was pleased with the way the boat cut through the water as he pulled on the oars. And in spite of the cool air and the persistent rain, it wasn't long before the assassin began to feel warm. So he brought the oars inboard and allowed the Whitehall to coast while he stripped the rain jacket off. That left him in a blue nylon top, matching pants, and running shoes. The Silverballers were invisible beneath the loose zip-up top. His garrote, plus a hypo loaded with an extremely effective sedative, were stashed in a waterproof knapsack that sat beside him.

It felt better without the jacket, and Agent 47 soon found that he was enjoying the exercise as he sent the rowboat north in a series of long, smooth spurts. The wind ruffled the surface of the lake, and the bow made a gentle smacking sound as it cut through the occasional wavelet. Gradually the Whitehall passed a marina, a dry dock, and the pier at which three NOAA ships were moored.

Water dripped off the tips of 47's oars, and left circles spinning in the boat's wake, as the skiff began to close with the houseboats ahead. It was perfectly natural for those who passed to eyeball the floating homes, so there was no need to be secretive, as the assassin took an occasional glance over his left shoulder. The first thing he noticed was that the waterborne structures came in a variety of shapes and sizes. Some were only one-story tall, while others had a second level, and were more spacious inside. Almost all of them were well maintained, and many boasted baskets filled with flowers.

One such home was of special interest to the agent because it was located at the end of the dock, directly across from the unit the target lived in. An elderly woman was kneeling on the front deck, tending a flower box full of bright red geraniums, as 47 directed the boat in toward her one-story houseboat.

"Your flowers are very healthy," he said, as the gap between the two of them closed. "What do you feed them?" The entire time he spoke, he remained aware of the target's houseboat, but saw no sign of activity.

Even with the weather, there were several rowers out on the lake, and the woman must have been accustomed to such compliments, because she registered no sense of alarm as the stranger allowed one of his oars to rest on her wooden deck. Her name was Grace Beasley, and wisps of gray hair stuck out from under the blue rain hat her dead husband liked to wear while golfing. Her eyes were like chips of turquoise mounted in sockets of wrinkled skin. A plaid shirt and a pair of black pants completed her outfit.

"I use regular fertilizer," Mrs. Beasley admitted. "But the key is to pinch off the spent blooms. That makes them flower again."

"Well, it certainly works," 47 said, admiringly. "By the way, might I have a drink of water? I should have brought some, but I forgot, and it's a long ways back to the dock."

The request seemed innocent enough, so Mrs. Beasley said, "Yes, of course. I'll be right back." She stepped through a sliding glass door that led into a comfortably furnished living room and the small galley-style kitchen beyond.

A moment later he found her there, removing a bottle of chilled water from her refrigerator. A large hand closed over mouth. Mrs. Beasley tried to scream, felt something bite her neck, and instantly began to fall.

Agent 47 caught the unconscious woman and carried her into the single bedroom, where he laid her out on the neatly made bed. To make doubly sure that she would remain immobilized for the necessary length of time, he bound her wrists and ankles with some of her own nylons. Confident that the elderly woman wasn't about to go anywhere, he set about his real task, which was to enter the neighboring houseboat and have a chat with its owner.

A task that would be easier said than done, he thought, since his target was an assassin herself, and was sure to have a variety of security measures in place. Just as he would.

So 47 turned out the lights in the living room, but left everything else as it was, knowing that the slightest deviation from the way the old lady normally did things could attract attention.

First, he subtly adjusted the position of what had once been Mr. Beasley's favorite chair, placing it where someone would have to actually press their nose against the glass in order to see him as he settled back to wait.

Finally, after an hour had passed, the assassin was reasonably certain of two things. The first was that the target didn't have any security guards to protect her. His position allowed him a reasonably clear view of the houseboat and the surrounding area, and even the most skilled surveillance would have given some sign of their presence, particularly within the small, close-knit floating community. There were no cameras, either. And that made sense, given her relatively low status within the *Puissance Treize* organization.

Second, based on the time of day and the complete lack of movement across the way, the assassin felt sure that the target wasn't home. This was something he could have confirmed simply by venturing out to check the parking lot, but he didn't want to take the chance, since one of the residents might see him exiting the old lady's home.

So all he could do was wait for the target to return, and make his move during the brief moment when her front door would be unlocked and she would least expect an attack. Having locked the gate behind her, and being on her own home ground, the target would feel safe.

Having formulated his plan, he checked to ensure that the houseboat's front door would open smoothly. The Whitehall was safely stashed behind Mrs. Beasley's boat, out of sight.

All that was left was the waiting.

The payoff came forty-five minutes later, when the target appeared on the dock, carrying two bags of groceries. She placed one of them on the bench next to the front door, slid the key into the lock, and gave it a turn to the right. There was a snicking sound as the deadbolt slid to one side; she turned the knob, and gave the door a gentle push. The telltale beep of a burglar alarm could be heard from the kitchen. That meant she had only a few moments in which to enter a PIN number, or the security company would call to check on her.

That was the moment when the *Puissance Treize* agent heard a series of quick footsteps behind her and began to turn. In one fluid motion 47 shut the door and gave her a violent shove. She tripped, lost the bag of groceries, and fell forward. The Walther was holstered under her left arm, but she had no opportunity to use it as she thrust out her hands in order to break her fall.

As the target went down, the assassin knew the situation was iffy at best. He had seconds, maybe a minute, in which to subdue an armed opponent and force her compliance before the alarm company reacted. The insistent *beep, beep, beep* served to emphasize that fact. So 47 was already moving forward, seeking to get a grip on her, when she rolled over onto her back. A can of soup was at hand so Marla threw it. The cylinder hit the assassin on the right cheek and caused him to stagger backward.

Marla instantly recognized 47 and felt a sudden stab of fear. The *Puissance Treize* agent had no doubt about her ability to deal with either a burglar or would-be rapist, but she'd seen this man in action, and knew his capabilities.

Which begged the question: Why was she still alive?

The answer was obvious. He wanted it that way!

The realization brought a new sense of hope.

Marla kicked with her feet in an attempt to put more distance between them, and thanks to the smooth wood floor of the living room, was able to push herself backward. A box of pasta lay within reach, so she threw it with her left hand and went for the Walther with her right.

But the spaghetti bounced off 47's left thigh. His right foot made contact with her gun hand, and the pistol went flying. There was a loud clatter as the weapon landed on the hardwood floor and slid away.

The maddening *beep, beep, beep* continued unabated.

Marla thought of herself as fast, but was shocked by the speed with which the man grabbed the front of her raincoat and jerked her up off the floor. A trickle of blood ran down from the point where the can had broken the assassin's skin, and she could see the cold determination in his eyes.

The phone began to ring.

"That's the alarm company," the agent said grimly. "Give them the code—and do it now."

"Or?" Marla demanded defiantly. "If you were going to kill me, you would have done so by now."

Agent 47 bared his teeth as the phone rang again. How long would the person on the other end of the line wait? For three rings? Perhaps four?

The ringing stopped.

There was a metallic whisper as the DOVO opened. Light rippled along the razor's stainless steel blade, and

47 brought the cold metal up to touch the side of the
Puissance Treize agent's softly rounded cheek.

"Answer the phone or I'll cut your face."

When Marla looked into the hitman's eyes, it was like
looking into a mirror. Here was someone just as ruthless as she was. She could feel the warmth of his breath
on her face, and the coiled strength of his body.

The phone rang again.

"Let go and I'll answer it," she said, the tension causing her to reveal a faint Irish accent.

"Use the phone in the kitchen," 47 ordered, and drew
a Silverballer as the woman crossed the room. Just because the Walther was lying on the floor didn't mean
the woman wasn't carrying a second weapon, or even a
third.

As Marla answered the phone in the kitchen he lifted
the receiver off the extension on her desk.

"Hello?" the *Puissance Treize* agent said, and the
ringing stopped.

"Ms. Norton?" a male voice inquired. "This is John
at the AJAX Alarm Company. Is everything okay?"

"I tripped and dropped my groceries, that's all."
Marla replied as she watched Agent 47 screw a silencer
onto his pistol. "But I'm fine."

"I'm glad to hear that," the man said cautiously. "So
you don't need medical assistance?"

"No," Marla said. And she hoped it would be true.

"Good," John replied. "Could I have your security
code, please?"

Marla turned her head toward the assassin and saw
that the silenced weapon was aimed at her right knee.

"My code is Indigo378."

"Thank you," John said politely. "Have a nice day."

She could have been lying, of course, but based on the speed with which the man on the other end of the line had accepted the code, 47 didn't think so.

He lowered the gun.

"Remove your clothes."

Marla raised a well-plucked eyebrow.

"Are you planning to rape me?"

She let the raincoat fall. The *Puissance Treize* agent had been forced to strip before. Once in Madrid, where it had been necessary to pose as an exotic dancer, so she could sit on her target's lap. Then in Paris, where the only way to steal the key she needed was to have sex with a French gangster. And most recently in Yakima, where the Big Kahuna insisted on a "show" the evening prior to the meeting.

So Marla knew her body could be used as a weapon—but was the man with the gun susceptible? Looking at his face it was impossible to tell.

He watched impassively as Marla's thong hit the floor.

"So," Marla said provocatively, as she completed a quick turn. "Are you satisfied?"

The agent ignored the question. "Who hired you to protect the Big Kahuna?" he demanded.

"Don't be absurd," the *Puissance Treize* agent replied contemptuously. "You know the rules. My superiors would kill me if I told you that!"

The assassin eyed her coldly.

"I'll kill you if you don't."

"No," Marla countered firmly, "You won't. Not as long as you need information, and there's a chance you might get it from me."

"True," 47 agreed as the DOVO reappeared. "Then

it looks like I'll have to torture the information out of you. . . .

"Which nipple should I remove first?"

Marla's hands instinctively flew up to cover her breasts. It was a sign of weakness she immediately came to regret, as she forced her hands back down.

"Torture doesn't work," she replied firmly. "People will say anything to make the pain stop. You know that, and I know that."

"That's what the experts say," 47 acknowledged darkly. "But I've had pretty good results. Perhaps that's because I enjoy it. Go over and sit on one of those chairs." Marla wasn't sure whether he was telling the truth or just trying to unnerve her more. He motioned with the gun.

The houseboat's interior featured a retro '50s theme, complete with lots of primary colors, plastic, and chrome. The chairs he referred to sat around a pedestal-style, circular table.

Fear tingled at the base of Marla's skull now, and with good reason, given the possibility that the assassin was a self-confessed sadist.

"Put your hands behind your back," he ordered sternly. He bound her wrists with phone cord. Her ankles came next, and by the time he was finished, Marla was helpless. Or nearly so, since the plastic-coated phone line was slippery, and difficult to knot.

"There," the agent said, as he stood. "Can't have any screaming . . . so all we need now is a gag. Or would you prefer to answer my questions?"

Marla remembered Mrs. Kaberov's cold blue eyes, and the bullet in the velvet-lined box.

"Go screw yourself!" she responded defiantly.

"Fine, have it your way," 47 said, and left the dining area.

The assassin returned a few moments later with a dish towel that he tied over Marla's mouth, and a pillowcase that he pulled down over her head. Then, much to Marla's relief, she heard a series of footfalls, followed by the sound of the front door opening and closing.

But the man with the gun would be back, and she knew her first opportunity to escape would most likely be the only opportunity to escape.

So rather than wait to see what would happen next, Marla went to work on freeing her hands. And thanks to the fact that the phone cord was slippery, it wasn't long before her bonds started to come loose. Thus encouraged, she struggled to work her hands free before her assailant could return.

After what seemed like endless minutes, the cord came off, and she reached up to remove the pillowcase. Once she could see, it was relatively easy to remove the line wound around her ankles. Finally, just as it seemed as if her heart were going to beat its way out through her chest, Marla's feet were free. She stood, got rid of the gag, and made for the door. The externally mounted slide-style bolt made a welcome snicking sound as it slid home.

The lock wouldn't be enough to keep a really determined assailant out, but it would buy some additional time, and that's all the *Puissance Treize* agent needed as she turned back into the room. The Walther was still there, lying on the floor, and never had the weapon's weight felt more welcome than when she lifted the pistol and pointed it at the door. Holding the semiauto with both hands, Marla waited for the assassin to return. Was the safety on or off? She should have checked but hadn't. A sure sign of how shaken she was, but an easy mistake to correct.

That was when she smelled smoke, heard her ceiling-mounted fire alarm go off, and saw flames in the kitchen. The fire immediately began to lick at the drapes before spreading across the ceiling, and there was barely enough time for her to slip into the raincoat, grab her purse off the floor, and exit the houseboat—gun in hand—as the flames continued to spread.

Marla had no desire to stay and explain everything to the authorities, so all she could do was shove the Walther into a pocket as she ran toward shore. Her bare feet made a slapping sound as they hit wet wood, and some of her neighbors emerged to shout instructions at one another as Marla entered the parking lot. Sirens could be heard as she fumbled for the remote and took refuge in the Mercedes.

Not knowing where 47 was, nor when he would return, she started the car and sped away. He might be following, but she would have to take that chance. She really had no alternative.

Her mind raced. The Agency knew where she was. That much was obvious, as was the fact that they were out to identify any of their employees who had leaked information to the *Puissance Treize* and put a stop to it. So, would they continue to come after her?

Yes, they almost certainly would. Except that the next attempt might be made by a specially equipped interrogation team that would use psychology, environmental conditioning, and drugs to break her.

That raised the obvious and most pressing question of what to do next. Would Kaberov provide support? Or punish her for incompetence? There was no way to be sure. But the odds weren't very good. Suddenly—through no fault of her own—Cassandra Murphy, aka Marla Norton, was on the run.

And whether she wanted to admit it or not, Agent 47 may have just flushed his prey.

PATRAS, GREECE

Though technically classified as a yacht, the 250-foot-long *Jean Danjou* had originally been designed to serve as a salvage tug, which was why she had none of the sleek grace that the other megayachts possessed as they lay at anchor on the sparkling waters of Patras.

But then, unlike her peers, the *Danjou* was expected to work for a living. Which was why she carried two armored SUVs, four BMW motorcycles, two snowmobiles, six personal watercraft, a four-place helicopter, scuba gear, a decompression chamber, a bulletproof Mercedes S500, and two forty-foot gunboats. Not to mention a great deal of very sophisticated communications and tracking equipment intended to support Agency activities worldwide.

The heart of the ship, and the place where Diana spent most of her time, was the communications and control room located deep within the *Danjou*'s armored hull. Her high-backed chair was located at the center of a U-shaped desk from which she could monitor twenty-four wall-mounted video screens, two side-by-side computer displays, and take satellite phone calls from all over the world.

Diana had a high forehead and eyes that were a tiny bit smaller than she would have preferred. Still, having been gifted with a straight nose, high cheekbones, and sensual lips, her face would have been considered beautiful had it not been for a certain hardness that was resident there.

"Say again," she said, as static rattled in her earphones. "You're breaking up."

"I have a message for Mr. Nu," Agent 47 replied. "Tell him I made contact with Marla Norton. And although I wasn't able to pry any information out of her, she's on the run. I placed micro-trackers in both her raincoat and her purse. With any luck at all, she'll lead us up the food chain, and to the person who has the answers we're looking for."

Diana glanced at one of the monitors to her right. Mr. Nu was taking part in a board meeting in Houston, where shipping magnate Aristotle Thorakis was halfway through a report.

"I'll tell him," the controller promised. "Take care of yourself."

"I will," 47 promised, and he returned the phone to his pocket.

That was when the crackling flames found the explosives that Marla Norton kept hidden in the crawl space above her living room, and the houseboat exploded.

There was a loud *boom,* followed by a spectacular fireworks display as chunks of fiery debris flew up into the gray sky and rained down onto the surface of the lake, where they made a hissing sound before bobbing on the surface. Mrs. Beasley's home was largely untouched, except for her geraniums, which were destroyed when a piece of wreckage fell on them.

The oarlocks creaked as the assassin pulled away. More sirens joined the already strident chorus, and the rain fell gently around him.

FIVE

The more than 7,000-square-foot suite took up the entire 16th floor of the Hotel France and had a sweeping view of Central Park. The reception area was dominated by a huge stained-glass window and the walls were covered with hand-painted depictions of the French countryside. All of which was quite familiar to Aristotle Thorakis, as he and his family had spent the Christmas holidays in the hotel just two years before, back when the $15,000-per-night price tag seemed reasonable.

But even with the 500-million-euro loan from the *Puissance Treize* in his pocket, equaling nearly 700 million U.S. dollars, the businessman was struggling to keep his shipping empire afloat, and he had come to view such expenditures as an indulgence. Especially when perfectly good accommodations could be had for $5,000 a night.

The cost of the suite included the services of a very proper English butler who was present to greet Thorakis as he stepped off the elevator. The man's hair was combed straight back, his long face was solemn, and the immaculate business suit fit his body to a tee. Judging from the way he greeted the shipping magnate, he was blessed with an excellent memory—or a very good set of files.

"Good afternoon, sir. Welcome back," he said smoothly. "My name is Bradley. Mr. Douay has asked me to direct you to the sitting room."

"Thank you," Thorakis said brusquely. "I know the way."

The formal reception area gave way to a hall that led past a formal bar, then a richly paneled dining room, into the large sitting area beyond. Picture windows opened out onto the park, a grand piano stood next to a tiny dance floor, and pieces of formal furniture were grouped to form discrete conversation areas, one of which was occupied by a pair of nattily dressed bodyguards. Both held magazines, but kept their eyes fixed on Thorakis.

Douay was seated behind a handsome replica of a French provincial desk. He was talking on the phone, and nodded as Thorakis dropped into one of the upholstered chairs that faced him.

The Greek couldn't help but take note of the fact that the Frenchman allowed what was clearly a routine business conversation to continue for a good five minutes before finally bringing the call to an end. Was Douay sending him a message? Seeking to emphasize the extent to which he was in control? Yes, the Greek decided, that was *exactly* what he was doing. And it served to amplify the anger Thorakis felt when Douay finally saw fit to acknowledge him.

"It was reckless of you to come here," Douay said sternly.

"Really?" Thorakis replied heatedly. "That's amusing, coming from you! Are you and your people *insane*? I just came from a board meeting where I learned that you and the rest of your morons sent a female operative to eliminate Agent 47, and she failed! That led to a very well-publicized massacre in Yakima, followed by an explosion in Seattle, and a great deal of unfortunate news coverage.

"So, how *dare* you lecture me on what is and isn't reckless!" he said, standing and placing his fists on the desk.

Both of Douay's security people were on their feet by that time, but the Frenchman waved them off. When he spoke, his voice was calm.

"The attempt to eliminate Agent 47 was a failure," the Frenchman acknowledged soothingly. "However, I assure you that the mistake will be rectified. And I want you to know that the decision to kill 47 wasn't made lightly. Comparative analysis shows that while he accounted for a mere three percent of the hits carried out by The Agency during the last fiscal year, those sanctions were the most difficult contracts the organization took on, and therefore constituted 37.2 percent of the organization's gross profit.

"That makes 47 the most valuable asset The Agency has. So, were the *Puissance Treize* to eliminate him, it would better position our company to compete for the lucrative upmarket jobs—those exhibiting a difficulty quotient of seven or better. That's where the serious money is. Do you follow our reasoning?"

Not only did Thorakis follow the man's cold-blooded

logic, he found that he admired the audacity of it, if not the ham-handed manner in which the plan had been carried out. And given the Frenchman's conciliatory tone, the shipping magnate felt his anger begin to melt away. But that left the fear, which, since he had just come from The Agency's board meeting, was considerable.

"Yes," he said gravely, "I follow your reasoning. And I apologize if my comments came across as being intemperate. But there is tremendous reason for concern. After the attempt on Agent 47's life, The Agency immediately went to work trying to find the leak. They're busy conducting an exhaustive review of the lower echelon people right now, but it's only a matter of time before they begin to look at senior management."

Douay started to say something at that point, but Thorakis threw up a hand.

"Wait. There's more. The decision has been made to send Agent 47 after your assassin . . . in the hope that she will lead him to a person who can reveal the traitor's identity. And that's why I'm here. According to the briefing they gave to the board, Agent 47 followed Marla Norton to Fez, Morocco, where she's living under the protection of a man named Al-Fulani. Does he know about our agreement? Because if he does, and if 47 were to gain control of him, then I'm a dead man."

"No, he does not," Douay lied smoothly. "Your identity is a closely guarded secret. Only three people know who you are, and Al-Fulani isn't one of them."

That was exactly what Thorakis wanted to hear, so the magnate felt a tremendous sense of relief, and even managed a smile.

"Good. None of us are immortal . . . I know that," he said. "But I'm not ready to go—not yet!"

"Nor am I!" Douay agreed jovially, as he rose to come around the desk. "So, now that you're here, will you join me for lunch?"

"Thank you, but no," Thorakis replied. "I have allergies, you know, and my chef is back at the hotel. Perhaps next time, though."

"Yes, next time," the Frenchman agreed politely. "Although it's important to be circumspect. And with that in mind, perhaps you would allow my security people to take you out through the basement garage."

"That would be perfect," Thorakis said gratefully. They shook hands vigorously, and moments later he was gone.

Douay waited until the elevator had closed on the Greek before opening an attaché case, activating a satellite phone, and entering a two-digit code that triggered a much longer sequence of numbers.

The truth was that Al-Fulani was fully aware of the shipping magnate's identity, which meant Marla Norton had an important job to do. She would have to protect Al-Fulani, or die with him.

$\underline{\text{SIX}}$

FEZ, MOROCCO

The French called Fez—or Fes—*la Mysterieuse,* and as Agent 47 pushed deeper into the oldest—and some said most dangerous—part of the city, he discovered what they meant.

About a quarter-million people were crammed into a maze of narrow cobblestone streets, busy *souks,* stately mosques, brooding blank-faced homes, and hidden gardens. And given the local propensity to not only change street names, but post them in a variety of languages, it was easy to understand why *Fes El Bali,* the old town, was sometimes referred to as "the most complicated square mile on Earth."

Tourists were well advised to hire a guide before setting foot in the area.

But Agent 47 was equipped with something more reliable than a human guide. He had a small global positioning device that was preloaded with data provided by The Agency. The handheld GPS unit showed Marla Norton's location, as well as that of The Agency's local armory, where he could pick up any weapons he needed.

The security measures put in place over the last few years as part of the worldwide effort to counter global terrorism made it nearly impossible to transport weapons on commercial flights like the ones 47 had been forced to use in order to keep up with Marla. So, with the exception of his undetectable fiber-wire garrote, the assassin was unarmed. A problem he would soon correct.

Thanks to its location directly across the Strait of Gibraltar from Spain, as well as its reputation as the gateway to Africa, Morocco was a favorite with tourists from all over the world. Which was why none of the people who lived along the edge of the old city gave the assassin so much as a second glance as he strode through labyrinthine passageways lined with small stores.

Further on the streets were lined with high walls, the iron-strapped gates that opened onto private courtyards, and the homes that embraced them.

As the faithful were called to prayer, and the melodic sound of the *adhan* issued from the city's minarets, the streets filled with locals and there were fewer and fewer European faces to be seen.

Unlike the young women who frequented the stores in the French-built *Ville Nouvelle* (new town), many of whom would have looked at home in New York City, most of *Fes El Bali*'s females wore the *burka* whenever they ventured forth to fetch food, buy clothes, or visit relatives. Men sat on white plastic chairs, stood in doorways, or congregated in open air cafés where many passed the time by playing cards.

Everyone, regardless of age, gender, or station, was forced to share the narrow streets with the heavily burdened donkeys. In the absence of motor vehicles, these beasts were used to haul everything in and out of the *medina* (city). And it was while he was taking refuge in a doorway, so that one of the sturdy animals could pass, that 47 noticed the scruffy-looking African.

A furtive figure ducked into a side corridor when the assassin glanced his way. A thief most likely, eager to steal a tourist's wallet, but the agent could imagine other scenarios as well, including the possibility that the *Puissance Treize* was somehow aware of his presence. The tail was a problem in either case, and would have to be dealt with before he could enter the armory.

With that in mind Agent 47 quickened his pace, passed a tiny shop stuffed with consumer electronics, and took a sharp right-hand turn into a narrow passageway. Despite the heat of the day, some of the cobblestones were wet, and the passage smelled of urine, though it was empty except for an overflowing trash bin. At the end of the alley, all further progress was blocked by a door covered with peeling paint. The barrier appeared to be at least a hundred years old and was equipped with an equally venerable lock.

The agent ventured a quick look over his shoulder before dropping to one knee and peering through the keyhole. The view was limited, but he couldn't see any sign of movement in the courtyard beyond, so he was inclined to take the chance. The pick made quick work of the worn tumblers, and it was only a matter of seconds before he heard a *click,* and the lock opened.

Another quick glance over his shoulder still showed no sign of pursuit.

Hinges squeaked as the agent pushed the door open and slipped inside. From all appearances, the small courtyard was being used to store construction materials. Scrap lumber was stacked next to a wooden box full of ceramic tiles and a rusty wheelbarrow. A short flight of stairs led up to a small landing, a palm in a large pot, and a second door. But 47 had no interest in entering the residence, as he heard the patter of footsteps out in the passageway and tossed a South African Krugerrand toward the stairs. The gold coin made a ringing noise as it hit, bounced once, and rattled into place.

The tail was at the door by that time, and having found it ajar, he gave the barrier a push. The African caught sight of the brightly glittering gold coin as the slab of wood swung out of the way, and he hurried to claim it.

The man was of average height, a good deal darker than most of the local population, and dressed in the pan-African uniform of a T-shirt and ragged pants. But what made this young man different from most was the fact that his right hand had been replaced by a rudimentary metal hook. The sort of prosthesis a village blacksmith might manufacture for a few dollars.

The African had covered half the distance to the gleaming Krugerrand when the fiber-wire noose dropped over his head. The assassin's plan was to choke the young man into submission, ask him some questions, and then decide what to do with him.

But 47's adversary brought the hook up so quickly that the prosthesis was inside the loop before the garrote could tighten. And because the inner surface of the hook had been honed until it was knife-sharp, the noose fell away.

Reacting to this turn of events, 47 pushed the African away, dropped into a crouch, and prepared to defend himself with whatever he could lay his hands on. The only implement that happened to be available was a rusty shovel that was leaning against the courtyard wall. He held it diagonally across his body where it could be used to block the other man's hook.

But if the assassin's opponent was intimidated, he showed no sign of it as the two men circled each other, looking for openings. A sheen of perspiration had appeared on the hook-man's forehead, but judging from the steady look in his eyes, he was quite confident. His prosthesis was held low and back, and one well-placed arc could sink the hook into 47's groin, where he would be able to jerk the blade upward, and thereby spill his victim's intestines onto the pavement.

But the hook-man would have to close with the assassin in order to accomplish such a move, and as long as 47 had the shovel, the African would be forced to keep his distance.

Suddenly the agent tripped on a loose paving-stone, which brought his opponent rushing forward in an instant. But it was a ruse, and before 47's opponent could react, the shovel was in motion. It made an audible *clang* as it came into contact with the African's left knee.

His eyes went wide, and both the hook and the man's remaining hand went to where the pain was, as he fell backward onto the pavement. Then Agent 47 was there, with the shovel blade pressing down on the man's throat, as the amputee whimpered in pain.

"Who are you?" the assassin demanded. "And why were you following me?"

"Jamal," the man on the ground choked out, as he tried to push the shovel away from his throat. "My name is Jamal. Please! I can't breathe."

"Okay, Jamal," the assassin said unsympathetically, as he put his right foot on the shovel. "Why were you following me?"

The response was little more than an inarticulate gurgling noise, so 47 was forced to remove his foot, and thereby relieve the pressure on Jamal's tortured windpipe.

"Now, try again."

"Money," came the raspy response. "I was going to take your money."

"That's one possibility," the agent allowed darkly. "But there are others. How can I be sure that you're just a thief?"

"My hand," Jamal said piteously, as he held up the hook for inspection. "They cut it off."

It had long been the Muslim practice to amputate hands, arms, and in some cases legs, as a punishment for thievery. While this approach was gradually falling out of favor in many Middle Eastern countries, it was still considered an effective deterrent in others. A fact that seemed to support Jamal's claim. So, having completed a quick pat down, Agent 47 backed out of reach.

"I suggest that you find a new line of work. You aren't very good at this one."

Jamal continued to hug his knee and moan softly as 47 put the shovel back where he had found it.

"I'll leave the gate ajar," the assassin promised, as he

bent over to retrieve the Krugerrand. "And don't bother to get up. I'll see myself out."

Having left the little courtyard behind, Agent 47 paused at the point where the side passage met the main thoroughfare, and took a moment to adjust his red silk tie. Then, having assured himself there weren't any additional Jamals waiting to attack him, he resumed his journey.

A right-hand turn took him down a short flight of stairs, under an arch, and past a group of boys who were playing with a soccer ball. It soon became clear that what had once been a residential area had gradually transitioned into a small *souk* with specialized stores slotted along both sides of the street. The establishment 47 was looking for lay about a hundred feet farther on, just around a gentle curve and opposite a family-run grocery. The sign out front read MEN'S CLOTHING, in both English and Arabic, followed by ABAZA TIRK, PROPRIETOR, in smaller letters, carved out and painted in gold.

Having stopped to inspect the overly ripe fruit displayed on the other side of the thoroughfare, and to make sure that he hadn't acquired a new tail, Agent 47 was forced to wait for a group of black-clad women to pass before crossing over to the store. Like the shops located to either side, the clothing store was quite narrow, which made it necessary to hang clothes in tiers, the highest of which were suspended just below the ceiling, and only accessible with a long pole. It was hot and musty, and there wasn't much light, but what there was came from ceiling fixtures that were at least seventy-five years old.

A well-worn aisle led straight back to where a man

with generally even features, slightly bulging eyes, and a servile manner stood waiting. He was dressed in a red fez, a well-tailored gray suit, and a pair of black Moroccan slippers. A young man sat behind the counter seemingly half-asleep.

"Good afternoon, *effendi*," the well-dressed man said, as he dry-washed his hands. "My name is Abaza Tirk. Welcome to my humble store. I can see that you are a man of taste and discernment. How can my family and I be of assistance?"

"Abd-el-Kader said, 'Death is a black camel, which kneels at the gates of all,' " 47 replied matter-of-factly.

"And Ben Sira said, 'Fear not death, for it is your destiny,' " the diminutive store owner replied, as the servile manner dropped away. "Welcome Agent 47—I was told to expect you. Please come this way."

The assassin followed Tirk past a small counter, and as he passed he noticed that the young man seated behind the till was cradling a mini-Uzi in his lap.

There was a momentary pause as Tirk entered a code into a keypad located at the back of the crowded store. It was concealed by a small scrap of cloth tacked to the wall. The metal door made no sound as it swung open. A motion detector activated two rows of lights, and Agent 47 felt the temperature drop as Tirk pulled the door closed behind them.

Unlike the dark, slightly musty clothing store, The Agency's armory in Fez was sleekly modern. Closely spaced racks of weapons took up both walls, all grouped by category, and labeled appropriately. Ammunition, accessories, and cleaning gear were stored below the firearms in stainless steel cabinets.

"So," the clothier said engagingly, "what will it be? A

Steyr AUG perhaps? Very stylish. An FR-F1 sniper's rifle? Or maybe you're in the market for something with more heft. I have a nice RAI Model 500 .50 caliber sniper's rifle. Agent Orbov made good use of it just two months ago."

"No," 47 replied simply. "The RAI is almost fifty inches long—which makes it very difficult to hide. Not to mention the fact that it's single action, and .50 caliber ammo is damned heavy. I'll take a Walther WA 2000, plus a Mossberg model 500 with a pistol grip, and two Silverballers. One short, and one long, with silencers for both. Plus a double holster rig, a dual-use drug kit, and a throwing knife."

"Of course," Tirk said approvingly. "A weapon for every occasion."

After they had collected the weapons, they moved through another door at the rear of the long, narrow room to a soundproofed range that lay beyond. Once he was satisfied that all of the guns were in good working order, 47 loaded them into a pair of lockboxes that looked like travel-worn suitcases. Each had its own alarm and self-destruct system.

"The cases are rather heavy, so my number four son will accompany you," Tirk said, as the containers were loaded onto a hand cart. "Not to mention the fact that we have our share of thieves in *Fes El Bali*."

"That's what I hear," the assassin commented soberly.

"Will there be anything else?" Tirk wanted to know.

"Yes," 47 said, as he eyed the store owner. "I want your hat."

Rather than allow Tirk's son to accompany him all the way to the hotel, Agent 47 opted to have the young

man take him to a point where a major street cut
through *Fes El Bali,* where it became possible to hail a
cab. Even though Tirk and his family were presumably
trustworthy, there was no need for them to know where
the assassin was staying. Furthermore, it would be unusual for a guest to bring luggage into the hotel on a
hand cart.

As it happened, there was barely room to squeeze
him, the gun cases, and a suitcase full of clothes into the
little Peugeot 205. But after much pushing and shoving,
the task was accomplished. Traffic was horrendous,
and in spite of the cabdriver's best efforts to bully his
way through the city's eternal gridlock, the sun was low
in the western sky by the time 47 arrived at the Sofitel
Palais Jamai Fes, paid the fare, and had his bags taken
up to his room.

As was his practice, the assassin allowed the bellman
to enter the room first. Once it was clear that he wasn't
about to walk into an ambush, 47 followed.

A quick glance told him that everything was just as he
had left it, so he gave the bellman a tip and closed the
door. A subsequent thorough inspection confirmed that
the room was free of threats. Having had to deal with
surveillance devices, explosives, and poisonous reptiles
at various times in the past, he was understandably cautious.

Thus satisfied, Agent 47 ordered a meal from room
service, and requested that the waiter leave the cart outside the door. Having watched the hotel employee depart through the peephole, the agent opened the door
and brought the tray inside. His dinner, which consisted
of roasted lamb and cooked vegetables on a bed of fla-

vored couscous, was delicious. Especially when paired with a sip of hearty burgundy.

Then it was time to strip down to his underwear and take the Silverballers apart while watching the *BBC World News*. He carefully examined each oil-slicked part for flaws, and automatically fingered for burrs prior to reassembling the weapons. This was a task he could perform blindfolded. Each nine-round clip made a comforting *click* as it slid home. With that accomplished, he found it a simple matter to pump a round into each chamber, set the safeties, and prepare the two-gun holster rig for the next day.

Then it was time to brush his teeth, push a chair in front of the door, and make a bed on the floor.

Sleep came quickly, as did morning, and the usual hunger pangs. But rather than seek out a good breakfast as he usually did, 47 was scheduled to break bread with a retired professor named Paul Rollet, who was said to be very familiar with Ali bin Ahmed bin Saleh Al-Fulani. The man Marla Norton was staying with—and might or might not be privy to the traitor's identity.

But first it was necessary to put together a disguise. He chose something inspired by a German tourist he had seen in the hotel's lobby. It took the better part of forty-five minutes to prepare, but the final "look" was quite convincing. It consisted of a *bollehatte,* a reddish beard, a loud shirt that Abaza Tirk had been happy to get rid of, a pair of knee-length shorts that matched the blue hat, and some sturdy sandals.

With his disguise in place the assassin went out on the street. The sun was up, but the air was still cool, and the city was still in the process of waking. All of which

made for a pleasant walk as 47 left the hotel for the
Paris Café, which was located six blocks away.

The agent had eaten in at least fifty "Paris Cafés"
over the years, most of which were little more than par-
odies of the real thing, and to be avoided if at all possible. But when 47 arrived in front of the Paris Café Fez,
and mounted the flight of stairs that led to a sun-
splashed terrace, he was pleased to see what looked like
an authentic Parisian restaurant, complete with awning-
covered tables, white-shirted waiters, and a personable
maître d'.

Having downloaded a photo of his contact the
evening before, it was easy for Agent 47 to pick the
Frenchman out of the crowd and saunter over to his
linen-covered table. A straw hat shaded a long, narrow
face, which was partially obscured by a bushy beard
and the top half of a newspaper.

"Excuse me," 47 said. "Are you Professor Rollet?"
The words were in French, just one of many languages
the assassin had been force-fed as a child.

The eyes that rose to meet 47's were blue and bright
with intelligence.

"Yes, I am," the academic confirmed. "And you
are?"

"I'm a friend of Bob Denard," the assassin lied, refer-
encing the infamous French mercenary.

"Ah, yes," Rollet responded. "Welcome to Fez, *monsieur*. Please, have a seat. Would you care for some
breakfast?"

"I certainly would," 47 replied as he took a chair.
"What would you recommend?"

"I like the gazelle horns," the Frenchman replied
equably. "They are shaped like a croissant, but filled

with almond paste, and flavored with orange flower water."

"I'll take two," Agent 47 said decisively, "and a cup of coffee."

The two of them made small talk until a waiter appeared to take the newcomer's order and refresh Rollet's cup. Then, once they were alone, the conversation began in earnest.

"I'm looking for some information about Ali bin Ahmed bin Saleh Al-Fulani," 47 stated, "and I hear you're quite knowledgeable about the man."

"I know what most people know," the expatriate said cautiously. "Al-Fulani is a successful businessman, a well-known philanthropist, and a devout Muslim."

"I think you're far too modest about the extent of your knowledge," the assassin said dryly, as he pushed an envelope across the surface of the table. "Because it's my understanding that in addition to your work on behalf of the American Language Institute, you spent twenty years working for the French Directorate of External Security. Please accept a small gift, which if properly invested, will make your retirement that much more pleasant."

The plain white envelope was thick with hundred-dollar bills, and without drawing any attention, the professor was quick to drop his newspaper on top of it.

"Both civil servants and educators are underpaid," Rollet observed. "So your gift is welcome. And yes, even though the public Al-Fulani glitters like gold, another man dwells just below the surface."

"How fascinating," 47 said, as his breakfast arrived. "Please tell me more."

So Rollet did, once the waiter had departed, and what

followed was the story of a man who had inherited his father's smuggling business and subsequently come of age while running hashish into Spain, where it was either sold or sent north to the Netherlands, Belgium, Germany, and other European countries.

Al-Fulani's success soon caught the eye of competitors from as far away as Colombia, and it wasn't long before some very unpleasant people began to call on the Moroccan, threatening to hijack his drug shipments unless he shared the profits with them. But, rather than cave in to the international cartels, Al-Fulani managed to maintain his independence.

At that point Professor Rollet paused to light a disreputable-looking pipe. A series of energetic puffs were required to get the moist, cherry-flavored tobacco going properly. But once the mix was alight, the academic took the fragrant smoke deep into his lungs, and smiled broadly.

"Ah!" he exclaimed. "It's a dirty habit, but oh, how I enjoy it!"

Having finished his second pastry, 47 took another sip of coffee. "So, how did he do it?"

Rollet frowned. "Do what?"

"How did Al-Fulani manage to maintain his independence?" Agent 47 inquired patiently. The Frenchman took a long, slow look around, as if to make sure that none of the other diners were listening.

"People began to die," the academic confided gravely. "People at the very top of the cartels, and it wasn't long before the pressure came off Al-Fulani."

"So, Fulani had them murdered?"

"*Someone* had them murdered," Rollet said darkly.

"But it wasn't clear who. Though Al-Fulani clearly benefited, none of the acts could be traced to him."

Perhaps Rollet didn't know, or was reluctant to say the name out loud, but Agent 47 was pretty sure he knew which organization had been responsible for the deaths. Either the *Puissance Treize* had been paid to neutralize the Moroccan's competition, or Al-Fulani had been co-opted by the organization. Not that it made much difference. All 47 cared about was the fact that Al-Fulani was in a position to know which one of The Agency's employees was providing their rivals with proprietary information.

"I understand he has a house here," the assassin said casually. "What else should I be aware of?"

Rollet's pipe had gone out again by that time, and the professor took a moment to strike a wooden match and relight it.

"Well," he said thoughtfully, as a new cloud of smoke formed a halo around his head. "That all depends, doesn't it? If you want to congratulate Al-Fulani on a life well lived, then you could walk up to his front door in the *Ville Nouvelle*, and deliver your message to one of the guards. But, assuming your intentions are a bit less straightforward than that, there's the orphanage to consider. He visits every Friday night. Usually in the company of close friends or business associates—but occasionally by himself."

Agent 47 raised an eyebrow. "He visits an orphanage?"

"Yes," Rollet said cynically. "That's what *he* calls it anyway. But some say the organization is a cover for other, less virtuous activities."

"Such as?"

Rollet looked away, as if reluctant to voice what he'd heard.

"I really couldn't say. But if you're interested . . . the orphanage is located in the *Mellah*."

"Which means?"

"The *Mellah* is the old Jewish quarter," the academic explained. "It dates back to 1438, when the Jews were forced to live in a section known as *Al-Mallah*, or saline area. A term that eventually became synonymous with salted earth, or cursed ground.

"Then, when Israel came into existence in 1948, most of the Jewish population left Fez," Rollet continued. "That created a vacuum that rural Moroccans rushed to fill. But the Jews left some beautiful homes in the *Mellah*—and the orphanage is in one of them. Ask anyone—they'll show you where it is."

The conversation continued for a while, but it soon became apparent that 47 had gained everything he was likely to obtain from Rollet, so the assassin stood, bowed, and took his leave.

The interaction was observed by a man who, like 47, looked like a tourist enjoying a light breakfast, but was actually employed by Ali bin Ahmed bin Saleh Al-Fulani.

The Moroccan was well aware of 47's presence—and the hunter was about to become the hunted.

Darkness had fallen on Fez, and Marla Norton felt frightened, as she looked out through the open window to the busy boulevard three stories below. The evening air was warm, heavy with the rich odors of the food that the street vendors were hawking, and busy with the sounds of the city.

While fear wasn't something she was accustomed to feeling, it was an emotion that the *Puissance Treize* agent had experienced a lot lately. Which was absurd, given the fact that it was *she* who was lying in wait for the man called 47. Not the other way around.

The trap consisted of the three-hundred-foot stretch of sidewalk located in front of Al-Fulani's brightly lit mansion. The twenty-six-room, eight-bath home boasted a Mediterranean-style ceramic tile roof, a white façade, and several ornate balconies. Clusters of bottom-lit palm trees bracketed both sides of the home, and provided the structure with a sense of glamour. They also lit the surroundings, making it more difficult for intruders to get past the guards.

The most important component of the trap, however, was a "retired" Royal Marine named Ted Cooper, who was a graduate of the British Army's famous Joint Sniper Training Establishment, and was officially credited with six confirmed kills in Iraq. An accomplishment Cooper had been advised to keep to himself, lest the Islamic militants catch wind of it, and decide to even the score.

Of course, Al-Fulani's chief of security—a man named Ammar—had other assets in place as well, three of whom were walking along the busy boulevard with him. Thus, if Cooper failed to spot Agent 47 from above, Ammar and his men would nail him down below.

That was the plan, but there were still dozens of people to screen as they came and went, and it was Marla's opinion that the members of Al-Fulani's security staff were far too cavalier where 47 was concerned. In spite of her repeated warnings, they clearly considered themselves to be superior to the European *abruti* (moron) that the silly female was so frightened of.

And maybe they were right.

In the wake of the disastrous shoot-out in Yakima, her unsettling meeting with Mrs. Kaberov, and the loss of her home, Marla's self-confidence was at an all-time low. And now, having fled Kaberov's predictable rage, Marla found herself dependent on Al-Fulani's goodwill, which, predictably enough, was based on her willingness to serve him both professionally and personally. Regardless of her own desires.

This had been the case the night before, when Marla was "invited" to participate in a *ménage à trois* with the Moroccan and a teenaged girl who had been snatched off the streets of Johannesburg a week earlier. It hadn't been an especially enjoyable experience, but far better than one of Mrs. Kaberov's .45 caliber "gifts."

The thought was sufficient to drive the young woman back to the powerful scope that had been set up next to Cooper's tripod-mounted 7.62 mm L96 sniper's rifle. The marksman seemed patient, *very* patient, which was good. As well he should be, since a single kill like this one could net him more money in a few seconds than the Royal-bloody-Marines would pay in a year.

Marla stared through the scope at the mostly young, upper-class men and women who continued to stream past Al-Fulani's home on their way to fashionably late dinners or one of the alcohol-free nightclubs that had sprung up within the *Ville Nouvelle*. Spotting one particular individual in such a crowd would be hard enough, but her target's tendency to use disguises would make the task that much more difficult, since each face had to be examined thoroughly before Marla could move on to the next.

As the hours dragged on, having examined and rejected hundreds of faces, Marla was beginning to wonder if 47 would ever appear when a man matching 47's height and build casually strolled into her field of view. A German tourist, judging from his clothing. But that meant nothing. When Marla put the spotting scope on the man's face her suspicions were confirmed! Beard or no beard, that was the man she'd seen in Yakima and Seattle! The very sight of him caused her heart to pound with excitement as her quarry turned to eye the mansion.

That was the moment when a second German tourist— dressed in identical fashion—arrived from the other direction.

Now, with two look-alikes on the street below, and both in motion, it would have been nearly impossible to tell Cooper how to distinguish between them. And to do so quickly enough to ensure the results she wanted. So Marla gave the only order she could logically give.

"The German tourists! The ones wearing the loud shirts! Kill *both* of them!"

Cooper's rifle was silenced, and there was plenty of background noise, so no one heard the subsonic 7.62 mm NATO round as it sped through the space that the first German tourist's head had occupied a fraction of a second earlier, and slammed into the second one.

The force of the impact threw the tourist to the ground and people ran every which way. Marla came unglued as the first man disappeared.

"You were too slow!" she shouted angrily. "You were supposed to kill *both* of them and you let one get away!"

"Don't be stupid," Cooper countered crossly as he continued to sweep the street below. "There wasn't enough time to acquire both targets."

"Well, acquire *this*," the furious *Puissance Treize* agent declared as she drew the Walther and began to fire.

The first shot wasn't fatal, so Cooper began to turn toward his attacker, but it was too late as four additional 9 mm rounds tore into his body. Finally, having put a final slug into the sniper's head, Marla provided the only epitaph the Brit was likely to receive: "Bloody idiot."

If the first tourist had truly been 47, Marla was convinced that she'd lost her only real shot at him. But then a voice crackled over the walkie-talkie clipped to her belt. The words came in short bursts—and were accompanied by the sound of heavy breathing.

"This is Ammar. He's on the run. But we're right behind him."

That was when Marla knew 47 was still alive. A real tourist might have taken cover, but wouldn't be on the run. "That's brilliant!" she said excitedly. "Don't lose him. Where are you?"

"We're heading in the direction of the *souk Dabbaghin*," came the confident reply. "He's running like a rabbit!"

"A very dangerous rabbit," Marla cautioned. "I'm on my way."

Idiot!

As he took a right, followed by a left, Agent 47 was angry. Not at the men who were following him. But at himself. He'd been stupid enough to walk right into their trap. Rather than prepare for the reconnaissance the way he normally would have, the assassin had gone for an after-dinner walk, and chosen to stroll past Al-Fulani's mansion on the way back to the hotel. A stupid impulse that had very nearly gotten him killed.

But how had she known he was coming? Had Marla caught a glimpse of him during the last few days? Had Rollet sold him out? Or was this latest fiasco the work of the very traitor he was looking for? There was no way to know, and no more time to think about it, as a bullet pinged off the wall to his left and forced him to concentrate on the business at hand. The assassin pushed a man out of the way and ran even faster. A woman went down as he slammed into her, a man swore at him in Arabic, and another gunshot sent people fleeing for cover.

Sirens had begun to bleat, but they were back in the *Ville Nouvelle*, where the real German tourist was being tended to and the police were trying to sort out the situation. The man he had modeled himself after—the one he'd previously seen in the lobby of his hotel—had unwittingly paid for 47's life with his own. The agent knew that he had to lose this particular disguise at the first possible opportunity.

Even though he was outnumbered, 47 still had some advantages, not the least of which was the fact that his pursuers had allowed themselves to become strung out. This provided the assassin with an opportunity to lay a quick trap of his own, as one fellow rounded a corner and came to a momentary stop directly beneath a streetlight. The long-barreled Silverballer barked twice. The target staggered and went down.

That was 47's cue to take off again, conscious of the

fact that reinforcements were on the way and might cut off his line of retreat.

Ammar began to round the corner, spotted the crumpled body, and pulled back again.

"He shot Dabir," the security operative said into the radio. "So be careful."

"Keep after him!" Marla's voice insisted through Ammar's radio. "Don't let him out of your sight!"

"You stay off the radio!" Ammar snapped arrogantly, as another man, Jumah, caught up with him. "We'll take care of this. Return to the mansion."

"What's going on?" Jumah wanted to know, his brown eyes alight with excitement. "Did you take a shot at him?"

"No, he was gone by the time I arrived," Ammar temporized. "You take the lead. I need to catch my breath."

Jumah, who was the youngest man on the team, and, Ammar knew, eager to establish his own reputation, took off at a sprint. Ammar waited for the telltale sound of a gunshot, and when none was forthcoming, followed in Jumah's footsteps.

As he did he glanced back at the body and watched as a pair of preteen boys materialized from the gloom, beginning to rifle through Dabir's pockets.

He swore bitterly. Dabir was his brother-in-law, and there would be hell to pay once he got home.

Fez was home to many *derbs,* or districts, each having its own epicenter with a mosque, bakery, and public fountain. And that's where Jumah found himself as the street he had been following delivered him into a square that boasted a large fountain.

But his quarry was nowhere to be seen, and since there were at least four other passageways that led out of the open area, he had no choice but to stop and look around. The security agent turned a full circle, noticed that the square was deserted, and wondered why.

Jumah was still pondering this when a voice came from behind him. The words were in French.

"Are you looking for me?"

Jumah whirled and was in the process of bringing the Jordanian-manufactured 9 mm VIPER up into firing position when he saw that a man wearing a brightly colored shirt had risen from the waters of the fountain and was peering down at him. Even worse was the fact that the stranger was holding two semiautomatic pistols.

"I'll take that as a 'yes,' " the man said evenly, and he fired both weapons. The heavy slugs pounded Jumah to the ground as gunshots echoed between the surrounding buildings, and the VIPER skittered away.

"Jumah?" A male voice inquired from one of the dead man's pockets. "What's going on?"

Agent 47 returned one Silverballer to its holster, jumped down onto the cobblestones, and carried out a quick search of Jumah's body. Having appropriated the walkie-talkie, the assassin fled.

More sirens had joined the chorus as Ammar entered the empty square. The Moroccan saw Jumah and felt a momentary pang of guilt, knowing it could have been *his* body lying there.

Then, having detected a flicker of movement on the far side of the square, Ammar ran over to the fountain. Careful to keep his head down, he began to circle it. Having lost two of his men, it was clear that Fulani's *sharmuta* was correct. The European *was* dangerous.

"Ammar? Fahd? *Answer* me!" The whore's voice came over the radio, thick with fear.

But Ammar knew the man they were chasing must have taken Jumah's radio, so he sent one last message to Fahd, ordering him to maintain radio silence. A strategy that was likely to work both for and against them, to the extent that it kept Ammar and Fahd from coordinating their movements.

To hell with the woman.

Having followed his prey's watery trail into a narrow passageway, Ammar felt cautiously hopeful. The ground was dry, and the infidel was wet, which meant Ammar had tracks that were easy to follow, at least temporarily. The wet prints led him up a long flight of stairs and under a two-hundred-year-old arch before they suddenly disappeared.

That brought the security agent to a cautious halt. He was examining the well-lit patch of ground in front of him when a fiber-wire noose dropped over his head and began to tighten around his neck.

Ammar dropped his gun and brought his hands up— but it was too late. He was jerked off his feet. The Moroccan attempted to scream, but discovered that he couldn't.

His legs kicked uselessly in the air.

After a few moments, the kicking stopped.

* * *

Time was of the essence.

47's sandals made a wet slapping sound as they hit the pavement, and his damp clothes began to rub his skin raw as the assassin followed a narrow street toward the tanner's quarter—an ancient section of the city where animal skins were left to soak in vats of dye before being hung out to dry. Lights had been rigged so that tourists could view the scene at night, and the air was heavy with the foul odor of the pigeon droppings that were used to make the leather more pliable.

And that's where Fahd was waiting.

While the operative was at least thirty pounds overweight, Fahd was smart and knew Fez like the back of his hand. Knowing which way Dabir's killer was headed, and being well aware of his own physical limitations, the Moroccan had cut over to a main street, hailed a cab, and arrived outside the *souk Dabbaghin* a few minutes later.

Thus, the moment Agent 47 appeared on the far side of the craterlike vats, Fahd began to fire. One or two of his VIPER's 9 mm slugs may have struck the assassin, but from what Fahd could tell neither did any real damage. Either way, Fahd had emptied his pistol and was busy fumbling for a second clip when the assassin fired in return.

What felt like a sledgehammer struck Fahd's shoulder, snatched the fat man off his feet, and dumped him into a vat full of blue dye. The liquid felt cold as it closed over his head and set fire to his wounded shoulder.

He struggled to right himself, and the moment that the Moroccan's feet made contact with the bottom of the vat, he pushed himself back up. Fahd spluttered as he broke the surface, opened his eyes, and immediately wished he hadn't as he found himself looking into the barrel of a shiny gun. There was a flash of light, and Fahd was gone.

The police arrived a few minutes later, but the mysterious European had disappeared, leaving four bodies in his wake. All of whom were tied to Ali bin Ahmed bin Saleh Al-Fulani; a man who gave generously to police charities and was known to place a high value on his privacy. So the corpses were given over to their respective families, funerals were scheduled for the following day, and the deaths were ascribed to gang activity. Which, sadly enough, was on the upswing.

SEVEN

FEZ, MOROCCO

Ali bin Ahmed bin Saleh Al-Fulani's study was quite large. Complex geometric designs had been painted onto the ceiling, and floor-to-ceiling bookcases covered most of the wall space not occupied by the three arched windows behind his desk. A set of six intricately carved, hand-painted, Moorish screens served to partition off the east end of the room, where a prayer rug and a day bed were kept, and three richly polished antique doors had been used to decorate the wall. They were made of cedar and bound with strips of brass.

But Marla Norton had other things on her mind, and was only vaguely aware of her surroundings, as she entered her sponsor's office and went to stand in front of his desk. There weren't any guest chairs, and wouldn't be, unless orders were issued to bring some in.

Al-Fulani was a big man with a broad forehead, heavy brows, and a prominent nose. He was at least fifty, and some said sixty, but his face was smooth and tight. He owned dozens of Western-style business suits, but it was rather warm that day, which was why he had chosen to wear a full-length, Gulf-style, white *thawb* instead. It made Al-Fulani look princely, which Marla suspected was one of the primary reasons why he wore it.

The Moroccan was genuinely fond of Marla, even if he considered her a Western whore, and smiled as he looked up from the report that he had been reading.

"Yes, my dear, what can I do for you?"

"Professor Rollet is ready for questioning," Marla answered evenly.

"Then it would be rude to keep him waiting," Al-Fulani replied cheerfully, as he rose from his executive-style chair. "Come, take my arm, and we will go down to greet him together."

Marla knew that both of the Moroccan's wives lived at his country estate, and were therefore blissfully unaware of what went on in Fez. So she allowed her protector to escort her down a flight of gently curving stairs and into the basement. Besides having six bedrooms, eight baths, a huge kitchen, large study, and sprawling living room, Al-Fulani's mansion boasted something none of the surrounding residences had: Its own medical clinic—and adjacent torture chamber. Which, like a similar facility at police headquarters, was equipped with ceiling-mounted hooks and a central floor drain.

Nor was the seeming contradiction lost on Al-Fulani, who while not the recipient of a formal education, was well read, and therefore familiar with the ancient Chinese concept of polar opposites. Which was why he called one room yin—and the other yang.

As the twosome entered the scrupulously clean yang room, the first thing they saw was Paul Rollet. The former spy and college professor hung spread-eagled at the very center of the chamber. Ropes connected his wrists to the hooks in the ceiling and his ankles to ring bolts sunk in beautifully tiled floor. The academic's partially bald pate gleamed under the bright lights, the bushy beard made him look much older than he actually was, and his long, obscenely white body was reminiscent of a skinned rabbit. Rollet's ribs were plainly visible, as was a shock of brown pubic hair, and a long wormlike penis. The bruises all over his body suggested that Rollet had put up a fight during his abduction, or been professionally beaten since.

Other than Rollet, Marla, and Al-Fulani, the only other person in the room was a man named Habib, who had been forced to drop out of medical school in Cairo because of his low grades, but had progressed far enough to learn a great deal about the human body, including portions that were particularly susceptible to pain. He liked to refer to himself as *Doctor* Habib, and affected a white lab coat, a pocketful of multicolored pens, and typically wore a stethoscope.

And, judging from the gleaming array of scalpels and hemostats laid out on a neatly draped Mayo stand, Habib was ready to both start and stop some bleeding, if ordered to do so. He was a sleek little man, with beady brown eyes and slightly protuberant ears.

"The patient is ready," the torturer said evenly as his employer entered the room. "As am I."

"Excellent," Al-Fulani replied coldly as he took up a position directly in front of Rollet. "So, Professor, are you ready to metaphorically spill your guts, or must Doctor Habib actually remove them? It's a process that won't kill you, at least not right away, but is *very* unpleasant."

The Frenchman's eyes had been closed until that point, but suddenly they popped open. Ironically enough, there had been occasions during the last twenty years when he had stood in Al-Fulani's position. Though for different reasons.

"So, if I tell you what you want to know, you'll allow me to live?"

"Yes," Marla agreed.

"Good," Rollet responded. "What would you like to know?"

A number of full-color photographs had been taped to a tiled wall. They were of good quality, and showed Rollet having breakfast with Agent 47 at the Paris Café.

"Tell us about the meeting you had with the man in those photographs," Marla instructed. "And leave nothing out."

Rollet complied, so that ten minutes later both Marla and her protector knew what the Frenchman knew, which was that 47 was extremely interested in Al-Fulani's activities. And given the match between the professor's story and recent events, there was no reason to doubt him. Al-Fulani was satisfied.

"I think we have it all," the Moroccan said. He turned to Marla. "Kill him."

"But you agreed to let me go!" Rollet protested.

"No," Marla countered reasonably. "We agreed to let you *live*. But we didn't say for how long."

The Walther spoke twice, two bullet holes appeared at the very center of Rollet's lightly haired chest, and his chin fell forward. Doctor Habib was left to clean up after the killing as Marla and Al-Fulani left the room.

Marla was the first to speak as they climbed the stairs.

"So, I have the job."

"Yes," Al-Fulani agreed soberly. "My men aren't used to taking orders from a woman, but Ammar was a fool to ignore your advice, and paid the price. So, from this point forward, you will be in charge of my personal safety, although responsibility for overall security will continue to rest with my cousin Rashid. Are we agreed?"

Marla didn't like Rashid, or the fact that he was still in the picture, but knew better than to overreach.

"Yes, and thank you," Marla said sincerely, as they reentered the study. "While we're on the subject of your safety, I would like to suggest that you stay away from the orphanage until we find 47. Rollet told him about it, and how you go there on Fridays. That means he could find a place to hide, lie in wait, and pick you off with a rifle."

Al-Fulani made a face.

"But the children will miss me!"

Marla had serious doubts about that but kept them to herself.

"Perhaps the staff could bring some of them here—but promise me you won't go there."

The Moroccan's face lit up.

"Yes! It shall be as you say. I will organize a party. And you will come."

Marla experienced a wave of revulsion, and could only hope that it wasn't visible on her face.

"Of course. Nothing would please me more."

EIGHT

Though slightly taller than the average Moroccan, there was nothing else to distinguish the man wearing the red fez, dilapidated business suit, and dusty black shoes from thousands of low-level bureaucrats and sales clerks as he made his way up the busy street, entered the run-down residential hotel located across from the Al-Fulani Orphanage, and carried two plastic bags bulging with groceries up three flights of stairs to apartment 301, where he paused to eye the thread that had been spit-welded across the doorjamb. It was intact.

Mindful of the fact that a truly dangerous adversary would not only notice the thread, but have an accomplice replace it once he was inside, the man in the red fez lowered his groceries to the floor. Then having eyeballed the other doors that opened onto the landing, the tenant drew a Silverballer with one hand, while he unlocked the door with the other. There was a soft *click*.

The man gave the door a nudge, saw it swing open, and backed away. But rather than a volley of gunshots, the only sounds to be heard were the muted babble from a television in 302 and the insistent bleat of a distant siren.

Having satisfied himself that it was safe to enter, the man in the red fez did so, weapon at the ready. But with the exception of the six flies that were chasing one another around the light fixture in the middle of the ceiling, the dingy apartment was empty of life.

The Silverballer slid back into its holster, the groceries were brought in from the hall, and the door was relocked.

The ceiling fan was broken, and there was no air conditioning other than that produced by the three vertical windows that opened onto the street, so he went over to open them. Outside air entered the room, but so did the acrid stench of exhaust fumes and the roar of traffic below.

Once the cold items were stowed in the gently wheezing fridge, Agent 47 removed both the fez and the suit that Mr. Tirk had given him. It would have been nice to remove the pencil-thin mustache, and the paste-on mole. But dangerous, because now that the move from the Sofitel *Palais Jamai Fes* was complete, it was important to stay in character as he kept Al-Fulani's orphanage under observation.

According to Professor Rollet, the Moroccan would probably visit the building on the far side of the street the following day. Which was when the assassin planned to enter the orphanage, drug the businessman, and make off with his unconscious body. Then, having driven the Moroccan out into the country, he would have an opportunity to ask some very pointed questions. But before he made his move he wanted to observe the comings and goings of the place.

So 47 sat down to eat the cold couscous salad with lemon dressing and feta cheese that he had purchased from a mom-and-pop grocery store. That was followed by six lamb-skewers from a street vendor, plus a piece of coconut fudge cake, and three cups of piping hot tea.

Then, as daylight gradually surrendered to darkness, the surveillance began anew. Thanks to the information provided by Rollet, 47 knew that the building across the street had once been the property of a wealthy Jewish family, which had chosen to emigrate to Israel—or been forced to do so, in the years immediately after World War II. The old mansion was solidly built, stood three stories high, and would have been at home in the Steglitz district of Berlin.

During the two days that Agent 47 had been watching the orphanage, he had never once seen children outside playing. There were plenty of adults, however, including household staff, security guards, and the well-dressed visitors who arrived each evening, almost all of whom were male, mostly European, and generally older.

There was a good deal of turnover where the visitors were concerned, or that's how it appeared, but there were regulars, too. Like the wheelchair-bound Mr. Wayne Bedo of Akron, Ohio, who had arrived in Fez three weeks earlier, and was delivered to the orphanage at exactly 7:00 each evening by a specially equipped van. All of which was information 47 had gathered by jumping into a taxi and following Bedo to his hotel the night before.

A breeze came up as the sun set, and the badly faded

curtains began to stir, even as the lights came on across the street. Having darkened his apartment so that no one could see in, Agent 47 began the evening's work, which consisted of memorizing everything that might be relevant to the coming mission.

That included taking note of the number of guards who were patrolling the grounds, where they were stationed, how frequently they were relieved, which ones had a tendency to goof off, where the surveillance cameras were located, how the floodlights were positioned, where the shadows fell, and much, much more. Each new observation was compared to the ones he had made during the past couple of days, in order to detect changes, variations, and patterns.

He noted the fact that at least three-quarters of the people who entered the orphanage were wearing masks, which seemed rather strange, unless the facility was being used to stage costume balls six nights a week. But, regardless of the reason, the practice might be beneficial to 47's plan, which was all that mattered to him.

Most of the visitors had arrived by 8:00 p.m., and Al-Fulani wasn't among them, so the assassin felt even more certain that the Moroccan would visit the orphanage on schedule the following evening. Later, about eleven or so, people began to leave. A process that continued into the wee hours of the morning before finally tailing off about 2:00 a.m. Which was when the agent put his binoculars away, took a tepid shower, and made a bed on the floor.

Then, with both Silverballers at hand, the assassin went to sleep.

*   *   *

The sun was low in the western sky, and the city's shadows were pointing toward the holy city of Mecca, as the man in the red fez made his way through the lobby of the Oasis Hotel, entered the elevator, and got off on the sixth floor.

Having checked his watch, he followed the blue and gold runner down the hallway toward the linen closet he had identified previously. After a quick look around to make sure that no one was watching, he dropped to one knee. The lock pick made quick work of the old tumblers, the door opened without protest, and 47 slipped inside.

Sturdy shelves took up most of the walls, all of which were loaded with clean towels, sheets, and blankets. There were a couple of carts, plus backup cleaning supplies, and a white plastic chair. The air was thick with the combined odors of soap, cleaning agents, and room deodorizer.

He was early, and intentionally so, lest something unexpected delay him. So there was nothing for 47 to do other than leave the door slightly ajar and wait. The second maid service of the day was complete, so there was no reason why members of the staff would bother him, but if they did, a syringe was ready and waiting.

That precaution proved unnecessary, however, because the next person to come down the hallway wasn't a member of the hotel's staff, but Mr. Nathan Ghomara, the English-speaking aide Bedo had engaged to take him where he wanted to go. Which, for the most part, was the orphanage.

Ghomara was of average height, but a bit overweight, causing him to waddle as he approached the closet. The Moroccan was dressed in a sports jacket, white shirt, and black pants. There was nothing especially remark-able about his features except for bushy eyebrows, a slightly bulbous nose, and a heavy five-o'-clock shadow.

Agent 47 waited for Ghomara to pass, stepped out into the hall, and took three running steps. He clamped a hand over the Moroccan's mouth and rammed the needle into his neck. Ghomara struggled weakly for a moment before becoming a dead weight as he col-lapsed.

The assassin was well aware of the fact that an eleva-tor full of people could arrive at any moment, or one of the hotel's guests might step out into the hall, which meant it was important to drag Ghomara into the stor-age room as quickly as possible. But the Moroccan was heavy, so it took quite a bit of effort to pull him through the door, and 47 felt a sense of relief once the chore was over.

The moment the door was closed he took a quick tour through Ghomara's pockets. The effort produced a key card that would get him into the American's suite, as well as the keys needed to operate the lift-equipped van parked in the hotel's garage. The agent toyed with the idea of taking the Moroccan's clothes, but couldn't see any benefit to doing so, especially given the fact that everything would be at least one size too big.

So he used hand towels to bind and gag Ghomara in hopes that he would remain undiscovered until the fol-lowing day.

Finally, after days of preparation, Agent 47 was ready.

The hotel suite consisted of a nicely furnished sitting room, a bedroom, and a bathroom. All decorated with the same beige Oasis-print wallpaper, beautifully framed black-and-white photos of the Sahara, and carefully set tiled floors. The room was equipped with air conditioning, which was set to a chilly 68 degrees, and blowing cold air into the room as the American readied himself for an evening out.

Wayne Bedo could walk, albeit with some difficulty, and was standing in front of the bathroom mirror buttoning his shirt when he heard a knock, followed by a familiar double-click as the door to his suite opened and closed.

"Nathan?" the American inquired. "Is that you?"

"No," Agent 47 replied from the entryway. "Mr. Ghomara is ill, so they sent me to replace him. May I come in?"

Bedo swore, dropped into the wheelchair, and propelled it out into the sitting room, where a tall man in a red fez stood waiting.

"My name is Kufa," the assassin lied solemnly. "Can I help with your shoes and socks?"

Bedo knew better than to trust strangers, but the man with the pencil-thin mustache was obviously acquainted with Ghomara, and in possession of the access card. That, plus the immediate offer to provide Bedo with some much-needed assistance, served to put the American's fears to rest.

"Yes," he replied. "They're in the bedroom closet."

It took the better part of an hour to get the rest of Bedo's clothes on, strap the American into his wheelchair, and push him out into the hallway. And that's where they were when Bedo ordered 47 to stop.

"My mask is in the bedroom closet," he said flatly. "Go get it."

So the assassin reentered the hotel room and went to the closet, where a Bacchus mask—complete with a wreath of stylized grapes—was waiting on the top shelf. Agent 47 was struck by the extent to which the heavily furrowed brow, the big staring eyes, and the prominent teeth resembled Bedo's actual appearance.

He returned to the hallway, after which it was a relatively simple matter to take the American down into the underground garage, load him into the lift-equipped van, and drive the vehicle out of the hotel. But due to the usual heavy traffic, it took a full forty-five minutes to complete the journey from the Oasis Hotel to the Al-Fulani Orphanage, where staff members helped unload their wheelchair-bound guest. And being familiar with the American by that time, the security guards waved both men inside, without so much as a glance at Bedo's ID card.

There was a loud *beep* as both the wheelchair and a pair of Silverballers rolled through the metal detector, but that was to be expected, given all the metal in the conveyance. So the two men were allowed to proceed without further inspection.

A valet drove the van away as 47 pushed the wheelchair into a large reception area. Formal stairs led up to the second floor, the walls were covered with red wallpaper, and a table loaded with drinks and appetizers had been set up at the very center of the entry hall. The setting was more appropriate to a bordello than an orphanage. And a bordello it was.

However, judging from the heavily made-up, scantily clad boys and girls who came forward to greet the American, this wasn't just any house of ill repute, but one designed to appeal to a clientele of pedophiles from all over the world, most of whom were wearing masks, lest they be recognized.

Bedo welcomed two little girls onto his lap as the assassin scanned the room. Having penetrated the orphanage, his plan was to take Bedo into the men's room, fiber-wire him, and park him on a commode. With that accomplished, he would wait for Al-Fulani and ambush him as he approached a urinal. Having shot the Moroccan full of sedatives, 47 would belt him into Bedo's wheelchair. Bodyguards, if any, would be invited into the restroom, and shot with the silencer-equipped Silverballers smuggled in along with the chair.

At that point, with the Bacchus mask covering Al-Fulani's face, it would be relatively easy to take the unconscious businessman out through security, load him into the van, and drive him into the countryside.

But if he and Bedo disappeared into the restroom for too long, it might draw attention. So he wanted to make sure Al-Fulani was present. He felt sure he would be able to recognize the Moroccan even if he were wearing a mask—thanks to the deferential manner in which the staff would interact with him. But there was no sign of the man.

Not yet, anyway.

So 47 was forced to push Bedo into what once had been a ballroom, as the so-called "guests" were invited to watch a "talent show." The walls were covered with mirrors that would multiply the images of whatever took place, and thereby intensify it. A lighting grid dangled above the low, circular platform at the center of the room, which served as a stage. Guests were invited to choose seats around the circumference of the platform, leaving two aisles via which the preteen performers could come and go.

Agent 47 felt his stomach lurch at the sight. The setup was reminiscent of the asylum's gymnasium, and he recalled the performances that had been held there. Rather than perform sex with adults, however, as the orphanage's children were clearly expected to do, the assassin and his clone brothers had been forced into brutal fights.

As the audience began to applaud, and a dozen half-naked boys and girls were sent out to engage in a highly sexualized parody of a beauty contest, the assassin found himself reliving a very different performance that took place many years before.

It was winter. The asylum's heating system had never been that good, and the air inside the gymnasium was cold. So much so that the boy named 47 could see his breath as he followed his brothers through double doors and out onto the worn hardwood floor.

Once they had lined up in front of the boxing ring, the boys were introduced to an audience that consisted of Dr. Otto Wolfgang Ort-Meyer's friends and associates. Ort-Meyer was the man who—along with four former legionnaires—was responsible for having created the clones. But even though the boys shared the same DNA, experience had exerted a profound impact on personality, granting each brother a decidedly different identity.

The visitors, some two dozen in all, wore ski parkas, expensive overcoats, and in some cases, furs. They were seated on padded bleachers, and each was equipped with a thermos filled with coffee, tea, or hot buttered rum. They clapped as each boy was introduced, took a step forward, and stood with his chest out and shoulders back while statistics regarding his past fights were read out loud. Each round of applause was followed by a rustle of activity as members of the audience placed bets on the various bouts.

47's record was well above average, and he was rewarded with more applause than most.

Yet that was nothing compared to the standing ovation reserved for number 6. Not only was he the asylum's most accomplished kickboxer, but 47's personal nemesis. No matter what the boy did to avoid notice, 6 consistently sought him out, called him names like "my little bitch," and constantly taunted him. Which was why 47, who was slated to battle 6 during the third round, felt a persistent emptiness in the pit of his stomach.

Once 6 had been introduced and collected his applause, he turned to wink at 47, as if to say, "Here it comes!" before taking a step back into line.

Some of the visitors laughed when they saw that, and the betting was brisk as they put even more money on 6.

The final introductions were made. Then, once the process was complete, the boys were ordered to sit on the cold metal chairs that lined one side of the elevated boxing arena.

The ring measured 20×20 feet square, stood three feet off the floor, and was equipped with an inch of canvas-covered padding. *Stained* canvas, because it was difficult to get the blood out of the material, no matter how hard the boys scrubbed. There were four posts, each of which stood a little more than four feet high, to which the side ropes had been secured.

Number 47 hated the ring—and more than that, he was afraid of it—but knew better than to let his emotions show. Fear equated to weakness within the closed society he lived in, and weakness invited attack. If not from 6, then from one of his toadies or a wannabe. So all he could do was sit there and shiver, as the headmaster gave the first two combatants their instructions, then left the ring.

As the name would suggest, kickboxing incorporated both the hand-thrown blows typical of boxing, along with the power kicks, knee strikes, and leg sweeps common to Asian martial arts. Which, to Ort-Meyer's way of thinking, meant kickboxing was the perfect form of unarmed combat for the clone-soldiers of the future to master. Each round of the competition would be supervised by the headmaster, Lazlow. He was a big man, one of the reasons the boys feared him and always did what they were told. Lazlow wore his hair in a comb-over that failed to conceal a large bald spot, and he stared out at the world through a pair of Coke-bottle-thick glasses.

Round one—which was intended as little more than an appetizer—ended quickly as Number 21 threw three rapid-fire volleys of head blows, spun, and delivered a reverse kick to 9's solar plexus. Then, as the boy known as "Niner" struggled to recover, 21 hammered the youngster to the floor.

Round two was a bit more entertaining, as the combatants traveled the length and breadth of the ring before 32 finally managed to run a younger boy into a post, thereby knocking his opponent unconscious.

That brought up round three as what felt like an ounce of liquid lead trickled into the pit of 47's stomach and continued to lay there as he scrambled into the ring. Lazlow's expression said that he already knew who was going to win the third round as he checked to make sure both boys had their protective mouthpieces, cups, and hand wraps.

"All right," the headmaster said, as 6 danced around the ring. "Don't kill each other." And with that admonition, he was gone.

47 had a plan—a fantasy, really—in which he would find a way to beat 6's defenses down and kick the other boy in the head. But that's all it was—a fantasy. Which quickly became apparent when the fight began. Even though both boys were made of the same genetic stuff, it was as if 6 had been imbued with an extra something that gave the bully a distinct advantage.

While 47 attempted to put Number 6 on the defense with a series of body blows, the other boy was able to reach around and grab him behind the neck, delivering a series of knee strikes to the groin.

"Take *that*, bitch," 6 said, "and *that*, and *that*, and *that*!"

He was going to lose, that much was certain, so 47 did the only thing he logically could. And that was to take just enough punishment to make the fight look convincing, take a fall, and walk away with the fewest number of injuries possible.

But 6 seemed determined to polish his image as the toughest student in the school. So rather than put his opponent down immediately, he pushed 47 away, and subjected him to a succession of front kicks, side kicks, and a fancy roundhouse that landed 47 on his back. A blow so hard, and so well delivered, it left 47 gasping for air.

That brought Ort-Meyer and his associates to their feet as 6 accepted a loud round of applause and grinned from ear to ear.

It took the combined efforts of Lazlow and another staff member to remove 47 from the blood-splattered ring, and load the injured youngster onto a squeaky gurney that carried him to the infirmary. It was there, while recovering from the beating, that 47 made a fateful decision.

After months of being victimized, the boy had arrived at the point where he was willing to do whatever was necessary to end the abuse. No matter what that entailed.

The decision produced both a sense of determination and a feeling of freedom as 47 left the infirmary and returned to the long, narrow dormitory he shared with eleven other boys. A pile of human feces had been left on his pillow, and there was no need to read the note to know which one of his peers had placed it there.

"Hey, shit head!" 6 said, as he and his toadies filtered into the area. "Oops! What's that? It looks like the turd fairy left you a present!"

That produced gales of laughter as the other boys left and went to dinner.

But even if 47 wasn't the fastest boy in the dorm, he was among the smartest, and he began to formulate a plan. From his training he knew how dangerous habits could be. And Number 6 had habits. One of which was to get up at roughly 3:00 a.m. every morning and take a pee before returning to bed.

With that opportunity in mind, 47 spent the next two days making careful preparations.

At the end of the second day he waited until everyone else had gone to sleep, got up long enough to get dressed, and returned to bed. At that point he set his mental alarm clock for 2:30, but was so amped up that he couldn't sleep, and was still awake when Number 6 padded by at 2:53.

That was the moment when the youngster slipped out from between the blankets, swung his still-bare feet onto the floor, and padded silently down the hall as he followed his enemy in the lavatory. Number 47 knew that one mistake, one errant sound, would be sufficient to alert the bully and cause him to glance back. And if that occurred, an even worse beating would come his way.

Adrenaline flooded his body, and his heart beat like a trip-hammer as he tiptoed into the dimly lit bathroom. And that's where 6 was, directing a powerful stream into one of the urinals, as the loop fell over his head.

Number 6 was fast, but he was sleepy, and his first instinct was to try to tuck his penis away. So his hands didn't come up until the ligature had already begun to constrict at his throat. The homemade garrote consisted of a length of cord from a window sash, affixed to two four-inch lengths of wood, both of which had been surreptitiously removed from one of the custodian's brooms.

Urine sprayed left and right as 47 pulled the handles in opposite directions, and the two of them performed a slow pirouette as the struggle continued. They turned toward the long row of sinks on the other side of the room. Suddenly the attacker could see both himself and his victim in the big wall mirror. Because the boys were identical in appearance, it appeared as though 47 were strangling himself. At that moment, he knew why 6 liked to brutalize people. It was all about control. He discovered how addictive such power could be as 6 made gargling noises and attempted to stomp 47's bare toes.

Then the bully's eyes began to bulge, his lips turned blue, and a long, drawn-out, farting sound was heard as he soiled himself. That was when 47 expected to feel a sense of regret. But there was nothing other than a feeling of satisfaction as all life departed the other youngster's body.

Number 47 wanted to release the garrote at that point, not out of a sense of revulsion, but to speed his escape. Especially since some other boy could enter the lavatory at any time and discover the grisly scene. But 47 knew that the only thing worse than a dead enemy was one who came back to life, filled with a burning desire for revenge. So in spite of the stench, the young assassin continued to pull the wooden handles in opposite directions, and counted to sixty.

Finally, confident that Number 6 was truly dead, 47 let go.

Then, in keeping with a boyish impulse to send a message to his clone brothers, he wrestled 6 into one of the stalls. The body was limp—a dead weight—so it was difficult to push the head into a toilet and make sure it remained there. But that's what the newly minted killer was determined to do.

Finally that chore was accomplished, and it was time to return to the dorm. There he gathered up two pairs of socks, plus his boots, and a heavily loaded daypack.

After having taken one last look around, Number 47 slipped out of the room.

A flight of stairs led down into the front hall, where Mrs. Dorvak was asleep behind the big desk, her head back, hands clasped over her protuberant belly. Number 47 smiled thinly as he tiptoed past. Maybe, if everything went especially well, Lazlow would fire the old cow for sleeping on duty!

Once in the hall beyond, he had to pause and pull on socks and boots before following a corridor to the side entrance. The much-abused door normally produced a horrible screeching sound whenever someone went to open it. But thanks to the grease lavished on its hinges the previous day, the door opened silently, and a blast of frigid air invaded the hallway.

But that was the easy part, 47 knew, because the real threat was patrolling the grounds outside, and his name was Bruno. The exact nature of the dog's ancestry was unknown, although he was huge and resembled a mastiff. A bad-tempered mastiff that prowled the asylum's grounds at night to keep intruders out, and to keep the boys in. Which Bruno managed to do with great efficiency. As far as 47 could remember, there had been only one escape attempt. It had concluded in a cacophony of horrible screams followed by a brief memorial service two days later.

So 47 had reason to be frightened as he left the protection of the asylum building and made straight for the pump house. That was where he had stashed a bow he had stolen from the gym—along with a single steel-tipped arrow. Dry snowflakes fell all around him, the air was bitterly cold, and his boots made a crunching sound as the ice-crusted snow gave under his weight.

Had Bruno heard him? Or caught his scent? There was no way to know, because everyone knew that Bruno's hunts were silent, until his jaws closed on something, and *it* began to squeal.

Of course, since he didn't want to attract any attention, that was good—or it could be, provided that 47 was able to pull the weapon out from under the pump house in one smooth motion, string the bow with cold fingers, bring the modified target arrow up into the proper position, pull the string all the way back, and let loose before Bruno could close with him.

After what seemed like hours of crossing the open ground, 47 skidded to a halt, fell to his knees in the snow, and stuck his right hand in under the dimly lit pump house. There was a brief moment of joy as his cold fingers closed around the arrow, but it was quickly followed by a sense of despair as he felt for the bow, and realized that it wasn't there! Most likely the groundskeeper or a maintenance worker had come across the weapon while performing some chore, missed the arrow during the process, and returned the bow to the sports equipment room.

It was a horrible break, but there was no time to think about that as 47 heard a deep growl and turned to confront the oncoming dog.

The brute was airborne by that time, so all the twelve-year-old could do was throw up his arms in a futile effort to protect himself while he waited to die.

But the arrow was clutched in his left hand, its knife-sharp tip pointed outward, and as Bruno's weight came down on it, the dog's own momentum inadvertently pushed the other end of the shaft into the frozen ground! There was a pitiful yelp as the improvised point penetrated the mastiff's skin, punched all the way through his heart, and emerged between his shoulder blades.

Number 47 took the full brunt of Bruno's weight, and produced a grunt as all of the air was forced out of his lungs. It took him a minute to recover, but finally, after gasping like a just-landed fish, the youngster managed to suck some oxygen. It was only then, as he battled to push Bruno off his torso, that 47 realized the dog was, indeed, dead.

The boy was too scared, and too cold, to appreciate the full extent of his good fortune, but there would be time later to marvel at how lucky he had been. Or *was* it luck? Because even though the bow was missing, the arrow had been wielded by 47's hand, which had made the "good luck" possible.

He shook his head to clear his mind of such thoughts. All 47 wanted to do now was turn and make a run for the metal fence that encircled the property.

It rattled as he leaped and his boots hit the mesh two feet off the ground. The boy's breath came in short gasps as he began to climb. Less than a minute later he was over the top, dropping to the ground below, and jogging along a snow-covered access road, then onto the main road. There weren't very many streetlights, but those there were wore halos, and led the way toward the highway, where he could hitch a ride to the city of Brasov.

The youngster's plans didn't extend much beyond that, although he knew Headmaster Lazlow would be furious and that all sorts of people would be out looking for him. So once in the city, it would be important to find additional transportation, and put as much distance as he could between himself and the asylum.

Yet like his clone brothers, 47 had never been allowed to venture outside of the asylum grounds, so after flagging down a passing motorist, and spinning her a lie about going to visit his sick grandmother, he quickly found himself in what amounted to an alien world. She took him into the city, where he asked to be dropped off.

Brasov had begun to stir by then. It was an ancient city, built on land that had been occupied since the Bronze Age, most recently by the Germans and the Soviets, and had long been regarded as Transylvania's gateway to the south and east.

He had been taught the city's origins in the course of his studies, and 47 could feel a deeply rooted connection with the past in the red-roofed merchant houses that surrounded Council Square and the tall watchtower located at the center of it. His boots left shallow impressions in the snow as lights came on in buildings around the perimeter of the square and the business day began.

There were all sorts of buildings off the main square, as well as store windows filled with things he had never seen before, all requiring money the runaway didn't have. Which was why 47 asked a passerby for directions, made his way to the local bus depot, and was busy trying to figure out a way to sneak on to a sleek-looking coach, when a heavy hand fell on his shoulder.

The boy struggled, but to no avail, as Headmaster Lazlow frog-marched him out of the depot and onto the busy street beyond. At that point the murderer-escapee fully expected to be turned over to the authorities. Or immediately taken back to the asylum for corporeal punishment.

But to the youngster's everlasting surprise, Lazlow led him down the street and into a busy restaurant. Once they were seated the headmaster ordered hot drinks and an enormous breakfast, which the two of them shared.

Then, as 47 went to work on a big mug of steaming cocoa, peering expectantly at his captor, Lazlow did something the boy had never seen before.

He smiled.

"Congratulations, son," the headmaster said warmly, glancing around to make certain no one was near. "That was your first kill—and it won't be your last! The problem with Number 6 was that he *enjoyed* hurting people, a flaw that ultimately would have limited his usefulness. Because pleasure skews judgment. So you did us a favor, freed yourself from tyranny, and proved what you can do. I'm proud of you, and so—for that matter—is Dr. Ort-Meyer."

"But from this point forward," he added, his expression turning grim, "you are not to kill without permission. Is that understood?"

Number 47, his eyes wide with wonder, nodded his head.

"Good," Lazlow said contentedly. "Now, have some waffles."

And, looking back over the intervening years, breakfast had been the most important meal of the day ever since.

A man dressed in a Nike sports outfit blew a whistle, which brought Agent 47 back to the present, and sent a team of mostly naked preteens tumbling across the floor. Though his face was hidden, Bedo seemed utterly enthralled, as were the other pedophiles seated around the low-rise stage, but the assassin was looking elsewhere.

While he had been reliving his youth, Marla Norton had slipped into the room, and was positioned on the far side of the platform. Agent 47 silently cursed himself for allowing his attention to drift.

The *Puissance Treize* agent wasn't alone. Two men, both armed with AK-47s, had taken up positions immediately behind her.

Judging from the manner in which the young woman was scanning the crowd, she was looking for someone. And there was very little doubt as to who that person might be.

The Silverballers were within easy reach, but 47 didn't want to shoot his way out of the building unless he was forced to do so, which meant he would have to rely on his disguise for protection. Thus, while the children performed handstands and made awkward tumbling runs, the assassin watched Marla out of the corner of his eye.

Then, as her gaze slid across him, 47 felt a tremendous sense of relief. The Kufa disguise had held!

For the moment, anyway.

Agent 47 felt his pulse quicken. If Marla was present—was Al-Fulani nearby? Waiting outside, perhaps? Ready to enter, once he got the all clear? That was the assassin's hope, but it wasn't to be. After a few more moments, Marla wrinkled her nose in what might have been an expression of disgust, and left the room. The security agents followed.

Almost immediately thereafter he heard the front

door open and shut, indicating that they had departed. Yet their very presence told him that they suspected he might be there. Knowing his target wasn't likely to appear, Agent 47 felt a keen sense of disappointment. But he was forced to suppress the emotion so he could focus his attention on extricating himself from the orphanage.

The last performance was coming to a conclusion by then, and Al-Fulani's customers were busy choosing which performers they wanted to take upstairs, when the assassin surreptitiously stabbed Bedo in the arm. The American produced a startled yelp, started to say something, then slumped forward as the sedative kicked in.

Staff members rushed to help—but 47 was quick to shoo them away.

"Don't worry," he assured them. "It happens all the time. I'll take Mr. Bedo back to his hotel and put him to bed. He'll be as good as new in the morning."

Having no reason to doubt the man in the red fez, and being understandably happy to rid themselves of what could have been a problem, the orphanage's staff hurried to escort the duo out through security, and load the unconscious Bedo into the van. It was dark by then, but Agent 47 discovered that traffic was a little bit lighter than before, as he drove the American back to the Oasis Hotel.

The question—and a rather important one—was whether Mr. Ghomara had been discovered, or was still lying in the locked linen room. Having circled the hotel twice without detecting any sort of police presence, Agent 47 concluded that no alarm had been raised. And since neither Ghomara nor Bedo had seen him without the Kufa disguise, it didn't matter what they told the police the following morning.

Not that Bedo was likely to be all that forthcoming, given his visits to the orphanage or his true reason for visiting Fez.

The assassin entered the garage without incident, chose one of the more remote parking spots, and shut the engine down. Thanks to the power lift it was possible to unload the wheelchair, move Bedo into an elevator, and return the American to his room without any assistance. Then, having removed the Silverballers from the chair's cargo pocket, he returned both weapons to their holsters.

Bedo's head came up at that point. The mask had fallen off.

"Where am I?" the American demanded groggily, as he blinked his eyes. "What happened?"

Agent 47 thought about his plan to kill Bedo and replace him with a heavily sedated Al-Fulani. The American had no idea how lucky he was. "You're in your hotel room," the man in the red fez answered evenly. "Which is all you need to know." And with that, the assassin was gone.

NINE

The acacia tree stood like a lonely sentinel on the vast windswept savannah, its large umbrella-shaped canopy of gnarled branches, small leaves, and needle-sharp thorns throwing a pool of welcome shade onto the bone-dry ground where a group of one hundred and twenty-three Dinka refugees had stopped to rest.

They had dark black skin, almond-shaped eyes, finely wrought features, and wore brightly patterned robes of red, blue, and gold. Many had traditional tribal scars on their foreheads. Some had children, who were so malnourished that they simply sat on their mother's laps, too tired to brush the flies off their eyelids. The group had a small flock of goats that hadn't been eaten because of the milk they gave. But except for the treadle-powered sewing machine that one elderly gentleman and his family had brought along, the group had very few possessions.

The Dinkas were just a few of the thousands of black Africans who had been forced to flee southwestern Sudan by the bloodthirsty Janjaweed militia. Though naturally tall and slim, many members of the group were emaciated due to a lack of nutrition and the intestinal diseases that eternally plagued them. Hope, such as it was, lay across the border in Chad, where the refugees might be able to find shelter in a European-run camp.

But first the Dinkas would have to reach Chad before the ruthless, camel-riding militia members could catch up with them. If that happened, the men would be murdered, the women would be raped, and the children would be killed or left to die. Which was why Joseph Garang, the group's unofficial leader, was squinting into the rising sun. If trouble found the group, it would arrive from the east, where the Arab-dominated government held sway.

Garang was a slender man, with richly black skin and intelligent brown eyes. Though only twenty-seven years of age, he looked older, and was considered to be an elder because so many of the real elders had been killed. Many of the Dinkas were Christians, and had just begun to sing one of their favorite hymns when Garang spotted a momentary flash of light low on the eastern horizon.

He stood, stared across the flat savannah, and wished he had a pair of binoculars. Had the momentary glint been produced by sunlight reflecting off a shard of broken glass? Or something more sinister? There was no way to be certain, but this was North Africa, where all who lived fell into two broad categories: The hunters and the hunted. Which meant that anything—even a wink of reflected light—could signal a predator's presence.

So he made his decision.

"*Up!*" Garang commanded sternly, striding through

the group. "Get up and walk. For he who walks, strives, and he who strives shall be rewarded. So saith the Lord."

There was no such passage in the tattered Bible that Garang carried with him, but only ten members of the group could read, and even they took comfort from the possibility that something good would come of their efforts.

Slowly, like reanimated skeletons, the Dinkas stood. And then, without giving the matter any conscious thought, they followed Garang out onto the savannah in exactly the same order as they had arrived. None of the refugees bothered to look back because there was nothing to look back at, except a painful past and the solitary acacia tree.

And the tree, like all of its kind, was content to remain where it was and worship the sun.

Mahamat Dagash lowered the powerful 10×42 HG L DCF Nikon binoculars, and brushed a fly off the bridge of his nose, the only part of his face not concealed by the ten-foot-long strip of white cloth that was wrapped around his head.

The refugees were a long way off, but his eyes were good, and the glasses made them better. So Dagash had seen everything he needed to see, and that knowledge brought a smile to his thin lips. Because there were many wonders of the world, including Toyota Land Cruisers, AK-47 assault rifles, and the fact that even the poorest people have something worth stealing: themselves. Flesh, muscle, and bone that could be put to work, or in the case of the younger ones, sold, sometimes for a great deal of money.

Satisfied that the Dinkas were on the move, and that he would be able to circle around and intercept them before they could reach the border, Dagash was careful to replace the lens caps on the expensive binoculars before pushing himself back off the ridge where he lay. Then, comfortable in the certainty that he wouldn't be seen, the Tuareg made his way down the reverse side of the dune using a series of well-timed leaps.

Two battered 4×4s and six robed men waited below. All were heavily armed, and with good reason. Even though the refugees lived at the very bottom of the North African food chain, Dagash and his slavers were only a few rungs higher up, and vulnerable to the government-supported Janjaweed, a group that was not only extremely jealous of their God-given right to kill, torture, and rape the peoples of the south, but could call upon helicopters and planes to attack anyone foolish enough to compete with them.

Which meant that as the Toyotas roared back to life and the sun continued to arc across the sky, there was no peace, or prospect of peace, except for that which was granted to the dead.

It had been a long hard day, but Garang and the refugees had covered nearly ten miles of barren ground since leaving the acacia tree's shade, and taken refuge at the foot of a rocky outcropping that promised to shelter them from the wind. There was a dry riverbed nearby, where by dint of considerable digging, the men had been able to coax a puddle of muddy water out of the reluctant ground. Small as it was, that was a blessing, as were the tiny fires the women had built and the vast wealth of stars that lay like grains of sand on the night sky.

Dinner consisted of lentil soup followed by cups of cinnamon tea, neither of which had much substance, but served to quell the worst of the hunger pangs and quiet the children. The little ones would fall asleep soon, the adults would talk for a while, and then they, too, would go to sleep.

Such were Garang's thoughts as he sat on a rock and stared up into the night sky. The moment of peace was shattered as engines roared, powerful headlights swept across the rocky ground, and the shooting began.

Judging from their targets, the slavers were only interested in children over the age of four and under the age of fifteen. For them, it was easier to shoot the rest rather than take them prisoner and be forced to feed them.

Garang and some of the other men grouped together and charged the attackers, hoping to overwhelm one of the evil men, and take possession of a gun. But it didn't work. Garang managed to get within five feet of the man who appeared to be the leader, before a burst of bullets cut him down.

By the time the shooting stopped, more than ninety Dinkas had been slaughtered. As soon as all resistance had been overcome, the more comely women were raped, often in front of their children, and then put to death.

With that out of the way, all the slavers had to do was corral the sobbing children and march them off to the town of Oum-Chalouba across the border in Chad.

Where, Allah willing, Dagash would be able to eat a decent meal and take a bath.

The thought cheered him as the Land Cruiser's right front tire rolled over one of the dead bodies. Life was good.

TEN

.

Several more days of surveillance from the apartment across the street from the orphanage led to the conclusion that Marla was keeping Al-Fulani away from the place. So Agent 47 had assumed a new persona and taken up residence in the ultramodern *Hôtel de Nouvelle Vague* located only two blocks from the Moroccan's mansion.

The "New Wave Hotel" was a small but exclusive hostelry that normally catered to young, well-heeled Europeans, and was currently jam-packed with musicians of many nationalities who were in Fez to perform in the week-long *Festival de la Musique* slated to begin the following evening. An event of special interest to the assassin because Al-Fulani was sponsoring it, as just one of many good deeds that kept local authorities happy and the orphanage in business.

So there the "record producer" was, lying in a chaise longue and soaking up the warm Moroccan sun when his phone began to beep. The assassin flipped the device open and brought it to his ear.

"Yeah? Talk to me."

Hundreds of miles away, deep within the *Jean Danjou*'s hull, Diana looked up at one of the twenty-four monitors arrayed around her. The shot was being relayed to her from a spy sat, and, thanks to lots of magnification, she could see 47 and the scantily clad young people sprawled all around him. Groupies, for the most part, who, having followed their favorite bands to Fez, were in need of a place to stay. Having been taken in by a free-spending producer known as "The Jammer," they had unwittingly become an important part of 47's cover.

"You look comfortable," Diana commented. "*Too* comfortable for someone who is supposed to be at work."

The assassin said, "Screw you," and directed a one-fingered salute up at the sky. If any of the young things sunbathing all around the agent thought that was strange, they gave no sign of it.

Diana chuckled.

"Sorry to bother you, 47, but it looks like you'll have to postpone the exercise scheduled for tomorrow, in order to deal with something more urgent."

The operative swore silently. Al-Fulani was scheduled to be present as the event got under way the next evening. He planned to kill the businessman's bodyguards as the Moroccan left the stage, hustle Al-Fulani into a stolen limo, and drive him out into the countryside. A workable plan with a decent chance of success.

"Whatever it is, it can wait," the assassin said evenly. "Opportunities like this one don't come along every day."

"No," Diana replied patiently, "they don't. And we're

sorry, but there won't be much point to snatching Al-Fulani if he's dead. Which will almost certainly be the case if the Otero brothers come after him."

Agent 47 took a sip of iced tea as one of his well-endowed guests stood long enough to drop her thong. Then, having straddled a long-haired musician, she began to lick his face.

"The Otero brothers?" the assassin inquired mildly. "Who are they? A new boy band?"

"No," Diana replied firmly. "They work for the Tumaco cartel in Colombia. They specialize in killing judges, government officials, and anyone else who gets in the organization's way. And based on the latest intelligence, it looks like they have orders to hit Al-Fulani. It seems the cartel wants a cut of the money the Moroccan makes by smuggling drugs into Europe, and he refused. That's where the Otero brothers come in."

The assassin felt a rising sense of frustration. No matter how hard he tried to move this assignment forward, it always seemed to slip back. Now, instead of abducting Al-Fulani as planned, The Agency wanted him to *protect* the miserable bastard!

But Diana was right. It would be pretty hard to pry information out of a dead man. And if the Oteros showed up in the middle of the snatch, then everything would go straight to hell. The risk factor had just ratcheted up to an eleven.

"So how's the internal audit going?" the agent inquired, as the couple to his right began to make noisy love.

"They haven't found anything so far," Diana admitted. "Which makes your initiative that much more important. Check your inbox. You'll find everything we have on the Oteros waiting there. Including their love affair with explosives. Bombs big enough to bring down entire buildings, blow up airplanes, and demolish bridges."

Someone else might have interpreted that particular approach as demonic overkill, given the amount of collateral damage that would be involved. But 47 saw the strategy for what it was. After all, why sneak into a well-protected casino and inject the owner with an overdose of insulin, if you can just hire some poor slob to drive a truck loaded with explosives into the parking lot underneath the building? And detonate the load from a hotel room blocks—perhaps even miles—away.

But that sort of thing wasn't tolerated everywhere. Sometimes the subtle approach was necessary. Which was why individuals like 47 were so sought after.

The woman was picking up the pace, her head was thrown back, and she was making high-pitched whining noises as her breasts flopped up and down and her friends looked on.

"I'll look forward to meeting the Oteros," the agent said dryly. "Is there anything else?"

"Yes," Diana said. "There are four brothers—and each one of them is worth $250,000."

"Then there's a client other than ourselves?"

"Yes," the controller replied. "A certain agency within the American government would *love* to see the Tumaco cartel fail. And they don't like the Oteros, either."

"Well, there isn't a whole lot of time, but I'll do what I can," he promised.

"Mr. Nu will be pleased," Diana said evenly. "And one other thing . . . "

Agent 47 looked skyward.

"Yes?"

"Tell the young woman to your right that she's getting a sunburn."

There was only one large public square within the city of Fez; that was where most of the main events involved in the music festival were scheduled to be held. And as Agent 47 exited a cab deep within the area known as *Fes El Bali,* he saw that preparations were nearing completion. The streets that emptied into the square had been blocked with police barricades, a huge stage had been set up at one end of the plaza, and the area was thick with workmen.

Having paid his fare, the assassin made a beeline for the closest security checkpoint. He wasn't carrying any weapons other than a garrote, and was relying on the ID card that dangled from his neck to get him in.

The queue continued to move ahead in fits and starts as a policeman examined the cards proffered by the people who had lined up in front of the operative. Then came the moment of truth as 47 stepped forward.

The ID was the rightful property of British folk singer Peter Samo, who was currently passed out on Agent 47's couch. It had been altered by the simple expedient of pasting a picture of the Jammer persona over the photo of a petulant Samo. It was an amateurish job by most standards, but the panoply of henna tattoos that covered the Jammer's hairless skull, face, neck, and bare arms proved such a distraction that the cop barely glanced at the card before waving him through.

Which, to 47's way of thinking, was a clear indication that if the Otero brothers wanted to sneak into the square, they certainly could. And quite possibly had, since the setup phase of the festival was the perfect time to plant a bomb for detonation the following evening. The easiest way to prolong Al-Fulani's life, at least for the moment, would be to remove the device. Or, if the bomb was too complex for the agent to handle, an anonymous call to the police would take care of the matter as well. Once that problem was out of the way, the assassin could turn his attention to finding the Colombians. A necessity if he were to prevent the Oteros from activating some sort of backup plan.

The problem was that there were literally hundreds of places to conceal one or more bombs on, under, or in the vicinity of the stage. Which meant there was lots of work to do. By far the easiest and most effective place to plant explosives would be directly under the performance platform, so the assassin resolved to begin his inspection there.

It was dark under the stage, and a maze of crisscrossed supports made it difficult to move around. But thanks to a penlight and his willingness to crawl through small spaces, 47 was able to thoroughly inspect the area under the platform. Half an hour later, without having found a bomb or any signs of suspicious activity, he was forced to brush off his clothes and return to the stage, where a team of electricians was working on the sound system.

Having checked to ensure that none of the workmen looked anything like the Otero brothers, 47 began to examine anything that might contain—or be—a bomb. He was stopped and questioned about his activities by a suspicious security guard, but the assassin explained that he was looking for his lost cell phone. That, plus a look at the Jammer's fake ID, was sufficient to put the guard's concerns to rest.

Just as 47 was about to give up and leave the platform, a couple of newcomers appeared. And unlike all of the other men in the area, they were wearing stylish sports coats on a very warm day. Why? *Because they're armed, that's why*—a problem he could relate to. Yet they weren't the Oteros, so who were they? Plainclothes police? Goons hired to protect the Oteros? Bodyguards for some mullah or another?

Then he had his answer, as a demurely dressed Marla Norton mounted the platform, closely followed by more men wearing sports coats. The assassin felt a jolt of adrenaline enter his bloodstream. Was Al-Fulani about to make an early appearance? Or had his security team simply come to check out the situation? Planning what to do if the shit hit the fan?

The second possibility seemed the more likely of the two, and as they moved closer, 47 went to one knee next to a row of spotlights, and pretended to inspect them.

Marla glanced at the tattooed man, wondered why anyone would do such a thing to his body, and turned to look out over the square.

If there were a worse situation to put her protector in, the *Puissance Treize* agent couldn't imagine what it would be. Buildings stood shoulder to shoulder all around the square, and any of them could provide cover to someone with a rifle or a rocket-propelled grenade launcher.

Then, as if that wasn't bloody well bad enough, there was the crowd to consider. It would be easy for an assassin like 47 to use the mob for cover, get in close, and bag Al-Fulani from twenty feet away. Or—given the fact that other dignitaries would be onstage—there was always the chance that somebody would try to eliminate one of *them* by lobbing a grenade onto the platform. Then there was the possibility of a suicide bomber, a riot triggered by religious fundamentalists, or a falling light, for God's sake. And those were only some of the possibilities.

Which was why the agent had done her best to talk her employer out of the appearance, only to be overruled. And why? Because Al-Fulani enjoyed the role of benefactor, and didn't want to miss out on his moment in the spotlight even if attending the event involved unnecessary risk. So she would have her people search the area for explosives prior to the opening ceremonies, dress her client in body armor, and station unsuspecting bullet catchers around the businessman in the hope that any incoming projectiles would hit one of them, rather than Al-Fulani.

Yet ultimately Marla knew that Al-Fulani's fate—and to a great extent hers—would depend on a great deal of luck, and the man called 47. Based on information that the *Puissance Treize* had given Al-Fulani, the assassin was still in Fez and eager to get his hands on the Moroccan. The thought sent a chill down Marla's spine as she turned to leave the stage.

It was late afternoon, and the sun had disappeared, leaving a bloody smear on the western horizon as Agent 47 guided the blue BMW motorcycle through heavy traffic. In contrast to the sleek chopped hog the Grim Reaper had been riding at the moment of his death, the

Beemer had a bulbous gas tank, controls that forced the
assassin to ride as if he were in a race, and a high-tech
aesthetic he liked. The only problem was that, even
though the bike was capable of going well over a hundred miles per hour, the jam-packed streets kept him
down to no more than twenty.

Stealing the BMW had been as easy as taking a
leather jacket that belonged to one of his house guests.
There were all sorts of useful things in the pockets, including two prophylactics, a plastic bag containing a
mysterious white powder, and the bike's ignition key.
The matching helmet and the guitar case slung across
his back were courtesy of the same musician. And because the jacket was long enough to conceal the short-
slide Silverballer, it served that purpose as well.

Most of the traffic consisted of smoke-spewing
trucks, buses, and dilapidated cars, all of which had
fully operable horns that honked, beeped, and brayed
as traffic continued to inch its way forward. But like the
rest of the scooters and motorcycles, the Beemer was
free to weave in and out of traffic. A potentially fatal
game were someone to open a car door unexpectedly,
but preferable to sitting in one place and sucking exhaust fumes.

Finally, having battled traffic for more than twenty
minutes, the BMW passed through one of the city's ancient gates, and was released into the countryside that
stretched beyond. Which, according to intelligence provided by The Agency, was where the Otero brothers
had set up shop.

The question was: *Why?* Especially given that their
target, and the best opportunity to kill him, lay deep
within Fez itself. Not that it mattered, so long as Agent

47 could locate the Colombians and kill them before they could carry out the hit.

Traffic opened up as the assassin left Fez behind. He followed a well-maintained two-lane road through a succession of small villages and into the hills. There, perched on a rise, stood an old Catholic church. It had been desanctified more than a hundred years earlier, and used for a variety of purposes since. The white-washed building seemed to brood over a hillside of weathered headstones, as if waiting for the dead parishioners to arise and worship again. There was very little light by the time he arrived. But what there was served to silhouette the variegated arch at the front of the building and the bell tower to the right of it. And that, according to Diana, was where the Oteros had chosen to stay.

Agent 47 downshifted, which caused the BMW to slow, giving the assassin the opportunity to observe that lights were on within the church. Then it was necessary to open the throttle and guide the bike up over a rise.

Confident that he couldn't be seen from the church at that point, 47 downshifted again, and turned onto a dirt track. The motorcycle's headlamp played across ranks of shadowy olive trees before the assassin turned it off, toed the transmission into neutral, and killed the engine. Having deployed the BMW's kickstand, Agent 47 swung a leg over the bike, and parked the helmet on the seat.

The countryside seemed unnaturally quiet after riding the noisy bike. In fact, there weren't any sounds to be heard, other than the occasional chirp of a cricket, the distant bark of a village dog, and the throaty growl that a heavily laden lorry produced as it made its way up a nearby incline. All of which were pleasant, but the silence also meant that gunshots would be heard if he missed a target and an all-out shooting war began.

Keeping that potential in mind, the assassin drew the short-slide, and took the time required to attach a silencer to it before returning the weapon to its holster. Branches grabbed at him as 47 passed between the trees, but did no damage, as he made his way toward the church. Local night creatures were out and about by that time, and the assassin heard an occasional rustle as other predators went in search of their prey.

The olive trees began to thin after a while, and 47 found himself at the very edge of the grove, which was about thirty feet from a five-foot-high wall, and the church stood beyond. A new sound could be heard by then: the muted but persistent beat of Colombian salsa, punctuated by occasional bursts of raucous laughter.

Noise won't be a problem, 47 mused gratefully.

Agent 47 was just about to cross the open ground that lay between the trees and the wall when he saw a sudden flare of light high in the bell tower, and realized a sentry had been posted there. That was a problem, especially since the moon had risen by then and was casting a ghostly glow onto the church and the area that surrounded it.

So 47 lifted the strap up over his head, lowered the guitar case to the ground, and knelt beside it. The catches opened soundlessly, as did the lid, revealing the Walther WA 2000 nestled within. The weapon was just under thirty-six inches long, which meant that the sniper rifle fit into the guitar case with ten inches to spare, leaving plenty of room for the silencer and extra magazines.

The first six-round clip was already seated, so all the assassin had to do was remove the rifle from a bed of dirty laundry and work the bolt before bringing the finely tuned weapon up to his shoulder. The Schmidt & Bender 2.5–10×56 mm telescopic sight was effective in spite of the low-light situation. Agent 47 inched the highly magnified circle up the white bell tower to the point where the red glow of a cigarette could be seen. It seemed to wink at the assassin as the sentry took a drag.

The heavily silenced rifle coughed and gave the assassin a solid nudge as the 7.62 NATO round left the barrel. The slug struck the sentry right between the eyes, passed through his brain at an upward angle, and blew the top of his head off. Gore splattered the ancient bell, but lacked the force required to ring it, as the dead body collapsed.

No one inside the church took notice, as a portable CD player continued to pump salsa music into the nave, where Pedro and Manuel Otero were drinking tequila and two half-drunk Spanish whores were attempting to dance.

Both brothers had thick black hair, dark brown eyes, and the best smiles money could buy. There was a strong family resemblance, though Pedro had a scar on his forehead, while Manuel was known as *Muchacho bonito* to his friends and associates.

Both women were topless, and their unrestrained breasts swayed to the music, as they stomped their feet in a clumsy imitation of flamenco-style dancing, and began to circle each other. The brothers shouted encouragement, and began to clap in time with the music.

*   *   *

Meanwhile, out in the olive grove, Agent 47 ejected the spent casing, and slipped the brass cylinder into a pocket. The Walther went back into the guitar case, which, if everything went well, would be retrieved on the way out. Then, concerned lest the dead sentry be discovered, the assassin took a run at the wall.

The jump was high enough that it took him cleanly over the top. As soon as his feet made contact with the ground, he dropped into a crouch, drew the Silverballer, and waited to see if a second sentry would reveal himself.

Which he did—but not in the way that the agent expected.

Thanks to a piece of very bad luck, the assassin had dropped into the garden only a few feet from the point where one of the guards had stopped to tie a shoelace. And the sentry must have been a very cool customer, because rather than shout for help, he remained silent. So much so that 47 was completely unaware of the fact that he'd been discovered until he heard a faint whisper of fabric, caught a whiff of cheap cologne, and felt the aluminum flashlight slam into his right forearm.

The pain was excruciating, and his pistol was still in the process of falling when a bony fist came around to connect with the assassin's head. That sent him reeling backward, which was almost a blessing, as it bought 47 some time. Not much, but enough to draw the DOVO with his left hand and flick it open as his shoulder hit the ground.

Certain of victory, the guard jumped onto his victim's chest and brought the flashlight up over his head. But before the smuggler could bring the weapon down, steel flashed in the moonlight.

Agent 47 saw the spray of black blood before he felt the warm liquid spurting from the cut. The sentry looked surprised. His head wobbled and slumped sideways, and the rest of his limp body followed.

The assassin rolled right, came to his feet in one smooth motion, and bent to wipe the DOVO clean. His right forearm wasn't broken, but it hurt like hell, and it would be a while before sensation returned to his hand.

That was when he noticed the guard's baseball hat and put it on, hoping that the piece of headgear might buy him a second or two, should a third sentry happen along.

Agent 47 had just reached down to retrieve the Silverballer when he heard glass shatter and the sound of drunken laughter. The steady *thump, thump, thump* of bass seemed to echo the beating of 47's heart as he made his way over to the building and followed the south wall toward the east. The back entrance was locked, so the assassin took a moment to peer through the ancient keyhole, and liked what he saw.

The church's kitchen appeared to be empty, so 47 was just about to pick the lock, when another sentry rounded the corner. Having caught sight of the ball cap, the man made the natural assumption.

"¡Hey, Jorge, *consigue de neuvo a trabajo! ¿O usted tienen gusto de Pedro para golpear su asno con el pie otra vez?*"

Agent 47 turned, the moonlight fell on his tattooed face, and the guard grunted his alarm. He was in the process of reaching for his Glock when the Silverballer spoke twice. Thanks to the weapon's silencer, the reports were no louder than a baby's cough. The heavy .45 caliber slugs threw the man backward, and dumped him onto the ground.

The assassin took the time necessary to drag the body over into an especially dark shadow before returning to the entrance and attacking the lock, which yielded seconds later. Once inside, he paused for a moment before passing through the kitchen and climbing the stairs beyond. By the time he arrived at a vantage point that allowed him to see into the nave, the entertainment had become quite intimate. Both women were seated astride their clients, both of whom were caught up in the moment, and nearing their respective climaxes.

Until Agent 47 shot Pedro in the head.

The prostitute who was seated on the Colombian's lap uttered a loud scream as her lover's head came apart, and continued to produce a series of short emphatic shrieks as her feet hit the floor and she backed away.

That caused the other woman to dismount as well, leaving Manuel seated on a chair, with his pants down around his ankles. The erection that had been so hard the moment before had already begun to disappear. But if the Colombian was embarrassed by his predicament there was no sign of it as he stared up at the man who stood in the choir loft.

"¿Quienes son usted? ¿Y por qué usted mato a Pedro?" he shouted at the intruder.

Agent 47 stared down the barrel of his weapon.

"No era personal. Mato para el dinero. ¿Donde estás sus otros hermanos?"

Manuel was at a disadvantage and knew it. Not only had he been caught with his pants down, his Beretta lay on a table three feet away. So the chances of grabbing it and getting off a shot were slim to none.

He had another weapon at his disposal, however, and when he brought his arms up as if to surrender, he thrust his right hand out in front of him. The sudden motion caused a spring-loaded mechanism strapped to his right forearm to shoot forward, delivering a double-barreled .45 caliber derringer into the palm of his hand.

It all happened so quickly that the tiny pistol had already been fired, and the fat bullet had already whispered something into 47's left ear by the time the assassin's brain registered a loud *bang*. So the reaction was involuntary, rather than conscious, as the Silverballer fired in response.

Manuel had triggered a second and final shot by that time, but the slug went into the ceiling as both the Colombian and his chair went over backward. The combination produced a loud crash as both women, still shrieking, backed toward the front door.

Agent 47 said, *"¡Parada!"* And they stopped.

It took the better part of a nerve-wracking half hour to lock the prostitutes into a storage room and search the building for explosives. Strangely, given the crime family's reputation for blowing things up, there wasn't so much as a firecracker to be found inside the church. And having been forced to kill Manuel, there was no one left to question. Not until the missing Otero brothers returned.

Which meant all 47 could do was dump the bodies into the cellar, collect the Walther from the olive grove, and position the BMW for a quick getaway. He parked it just inside the main door, where it wouldn't be seen.

Those chores kept the assassin busy for a while, but they were followed by a long stretch of inactivity, and Agent 47 soon began to tire. By the time three hours had passed, it was clear that José and Carlos were on something more substantial than a beer run. Still, having no idea what the brothers were doing, or how long it might take, the assassin was forced not only to stay awake, but to keep his wits about him as well.

He called Diana, who would be monitoring the situation back in Fez, but there was nothing to indicate that the brothers were there, either. Which was a relief, though it brought him no closer to discovering their whereabouts.

So 47 waited, and waited, and when the first blush of dawn appeared in the east he was still waiting. Another call to Diana yielded no useful information. The Agency had no idea where José and Carlos were—or what the brothers were up to.

By now, however, he had to admit to the very real possibility that the Colombians were in Fez, perhaps even planting bombs all around the main plaza, and wouldn't be back until Al-Fulani was dead. Yet there was only one of him, and while The Agency had other assets, none were close enough to intervene prior to the coming ceremony.

Rather than remain in the nave, where his field of vision was limited, 47 took his binoculars, the Walther WA 2000, and a thermos of hot coffee scrounged from the kitchen up into the blood-spattered bell tower. The dead sentry's blood had attracted flies, which were a constant annoyance, but the vantage point was excellent— one that provided a view of the highway that fronted the church, the olive grove he had passed through the night before, and the hills to the east.

The cool breezes that blew down from the north, combined with the opportunity to examine the surrounding terrain, were sufficient to keep the assassin occupied for a while. But shortly after he sat down on the white plastic chair, his eyelids grew heavy, and his mind began to drift.

When he awoke, four minutes later, it was to a sense of fear, and pangs of guilt.

A cup of black coffee helped keep him awake for a while, and he observed the passage of an old man and a flock of bawling goats. But the siren call of the chair and the warmth of the morning sun were too much to resist, and even 47 eventually had to give in to sheer fatigue.

The next time he awoke it was to the sound of a bleating siren.

He was already reaching for his gun as he came to his feet. But the ambulance blew past as it continued on its way toward Fez.

Agent 47 glanced at his watch and realized that while more than three hours had elapsed, the Otero brothers had yet to return. More than ever, he was certain they were in Fez, preparing to assassinate Al-Fulani. The Agency's suits would be pissed off, but such was life, and there wasn't much he could do about it.

And besides, José and Carlos would return to the church sooner or later. Each of them was worth $250,000, which when added to the kills he had already pulled off, would constitute a solid payday.

So Agent 47 went down to scrounge some food from

the kitchen, where he brewed a fresh pot of coffee before returning to his post.

Then, somewhat refreshed, he continued his vigil. Finally, when the shadows cast by the tombstones had grown into long, thin fingers, and the sun was hanging low in the western sky, the Otero brothers returned.

But not in the fashion 47 expected them to. Hundreds of trucks had passed his vantage point during the day, rumbling along the highway, so the fuel tanker was of little interest until the rig began to slow.

It turned onto the pull-through driveway that fronted the church, where it produced a loud *blat* of sound as the driver braked to a stop.

That was the moment when 47 understood why there weren't any bomb-making materials in the church. And why José and Carlos had been gone for so long. They had been sent to buy—or steal—a tanker truck loaded with petrol. Which, when delivered in the proper manner, would have enough explosive power to kill Al-Fulani and everyone else in his vicinity! Unfortunately for the Colombians, the process of acquiring the tanker must have taken longer than expected and left them with barely enough time to carry out the hit.

Had José and Carlos been trying to raise their dead brothers by phone? Most likely, and having failed to do so, they were probably hoping that Pedro and Manuel would come running out. Speed would be of the essence, if they were to enter Fez on time.

But as José stepped on the clutch and threw the big rig into neutral, 47 fired. Though dead-on, insofar as the assassin could tell, the true purpose of the first bullet was to blow the truck's windshield out, thereby exposing the man behind the wheel to a follow-up shot.

And the strategy worked perfectly, because the avalanche of safety glass was still falling when the second 7.62 mm slug struck José square in the face. The Colombian probably was already dead, but it paid to make sure, especially at long range.

The sole surviving Otero reacted instantly. Rather than bail out of the truck and expose himself to fire the way the assassin wanted him to, Carlos threw himself across his dead brother's body and opened the door. That decision saved the Colombian's life as a bullet thumped into the passenger seat.

Then, with a strength born of desperation, Carlos shoved José out onto the gravel driveway. It took some effort to clamber over the gearshift, but the Colombian made it, and was already behind the wheel by the time the inside rearview mirror shattered. Carlos swore bitterly, as he slammed the truck into gear, and put his foot on the accelerator.

Agent 47 frowned as the tanker began to pull away. Was the Colombian simply trying to escape? Or head into Fez and complete the contract? He took a shot at one of the truck's tires, and had the satisfaction of seeing it go flat. But the rig had more tires, plenty of them, and kept right on going as Carlos sounded the horn and bullied his way out onto the two-lane highway.

Plumes of dark blue smoke jetted up out of the tanker's twin stacks, and the engine roared as 47 put a bullet into the silvery fuel tank. But, rather than the massive explosion the assassin was hoping for, there was no visible reaction as the double-hulled safety tank managed to absorb the 7.62 mm round.

So Agent 47 still had to prevent the assassination, and he could score an additional quarter-million, so he threw the rifle into the open guitar case, snapped it closed, and slipped the strap over his head.

Then, rather than descend the ladder normally used to reach the top of the tower, 47 slid down the bell rope into the vestibule below. That caused the bell to toll, and it was still ringing as the assassin entered the nave. He hopped on to the BMW, which was parked just inside the main entrance. He didn't want to waste the time it would take to don the helmet, which clattered as it hit the floor. The engine roared as it came to life, and there was a solid thump as the front wheel made contact with the partially opened door.

Then the way was clear as 47 opened the throttle and stood on the pegs while the BMW flew through the air. The big bike hit the pathway hard, but kept right on going, as the agent skidded onto the driveway and sent a wave of gravel flying toward the wall. There was a momentary screech as the Beemer hit the pavement, followed by a loud roar as the assassin twisted the throttle.

Off in the distance, the fueler vanished into a dip, so 47 put his head down and took up the chase.

He eyed the road ahead, swerved into the left lane in order to pass a heavily loaded flatbed truck, and went back again to avoid a head-on collision with a red sedan. Then he was in the dip—with the wind pressing against his face. By that time the assassin was sorry he had left the helmet behind. But there was nothing he could do but let the tears stream back along both sides of his face and tough it out.

Meanwhile, half a mile up the highway, Carlos Otero was experiencing a similar problem, as a wall of wind pushed in through the shattered windshield. Fortunately both of the truck's front tires were intact, but one of the right-side duals had been punctured. *By a bullet?* Yes, the Colombian thought so. Which meant the tire was tearing itself apart, and the Colombian was forced to grip the huge ivory-colored steering wheel with both hands in order to keep the rig on the road.

That was when Carlos glanced at the outside rearview mirror, saw the motorcycle appear out of the dip behind him, and knew someone was after him. Not the police, who would have converged on the fueler in force, but by a *lobo solitario*, who—for reasons unknown—was determined to stop him.

But what about Pedro and Manuel? Where were they?

Dead, the Colombian concluded soberly, *just like José.*

Carlos downshifted to take some speed off the juggernaut, gave the van in front of him a blast from the air horn, and pulled out to pass. The tanker truck's right flank barely brushed the smaller vehicle, but that alone was enough to send the van flying off the road and into the ditch, as Carlos jerked the wheel to the right.

Agent 47 blew past the wreck as the distance between the BMW and the tanker began to close. It was his intention to pull up alongside, shoot the surviving Otero brother in the head, and let the big rig go wherever it wanted. But that plan was easy for his prey to anticipate.

As 47 pulled out onto the centerline and opened the BMW's throttle, the Colombian countered by swinging left. The trailer came within inches of swatting the bike off the road as a bus appeared up ahead and the assassin was forced to drop back behind the smoke-belching behemoth.

Carlos smiled thinly as the pursuer was forced to eat exhaust, and he took a moment to consider his options.

Originally, back at the church, his only motivation had been to escape what seemed like certain death. But now, as darkness began to fall, another possibility occurred to him.

The music festival would begin soon, and the motor-cyclist was powerless to stop him from entering Fez. He would be even more powerless as they approached the city, and the roads narrowed.

So why not complete the hit, avenge his brothers, and collect the second half of the fee that the Tumaco cartel had promised them?

It was a good plan, a *macho* plan, and the thought pleased him.

The air horn blared, a car veered onto the shoulder in order to escape the oncoming monster, and the outskirts of Fez appeared ahead.

Agent 47 felt a grim sense of satisfaction as city lights appeared in the distance. The tanker was about to hit the usual traffic jam. Once it did, the assassin would be able to pull up alongside the truck and empty the Silver-baller into the cab.

That would leave plenty of time for a hot shower, a decent dinner, and a full night's sleep.

But to his astonishment, there was no traffic jam, because that particular access road had been set aside for official use during the music festival. A fact that

Manuel Otero must have been aware of when he chose the route.

There were wooden barricades, however, which shattered into a thousand pieces as the truck's massive bumper struck them, and half a dozen uniformed policemen sprinted to get out of the way.

Pieces of debris were still falling as 47 roared through what had been a checkpoint, and a chunk of wood struck his shoulder a glancing blow. The impact hurt, but the leather jacket offered some protection as the Colombian upshifted, and the truck accelerated. But if the oncoming traffic along the open road had provided Carlos with an advantage, Agent 47 benefited here, since there was no traffic to worry about. That allowed the assassin to pull out, twist the throttle, and surge forward.

The Colombian saw the move in the truck's huge side-view mirror and swerved to block it. But with no traffic to worry about, and a nimble bike, 47 had plenty of room to maneuver.

So he guided the BMW to the left, and was just about to reach for the Silverballer with his right hand when he realized he couldn't do so without releasing the throttle! And having left the long-slide back in the apartment, there was no other weapon at his disposal. That forced Agent 47 to drop back and release the throttle long enough to pull the .45 and transfer the weapon to his left hand before resuming the chase, a task made more difficult by the fact that he could no longer operate the clutch or shift gears.

Both the tractor-trailer and the motorcycle had passed through the open gate, and were well within Fez by that time. As another checkpoint appeared up ahead, the police opened fire. They had been warned by radio and had realized what could happen if 8,000 gallons of gasoline were detonated within the city's walls. But their puny service pistols and a few assault rifles weren't enough to stop more than 90,000 pounds of rolling metal. Thanks to the mirror, 47 could see Carlos laughing into the wind as bullets pinged around him.

The laugh was cut short as the BMW appeared next to the cab; the tattooed man pointed his semiautomatic pistol upward and began to fire. Both vehicles were still in motion, so precision was impossible, but there were nine rounds in the extended clip and 47 planned to use all of them.

Carlos uttered an involuntary grunt of pain as a .45 caliber slug punched a hole in the driver's side door and buried itself in his left thigh. But the motorcycle rider was forced to back off as the Colombian stuck his 9 mm Beretta out through the window and triggered three rounds.

The truck was becoming increasingly hard to control, especially with the missing tire, and the street was beginning to narrow as it wound its way toward the plaza. It was time for him to downshift.

That forced the Colombian to bring his arm back inside and park the pistol on his lap. There were people now, lots of people, all streaming toward the public square. There were screams and curses as they scattered. Or tried to, but there was a sickening *thump* as one man fell, and the big wheels rolled him under.

Agent 47 dropped back, and brought the Beemer up next to the passenger side door, where he stood on the BMW's pegs. Then, by bringing his right foot up onto the seat and pushing off, he was able to launch himself at the tanker.

The BMW fell away, hit a curb, and flipped end-over-end before crashing onto the pavement and sliding for another thirty feet.

Meanwhile, with both feet on the step, and having secured a grip on an external grab bar, Agent 47 fired through the open window.

Carlos jerked his head back as the bullet removed most of his nose, blood sprayed the steering wheel, and blew back into his face. Having heard the unsilenced report, the Colombian realized that the man with the gun was off to the right, and was fumbling for the Beretta as he turned to look.

Most of the Colombian's face was obscured by a bloody mask, but his eyes were visible, and it was during the brief moment that they were looking at each other when 47 pulled the trigger. Then, certain that the job was done, he jumped clear.

Having been left to its own devices, the driverless tractor-trailer rig missed an important curve and sent music lovers running for their lives as the Colombian's lifeless hands and heavy foot sent the fueler racing toward a spot where a block of substandard apartments had been torn down to make way for what the government promised would be something better.

There was a loud crash as the truck broke through the plywood panels erected to protect the construction site, followed by a brief moment of silence as the tractor-trailer rig sailed out over the pit, and a resounding *BOOM!* as the big gas tank finally exploded.

*   *   *

The opening ceremonies had just gotten under way, and Marla was on the stage with Al-Fulani when they heard the explosion and saw a huge fireball rise over the buildings to the north.

A chorus of discordant sirens began to bleat a few moments later, the music festival came to an abrupt end, and Al-Fulani was still alive.

It wasn't until the next morning, when some of the facts surrounding the explosion appeared in the news, that the true nature of what had occurred became clear. A group of Colombians, all of whom were wanted for murder, had stolen a tanker filled with petrol. And given their histories—not to mention the fact that they were in the country illegally—it was clear that they had been planning an attack on the music festival. A political act, according to some accounts, but Marla and Al-Fulani knew better. The Otero brothers were well known to the *Puissance Treize*.

Of more interest to Marla was the man on the motorcycle who, according to most reports, was heavily tattooed. She had seen such a man the day before, had passed within a few feet of him, and never suspected a thing.

The air was warm out on Al-Fulani's well-screened terrace, but the *Puissance Treize* agent felt a chill run down her spine, and knew why. It appeared that Agent 47 had orders to take Al-Fulani alive. It was her job to stop him, and she wasn't certain she could.

"It's time to come inside," Al-Fulani called, as he appeared in the doorway of his darkened bedroom. "We're ready!" A child could be heard sobbing somewhere behind him.

Marla swore silently as she stood, and let the white robe fall to the floor. There were moments when she would have been perfectly happy to shoot Al-Fulani herself. But he was the only person who stood between her and Mrs. Kaberov's wrath. Which meant that the *Puissance Treize* had to do whatever the Moroccan wanted her to.

The screams lasted for a long time.

ELEVEN

BLACK CORAL KEY, THE GULF OF MEXICO

The deHavilland Twin Otter DHC-6 circled the small, kidney-shaped island as the pilot sought clearance from the ground. Reefs of dark rock could be seen just below the surface of the gulf's sparkling blue water, where they served to protect the tiny bay from intruders, all but guaranteeing the island's privacy.

Most of the key was brown and desolate, but The Agency's retreat was marked by an oasis of green, made possible by a state-of-the-art desalinization plant. Aristotle Thorakis, like all the members of The Agency's board, had been a guest on previous occasions. Back during happier times, before he'd been forced to borrow money from the *Puissance Treize*.

Now, rather than enjoy the comforts to which he otherwise would have been entitled, the shipping magnate was a hostage to his own fear. A terrible gut-wrenching worry that seeped into his mind during the day, haunted his dreams at night, and had grown steadily worse with the passage of time. The Agency knew it had been betrayed and was determined to identify the person or persons who were responsible.

Hence the surprise summons to Black Coral Key.

Thorakis could have refused, of course, but to do so would have been to focus more attention on himself rather than reduce it, and potentially hasten exposure. Not to mention the fact that Pierre Douay had insisted that he attend, so that he could find out what The Agency was up to. It was a truly hellish cycle from which there could be no escape until he found the means to repay the *Puissance Treize,* they destroyed The Agency, or he was assassinated.

Which, all things considered, he richly deserved.

Such were the businessman's morbid thoughts as the twin-engine plane banked, began a steep descent, and came in for a picture-perfect landing on the key's pristine bay. There was a gentle *thump* as the aircraft put down, followed by a loud roar, as the pilot put both props into the reverse—or "beta"—position in order to slow the seaplane down.

No sooner had the deHavilland touched the surface than a sleek launch was dispatched to meet it. The boat's bow split the gulf water into two creamy waves and the inboard engine rumbled gently as the coxswain cut power and allowed the classic Chris-Craft to coast up to the plane. Cheerful greetings were exchanged between the copilot and the boat's neatly attired crew as the businessman's TUMI suitcase was transferred to the launch.

Then it was time for the shipping magnate to step across the narrow strip of water that separated the plane from the boat. Something he did without assistance, thanks to all the years he had spent on and near the water.

Once seated in the Chris-Craft, with the wind whipping through his hair, Thorakis was able to enjoy a brief interlude of worry-free pleasure as the boat cut across the bay and pulled up alongside a floating dock. A smartly uniformed member of the retreat's staff was there to welcome him with a casual salute and an ice-cold glass of lemonade.

Three minutes later he was in an electric golf cart, with his bag in the back, being driven up a path paved with crushed seashells toward the ultramodern house above. The twenty-six-room mansion had been built for a Hollywood film actress and her husband before they were killed in a strange car crash. That was when The Agency had acquired the place for a bargain-basement price. Five-million had gone into improvements, many of which were invisible to all but the most discerning eye. They had to do with the murder-for-hire organization's need for privacy, real-time global communications, and—if absolutely necessary—self-defense. Which was why the Hollywood House, as the staff commonly referred to it, was ringed with carefully concealed surface-to-air and surface-to-surface missile launchers.

More staff hustled out to greet Thorakis, including the lovely but somewhat enigmatic Diana, who was dressed in a crisp white halter top and sarong-style skirt. Her well-toned midriff was bare, as were her shapely legs and pedicured feet. It was an elegant yet slightly provocative look, which very few women could pull off.

"Aristotle!" the controller said warmly, as she came

over to plant a kiss on his cheek. "It's so good to see you. The rest of the board is already here, and we were just about to have some drinks. Will you join us?"

Search as he might Thorakis couldn't detect any signs of distrust in the way Diana greeted him, the look in her eyes, or the positioning of her body. That was a relief and the shipping magnate forced a smile.

"Of course!" Thorakis said, as he offered his arm. "Especially if I will be free to feast my eyes upon you!"

Diana smiled as she took his arm.

"No wonder you have so many women. You're not only handsome, but charming, as well."

The truth was that there were only two women in the shipping magnate's life. His wife, who was currently at home in Athens, and an Ethiopian mistress, who lived in Portugal. But the businessman always enjoyed compliments, especially from beautiful women, and took pleasure in being the one who got to escort Diana into the well-appointed boardroom.

A huge chunk of black coral sat next to the entry, where it was supported by a pedestal made of turned granadilla wood. Beyond that a bar stood to the right, the table occupied the center of the room, and a huge picture window filled the wall opposite the door. It was perfectly positioned to frame the well-watered green lawn, the picturesque bay, and the surf beyond.

There were all the usual greetings, as the twosome was absorbed by the gathering of international movers and shakers, all of whom knew each other well. Most of the conversation was centered on money, but other topics were under discussion as well, including the results of a hard-fought cricket match between India and South Africa.

The group included Mr. Nu, who was there to represent management; Aheem Shbot, the onetime Iraqi minister who was sitting on more than $25 million stolen during the early days of the war; José Sosa, a Venezuelan oil minister whose enemies had a marked tendency to die in car accidents; Frank Tang, a senior member of a successful Chinese tong; Lalu Khan, who was known as "The King of Whores" in his native India; Dr. Natalia Luka, who ran a profitable business peddling Russian nuclear technology to third-world countries; Hans Beck, a German industrialist with lofty political ambitions; Mary Minnarr, a South African whose fortune had been made selling blood diamonds; Mustapha Nour, an Egyptian arms merchant with valuable contacts inside the Tamil Tigres, the PKK, and other terrorist organizations; and Goto Osami, a member of the Japanese yakuza.

Thorakis watched their eyes, as the various board members turned to greet him, but found no signs of suspicion. So the gut-wrenching fear the shipping magnate had experienced on the plane had begun to abate by the time he and his peers took their respective places around the long, glass-topped table. Mr. Nu sat at the west end, with his back to the window, five members on his right, five on his left, and an empty chair opposite him. That was the seat traditionally reserved for the mysterious Chairman, whose identity was unknown, but was very much in attendance via a one-way video hookup.

It was he who called the meeting to order.

"Thank you for coming," the deep melodious voice said. There were speakers in the ceiling, walls, and floor, so the words seemed to originate from every-where and nowhere, all at once.

"I know how busy you all are," the voice continued smoothly. "And because of that, I was hesitant to add another meeting to your already demanding schedules. However, I'm sorry to announce that the efforts to iden-tify the traitor within our organization have been unsuc-cessful thus far. All of our lower-ranking administrative personnel and field agents were rescreened," the Chair-man added soberly. "And, while three individuals ap-pear to have been engaged in various types of theft, the effort to find the leak has been fruitless, evidence of which can be seen on the screen."

A huge flat-panel screen was mounted on the inner wall over the sleek mahogany bar. Nu and the other board members turned to look as a professionally edited video montage began to roll. There was no nar-ration, other than that provided by television reporters in a variety of countries. Subtitles had been added where necessary, and each clip was different from the others, except for the one element that tied all of them together.

There was an unsolved murder at the core of each story. Three individuals had been shot, two had been knifed, and the last victim had been pushed into the path of a train. An especially gruesome affair that dom-inated two news cycles in the United States.

When the five-minute-long compilation came to a close, the Chairman picked up where he had left off. There was anger in his voice now.

"*Each* of those people worked for us, *each* was a valuable asset, and *each* left a hole that will be difficult to fill. Some were field agents, but three were technical experts, who weren't even armed.

"So," the disembodied voice continued ominously, "it seems that someone—or some*thing*—has declared war on our organization. The attacking entity could be a criminal organization out to get revenge, a competitor that wants to level the playing field, or a disgruntled former client. All of which can be dealt with. But it's extremely difficult to fight back without knowing who the enemy is. So Mr. Nu and his staff have been authorized to rescreen both senior management and the board in an attempt to find the traitor.

"That means your movements, phone calls, and email will be subject to expert analysis. Of course, all of you utilize multiple layers of encryption, some of which may be good enough to keep even our experts at bay. If so, please provide our people with full access. Failure to do so will be interpreted as a hostile act. Especially since you specifically agreed to such transparency when you joined the board. You have my word that any and all proprietary information related to your affairs, having nothing to do with The Agency, will not be altered, copied, or shared.

"Are there any questions?"

Heads swiveled as board members turned to look at one another, but no one chose to respond, so the Chairman brought the meeting to a close.

"Unfortunately, it's quite likely that the traitor is right here in this room. If so, then know this. When we identify you, and we will, The Agency will kill you, eliminate your entire family, and all of your friends.

"Have a nice day."

There was a click as the line went dead, and Aristotle

Thorakis battled the dizziness that threatened to overwhelm him, as he visualized various members of his family being gunned down. *I did it to protect you,* he thought forlornly. *To preserve what is rightfully yours.*

But it isn't over yet, the shipping magnate told himself. *You have the* Puissance Treize *to protect you, and they are powerful, as well! So powerful that The Agency may be a thing of the past within a matter of months.*

But such thoughts offered cold comfort, as fear trickled into the shipping magnate's belly, and the vetting process began.

TWELVE

FEZ, MOROCCO

Waleed Abadati was a true believer, a dedicated husband, and a good father. Virtues built on a foundation of good habits that began with a regimen of personal hygiene before breakfast, followed by early morning prayer, and a brisk three-mile walk to work.

That journey began deep within the *Fes El Bali*, and took him to the *Ville Nouvelle* district, where thanks to four years spent in the army, he worked as a low-ranking security guard at Ali bin Ahmed bin Saleh Al-Fulani's mansion.

It was a boring job for the most part, but a relatively well-paid one, and Abadati felt fortunate to have it. The security guard was in a good mood as his feet followed the same path they walked every day and his mind contemplated the purchase of a secondhand car. It was a big step, but the money had been saved and was waiting in the bank. *But what kind to buy?* There were so many possibilities. Perhaps that was why the Moroccan didn't pay any attention to the scrape of shoe leather behind him, and was completely unprepared when a hand covered his mouth, and a strong arm jerked him into a heavily shadowed passageway.

That was when the needle bit his neck, the sedative entered his bloodstream, and the arms of darkness opened to receive him.

Having followed Abadati the previous day, Agent 47 had chosen the spot with care, and knew that the sloppily constructed lean-to that half-blocked the walkway would provide cover while he stripped the security guard of his belongings, including his photo ID, access card, and a U.S.-made Colt Python revolver, complete with gun belt and twelve extra rounds of .357 Magnum ammunition.

The clothes fit fairly well, which wasn't too surprising, since Abadati had been chosen for his height and build. Once the transformation was complete, 47 took time to bind and gag the security guard before piling musty burlap sacks on top of him.

Then, having assumed Abadati's persona, including the guard's peaked hat and sunglasses, the assassin continued the walk to work. The henna tattoos had started to fade by then, and were covered over with makeup that served to darken 47's skin. The impersonation was so good that merchants waved to the familiar figure, and one of Abadati's second cousins shouted a greeting from a second floor window as the guard passed below.

Fifteen minutes later Agent 47 entered the *Ville Nouvelle*. From there it was a short walk to the Al-Fulani mansion, where 47 made his way to the main gate, and waved Abadati's ID card as he passed the guardhouse. The operative waited for what seemed like an inevitable challenge, but the gate guard had seen what he expected to see. Which was the eternally dependable Waleed Abadati, showing up early for work.

Now that he had successfully penetrated the outermost layer of Al-Fulani's security, a single swipe of Abadati's key card opened the basement door. That provided 47 with access to the locker room where staff stored their personal belongings, and ultimately the subsurface corridor that would take the assassin to his real objective—a stairway that led from the basement up to Al-Fulani's study. The passageway, which was intended to function as an emergency escape route should the mansion come under attack, was to see on the diagrams downloaded from The Agency.

Which meant the assassin should be able to enter Al-Fulani's private office, overpower the businessman, inject him with Sodium Pentothal, and ask two extremely important questions: Who had penetrated The Agency—and who were they working for? It would be awkward, since time would be limited, but with Marla running Al-Fulani's personal security detail, 47 had given up all hope of spiriting the Moroccan away. Ever since the incident with the fuel truck her precautions had been extremely thorough.

Since Abadati was habitually early for work, Agent 47 had a full thirty minutes to enjoy before anyone would question his whereabouts, and perhaps another fifteen minutes before a search began. With that in mind, he entered the employee lounge, gave thanks for the fact that it was empty, and proceeded out into the hallway. An elderly janitor was swabbing the floor, but he didn't bother to look up as the uniformed guard passed and slipped around a corner.

Agent 47 knew where the hidden door was supposed

to be, but when he arrived there, it was to discover a wall covered with panels of gold fabric. After a quick scan to ensure he wasn't being observed, 47 began to push and prod at the panel where the door was supposed to be.

There was no response at first, and the agent had begun to worry when he heard a click followed by a whir as the door swiveled open. That released a rush of air laden with the faint odor of incense. He stepped through the portal, and was about to turn and close the door when a sensor took care of that task for him. Pleased with his progress so far, Agent 47 paused to remove his shoes before climbing a flight of narrow wooden stairs to the floor above.

Ali bin Ahmed bin Saleh Al-Fulani was seated behind his desk, with his back to three arched windows, as Marla stood in front of him.

"There's no doubt about it," the *Puissance Treize* agent said earnestly. "The Otero brothers were sent to kill *you*. Not one of the other VIPs who occupied the stage."

"Yet they failed because this Agent 47 person managed to stop them," the businessman mused. "Why would he want to do that?"

Six intricately carved Moorish screens served to partition off the east end of the office. Beyond them, in the alcove where Al-Fulani took his naps, one of the richly polished antique doors that decorated the back wall opened on silent hinges as Agent 47 entered the room. The assassin's feet were silent as he padded over to the screens and peered through one of them onto the scene that lay beyond.

Damn it! Al-Fulani was present, all right, but so was Marla, and the clock was ticking. Still, there was always the possibility that she would leave, so it made sense for the operative to wait.

"There's no way to know for sure," Marla replied gravely. "But it's my opinion that he wants to capture you, perhaps to interrogate you. And that would be difficult if you were dead."

"Yes," the Moroccan agreed bleakly. "It would. But I have news for you. *Good* news. We're about to leave Fez, which will make your job much easier!"

Marla wasn't sure whether leaving Fez would make her job easier, but she could hope. So she forced a smile.

"Really?" she responded. "Where are we going? Somewhere cool, I hope."

"No, I'm sorry," Al-Fulani answered sympathetically. "It's pretty warm in N'Djamena this time of year. But the desert in Chad has its own kind of beauty—and Agent 47 will have no idea where I am."

Having said that, the Moroccan businessman rose and circled the desk.

"Come, my dear," Al-Fulani said playfully, as he offered his arm. "My limousine awaits!"

"But I don't have the appropriate clothes!" Marla objected.

"Ah, but you will," Al-Fulani assured her soothingly. "We'll stop by your apartment on the way to the airport."

There were other things to worry about, including

her team's readiness for such a journey, but Marla knew her sponsor well, and he wouldn't want to wait, so she'd have to make arrangements on the fly.

The twosome were gone a few seconds later, which left 47 with no choice but to retrace his steps, and escape the mansion as quickly as he could. Fortunately the stir caused by Al-Fulani's sudden departure was such that the assassin was able to exit the basement undetected, and make his way to the south side of the property where Abadati was normally stationed. What could have been a tricky moment was eased by the fact that the other guard was tired, and eager to go home. He said something in Arabic, then laughed at his own joke, as he turned to leave.

The assassin waited for a full minute before he slipped out through the very gate he was supposed to guard, and faded into the foot traffic beyond.

He had been forced to abandon the Jammer identity in the wake of the truck explosion. His new base of operations, which consisted of a room in a seedy hotel, was about a mile away.

The real Waleed Abadati called in shortly after 47's departure, which triggered a full-scale search of the property. But having found nothing amiss, the way in which Abadati had been waylaid was ascribed to thieves, and the hapless guard was ordered to pay for both the uniform and the stolen weapon.

It was a significant setback that meant the car would have to wait. But Abadati was a good man, a righteous man, who knew that Allah promised those with patience a reward without measure.

A reward that, with the passage of time, would eventually be his.

East of N'Djamena, Chad

There was no direct air service to the city of N'Djamena—not from Fez—so unlike Al-Fulani, who had a private plane to call upon, Agent 47 had been forced to travel via a number of commercial connections, thereby losing quite a bit of time in the process. But thanks to some assistance from The Agency, a driver and a vehicle were there waiting when he landed.

And now, some six spine-jarring hours later, the operative and his paid companions were closing in on the spot where Al-Fulani and his party had probably spent the previous night. Would the Moroccan still be there? That seemed unlikely, but 47 hoped to confirm that he was on the right trail. Especially since the desert was a big place, and The Agency's spy sats had lost Al-Fulani's convoy during a dust storm.

The sub-Saharan landscape was divided between the bright, almost searing blue of the sky and the khaki colored landscape that lay sprawled below. The growl of the Unimog's engine dropped a full octave as Pierre Gazeau shifted down, released the clutch, and guided the truck up the sand-drifted track toward the next rise.

The Libyan freelancer had thick black hair, a hooked nose, and a three-day growth of beard. He wore wraparound sunglasses, a sleeveless khaki shirt, and a pair of matching slacks. Black hair crawled down his arms and darkly tanned legs to a pair of beat-up desert boots. Though born in Tripoli to an ex-legionnaire and a Tuareg mother, Gazeau had been educated in France, and spoke English with only a slight accent.

"There are tracks, my friend. Someone else has passed through the area, and recently, too."

The snub-nosed U90 Mercedes Unimog lurched as the right front tire mounted a large chunk of rock, the vehicle tilted to the left, and an avalanche of junk slid across the dashboard, ran out of room, and tumbled into Gazeau's lap. Only the statue of St. Francis remained where it was, his feet anchored by a dollop of glue, his eyes firmly on the track ahead.

The Libyan rescued one of his many pairs of sunglasses from his lap, placed them on the center console, and brushed the rest of the mess onto the already littered floor.

Agent 47 held on to a grab bar, and waited for the right tire to pass over the obstacle, before making his reply.

"I'm glad to hear it. That's a good sign."

"So," Gazeau said out of the side of his mouth, "how close are we?"

Agent 47 consulted the Garmin eTrex Vista GPS receiver, checked the readout against a map, and eyed the dry, rocky landscape ahead.

"The village should be about half a kilometer away."

Gazeau took his foot off the accelerator, engaged the clutch, and stepped on the brake. The truck came to an abrupt stop. Dust swirled up and drifted to the east.

The Mog was equipped with a crew cab. The assassin heard one of the rear doors close and turned to discover that Gazeau's assistant was no longer in the vehicle.

"Where did he go?"

Gazeau shook his head and laughed.

"You've seen him . . . Numo goes wherever he *wants* to go." And with that, the Libyan let out the clutch, fed fuel to the 5-cylinder diesel, and guided the big 4×4 up past the skeletal remains of an ancient VW bus. The path rose, turned toward the right, and disappeared over a rise.

Mahmoud heard the chatter of the big diesel engine and spotted the plume of blue-black exhaust long before he actually saw the blocky-looking Mercedes truck lurch up out of the ravine. It was white with a chromed star over the radiator, a tow rope that was looped back and forth across the front bumper, and the usual roof rack loaded with gear.

His own vehicle, an ancient Toyota Land Cruiser, was hidden a half klick to the east, well out of sight behind a chunk of weathered sandstone. Now, lying on his stomach, he felt the full force of the North African sun. It was uncomfortable—very uncomfortable—but would be well worth it if he and his men came away with a nearly new Unimog and whatever the vehicle was carrying.

The bandit had been tempted to attack the caravan that had camped in the abandoned village the night before, and steal all three of their vehicles, but there had been more than a dozen guards. So it had been necessary to let the group pass. But now, as a reward for his patience, Allah was about to deliver a different bounty.

What remained of the village became a blur as the Arab swept his binoculars from left to right. Many years before, previous to the Sahara's latest incursion into the semiarid grassland called the *sahel*, the *guelta*, or waterhole, had been the heart of the village. Trees,

long since cut down, had served to shade the depression
and protect the water from the sun. But the *guelta* de-
pended on rainfall for its sustenance, and with even less
precipitation than before, the waterhole dried up.

Having no water for themselves or for their animals,
the villagers had been forced to leave. It was an old
story, and a painful one, since it was unlikely that the
displaced population had been welcome anywhere else.
Not that it mattered to Mahmoud, who had other
things to worry about, as the diesel died and a couple of
doors slammed.

A thick layer of windblown sand gave way under the
soles of 47's boots. It parted occasionally to reveal the
rocks that lay below, as well as the detritus of human
habitation. The assassin saw a well-rusted wheel, what
looked like the remains of an old hand-cranked wash-
ing machine, and a partially exposed camel skeleton.
All of which had been there for a long time.

But there were more recent signs of habitation, as
well. Including a lot of tire tracks, what remained of
footprints, and three fire pits from which wisps of gray
smoke still issued.

"It looks like they were here," Gazeau commented, as
he bent to examine an empty Coke can.

Agent 47 was about to reply when he heard gravel
crunch, and turned to see a man with an AK-47 standing not ten meters away. He wore a billed cap with a
French Foreign Legion–style flap that hung down the
back of his neck, a white short-sleeved shirt, a pair of
khaki slacks, and lace-up boots. His skin was nearly
black, a pair of pink shoelaces had been tied around his

left arm just above a powerful bicep, and the sun glinted off his Rolex Submariner watch.

There was no doubt as to the familiar way in which the man held the assault rifle or the hardness of his eyes. His French was quite good.

"Good morning, gentlemen. Please place all of your personal items on the hood of the truck, and take three steps back."

Gazeau made as if to move, but stopped when the gun barrel jerked in his direction.

"There are worse things than being robbed, monsieur. Look to your left."

Both 47 and the Libyan turned. Two additional men had appeared—Tuaregs by the look of them—both dressed in indigo robes. They, too, were armed with assault rifles and appeared ready to use them. When the bandit saw how surprised his victims were, he laughed.

Numo liked working for Pierre Gazeau, especially since the pay was good, and the long trips into the desert meant he could escape from the friendly chaos that surrounded his steadily growing family. And the work brought him simple pleasures. The way that the sun beat down on his back, the shadows pointed away from the rocks, and a *hamada* (stony desert) seemed to float at the very edge of the sky. It was during moments such as this that his mind, spirit, and *jesm* (body) were all in one place.

Numo snuggled the rifle up against his shoulder, allowed the barrel to rest on the jacket-wrapped rock, and poured the sum of his intelligence into the telescopic sight. The targets—and there were three to choose from—were approximately 600 meters to the east of his position, well within the rifle's 800-meter range, and two of them were facing in his direction. The third, the AK-47 man, was looking toward Gazeau and the man who called himself Taylor.

The situation presented a number of technical difficulties, none of which were insurmountable. First were the capabilities of the weapon itself. Having first learned to fire it during his time with the Libyan army, Numo knew that the Mauser 7.62 mm SP 66 sniper's rifle was a fine weapon, especially against a single target. The problem was that the bolt-action rifle came equipped with a three-shot magazine.

Yes, he *might* be able to work the action quickly enough to hit all three targets, but what were the odds? The first target would fall, that was a given, but the others would immediately spring into motion. Would he be able to work the bolt, acquire the second target, and achieve another kill?

And what about target number three?

No, the best thing to do was prioritize the targets, and count on them to react in the manner he thought they would. Kill the leader first, then the man wearing the bush hat, and trust to luck after that. Satisfied that he had a plan, and that it stood a good chance of success, Numo drew a deep breath and let it out.

Agent 47 heard the flat *whip-crack* of the rifle shot, knew it was Numo, and turned in time to see the explosion of blood and brains.

Then came a second shot. And as the Tuareg who was wearing the bush hat fell, the other brought his AK-47 up. He was about to spray the foreigners with bullets when the agent shot him in the head.

The Silverballer was on its way back to the shoulder holster hidden beneath a safari-style vest even as the thief went down. Gazeau had seen his share of violence in North Africa, yet he was clearly impressed by the speed and accuracy demonstrated by his newly acquired client, and allowed his eyebrows to rise.

"You travel armed."

The assassin nodded. "So do you."

The Libyan laughed. "Yes, and it's a good thing too! Come . . . we have work to do."

It took the better part of an hour to dump the bodies into a gully and cover them with soil. The beat-up Toyota Land Cruiser would be impossible to hide, however, so Gazeau did the next best thing: he left the key in the ignition.

"It will be gone by tomorrow morning," the Libyan predicted. "And I can assure you that the new owner won't file any reports with the local police!"

Confident that he was less than a day behind Al-Fulani, Agent 47 instructed Gazeau to drive him to Mongo, the next logical destination for Al-Fulani and his party. The trip required another six-hour journey, then an overnight stay in a convenient *wadi,* and a two-hour drive the following morning. But finally they were there.

Gazeau downshifted, and the diesel belched black smoke as the Mog eased its way down Mongo's main street. It was cool in the cab, thanks to the air conditioning, but Mongo shimmered in the midmorning heat.

Agent 47 noticed that there were two styles of architecture in town. Some of the locals favored flattopped structures made from concrete blocks, while others preferred buildings with peaked roofs that were sheathed in rusty metal. None, with the exception of a single white mosque, exceeded two stories in height.

However, disparate as the two styles were, there was a common tendency toward garish paint, piles of festering trash, and brand-spanking-new Coke signs that not only served to advertise the product, but plugged otherwise gaping holes in the buildings.

The much abused structures stood shoulder to shoulder, like drunks who rely on each other in order to remain upright, and bled rivulets of brown wastewater into the unpaved street. The effluvium stank to high heaven, and merged into sluggishly flowing streams that followed the gentle gradient down toward the other end of town.

None of which seemed to bother the men of Mongo, most of whom appeared to be unemployed and stood in doorways, sat on stoops, or perched on the hoods of half-stripped vehicles. They watched the Mog pass with the same alert intelligence possessed by scavengers everywhere, as they listened for early signs of mechanical distress, and calculated what such a handsome vehicle would fetch on the black market.

In the meantime their women, busy in the way third-world women are always busy, struggled to cope with hordes of quarreling children, tons of filthy clothes, and an endless succession of meals. Some were Arabic, commonly referred to as "northerners," and wore conservative clothing. Others—those dressed in more colorful attire, and commonly referred to as "southerners"— were generally non-Islamic.

But regardless of their origins, all were locked in a battle with poverty, ignorance, and disease and went about their chores with downcast eyes, as if fully aware of the forces that opposed them, having already conceded defeat.

Gazeau glanced at the man seated next to him.

"It's depressing, isn't it?"

The operative shrugged.

"I've seen worse." Again the Libyan's eyebrows rose.

"There's the police station," Gazeau said, and he pointed through the dirt-smeared windscreen.

Agent 47 looked. The police station was a squat-looking affair, set apart from the other buildings, and surrounded by a nine-foot-tall cyclone fence topped by coils of razor wire. Three desert-equipped 80-series Land Cruisers sat by the gate. Two appeared to be operable, and the third was up on concrete blocks. Judging from the scattering of mismatched tools that lay about, not to mention the scrawny legs that protruded from under the vehicle, it appeared that one of the local mechanics was hard at work trying to repair it.

Of more interest was the police model Eurocopter EC 135 that sat on a pad within the enclosure. The aircraft was so new, so valuable, that it rated its own sentry.

Gazeau braked, pulled into the parking area, and killed the Mog's engine.

"You're sure this is a good idea," 47 said doubtfully.

"No," Gazeau answered cheerfully, "I'm not. But *real* geologists would stop and pay for a permit to take samples out of the country. And if Al-Fulani passed through here, the police will know about it. The problem, if we run into one, will relate to the size of the bribe. If the fee is reasonable, which many are, we pay and go. But, if the *Sous-Prefet* is greedy, we'll make some sort of excuse, and take our chances with the locals. Unfortunately, whatever information they give us may be a pack of lies."

"Okay," the assassin agreed. "You're the expert. Let's do it."

Gazeau nodded, ordered Numo to guard the truck, and opened the driver-side door. Heat flooded in, along with the choking smell of sewage and bright sunlight. The Libyan jumped to the ground, slammed the door, and hooked a pair of aviator-style sunglasses over his ears. Then, with the shades in place, Gazeau led 47 up to the gate.

The sentry, who looked as if he had only recently graduated from the police academy, was proud of his new khaki uniform and the huge revolver strapped to his hip. He spoke serviceable French.

"Good morning, how can I help you?"

Agent 47 listened absently as Gazeau answered in the same language, wondered why the front of the pale blue police station was pocked with what looked like bullet holes, then followed the Libyan inside.

The interior was only a few degrees cooler, but it still felt good to step out of the sun, even if the ancient ceiling fan was turning too slowly to do much good. There were benches on either side of the room, both filled with pitiful-looking supplicants, many of whom had brought food with them, as if expecting a long wait.

The counter, which was manned by a flat-eyed corporal, was made of plywood. The front had been decorated with a carefully rendered likeness of the blue, yellow, and red national flag. A Michelin map covered most of the desk's surface and was protected by a sheet of scratched glass. The Libyan leaned his arms on it and inquired as to the availability of export permits for the worthless rocks that occupied the back of the Mog. The corporal countered by demanding to see a valid *Autorisation de Circuler,* which Gazeau pushed across the counter.

Then, having examined the document for what seemed like an extraordinary length of time, the policeman issued what might have been a grunt of approval, whispered something to a grubby little boy, and sent him scurrying away.

"You will wait," the corporal said, gesturing to the already packed benches. "The *Sous-Prefet* will be available shortly."

"Shortly" turned out to last for the better part of an hour as the corporal worked his way through a large stack of forms, hitting each one with a decisive thump from his poorly inked stamp. In the meantime, the fan turned in meaningless circles, the flies searched for new territory to conquer, and the locals waited to learn what fate had in store for them. Finally, just as 47 was about to suggest that they pull out, the grubby little boy scampered up to the corporal, whispered in his ear, and eyed the foreigners as he did so.

The corporal nodded gravely, cleared his throat pretentiously, and relayed the message.

"The *Sous-Prefet* will see you now."

Omar Al-Sharr was an intelligent, if not very energetic, man. That was why he had chosen a career in the public sector, rather than try to eke out a living by running his own small business. Even so, having applied to the police, Al-Sharr had used what savings he had to grease the correct palms, and was accepted onto the force.

After that the ambitious young man had spent many years bribing, blackmailing, and charming his way up through the ranks until finally achieving the rank of *Sous-Prefet* of Mongo. Not the final prize—but within a few steps of where he wanted to end up.

He had been extremely thin back in the early days, malnourished even, but not anymore. Now Al-Sharr weighed in at a hefty 160 kilos, which meant that his body was a good deal less agile than it had been.

There was nothing wrong with his mind, however, which was why he had stalled the foreigners long enough to have the boys he often referred to as his "operatives" perform a little research. The results were curious, to say the least.

After swarming around the foreigners' truck, a rather fine specimen that would fetch a hefty price on the black market, and peppering the Libyan guard with dozens of seemingly innocent questions, the operatives had learned that the Unimog was loaded with mineral samples that the foreigners wanted to take home and analyze.

A seemingly plausible story, and one that Al-Sharr would have been inclined to believe, except for one thing: Outside of sodium carbonate and the Doba oil field, Chad had no natural resources to speak of. So, if the foreigners weren't geologists, as they claimed to be, then what were they?

Smugglers? Quite possibly. But there were other possibilities, as well. And it would be interesting to see what he could learn from them.

Agent 47 followed Gazeau into the police official's office, and was struck by how dim it was. What little bit of light there was emanated from a narrow, window located high over the *Sous-Prefet*'s head, and the lamp on his well-polished oak desk. The massive piece of furniture was an antique, something salvaged from the French Colonial government, most likely, and preserved by a succession of proud civil servants.

The man who sat behind the desk was huge, a fact which even his baggy XXXL jogging outfit couldn't conceal. It was blue, with white stripes that ran down the arms, and decorated with so many Nike swooshes that it couldn't possibly be genuine.

The official gestured toward two orange injection-molded chairs. His words were spoken in slightly fractured English.

"Please to sit down. My name is Omar Al-Sharr. I would get up, but my knees offer trouble."

"Taylor" and Gazeau introduced themselves, sat on the hard plastic seats, and waited to see where the conversation would go. It was warm in the office, very warm, in spite of the best efforts of an emaciated boy. He was too short to sit on the bicycle's seat, so he stood as he pedaled. Each downward stroke turned a chain, which turned a series of old automobile belts, which powered a makeshift fan. Whether this was by way of job creation, or to compensate for Mongo's iffy power grid, the rear wheel whirred, the chain rattled, and the fan squeaked as it pushed a steady stream of warm air toward the monumental desk.

"So," Al-Sharr said as he picked up Gazeau's *Autorisation de Circuler* and pretended to examine it, "tell me about these mineral samples."

Agent 47 had expected the question, or one like it,

and launched into a cover story that involved the possibility of commercial-grade iron ore deposits near Mongo. A fabrication that was consistent with the rusty red rocks in the back of the truck.

Al-Sharr's expression said that he didn't believe a word of it, but he nodded as if he did, and reached down into a galvanized tub that was located next to his oversized chair. It contained some reasonably cool water, plus a dozen cans of Diet Coke. He held one up for his visitors to see.

"Would you drink something? No? Please let me hear if you change your minds."

So saying, the police chief popped the tab, took a long pull, and wiped his mouth with the back of a hand. A gentle belch served as an exclamation point.

"Now, where were we? Ah, yes, the possibility of iron ore deposits. Once you confirm the presence of these deposits, and obtain permissions to exploit them, Chad will greatly benefit. In the meantime the government will have to rely on more modest sources of revenue, such as export fees. So, if you would be so kind as to submit 10,000 euros, or 9,165 U.S. dollars, we will fill out the necessary paperwork and get you on your way."

It was an outrageous sum, much more than the government would require, or a legitimate business would be willing to pay. That being the case, 47 frowned. "Really? That's a good deal more than we had anticipated. So much more that it will be necessary for us to contact our employer, and request instructions."

Al-Sharr was surprised. Maybe his instincts had been wrong. Maybe the men were exactly what they claimed to be. Or maybe they were too greedy to pay a reasonable bribe. He took another sip of Coke, put the can down, and felt the first pangs of hunger. It was time for his lunch, followed by a nap and a cooling bath. "Here are your papers. Please let me know if there is anything else you need. Have a good day, gentlemen."

"There is one other thing," 47 said, as both he and Gazeau came to their feet. "Could you tell us if a party of three vehicles and about fifteen people passed through Mongo within the last twenty-four hours? They're friends of ours, and we were hoping to catch up to them."

Given the fact that Al-Sharr had hosted Al-Fulani and his party with an enormous feast the night before, and had been on the Moroccan's payroll for the past three years, there was little doubt as to who the foreigner meant. But were the men in front of him friends of Al-Fulani's? Or were they enemies? There was no way to know. Regardless, given that the information could be had in the local market, he thought it best to tell the truth.

"Yes, as a matter of fact there was. A Moroccan, if I'm not mistaken. He and his party left early this morning."

Agent 47 thanked the policeman, and together with Gazeau, left the *Sous-Prefet*'s office.

The two men had just exited the building, and were halfway to the gate, when Al-Sharr summoned the corporal into his office. They were related, so there was no need for pretense.

"Have someone follow them. Someone reliable. And keep me informed. Maybe they are what they claim to be . . . and maybe they aren't. Call me if you discover anything. I'm going to lunch."

The corporal nodded, sent for his brother-in-law, and returned to his desk.

The fan turned, the flies buzzed, and the people who lined the benches continued to wait.

THIRTEEN

Darkness had fallen over the desert, leaving only half a dozen small fires to hold back the night, as the ragged children ate what little bit of food they had been given. The air was starting to cool, making travel possible once again, so it was time to move.

Allah willing, Mahamat Dagash and his men would deliver the children to the market in Oum-Chalouba just before dawn. Even though the ambush had gone extremely well, there had been problems ever since. First with one of the Land Cruisers, which took a full day to repair, and then with the children, because their legs were short, and they were suffering from malnutrition, which made them unbearably slow.

Whipping the little beggars was always good for a momentary increase in speed, but the orphans soon began to slow once again, forever testing the slaver's patience. Yet now, with only hours to go, Dagash felt his spirits begin to rise.

"Extinguish the fires!" he ordered brusquely as he

made the rounds. "Load the trucks! And give each child a drink. We're almost there."

That announcement was sufficient to elicit a cheer from the slavers, all of whom were looking forward to a good meal, hot baths, and a rich payday. Money with which to support their families, purchase a vehicle, and to possibly open a business.

They went to work with enthusiasm.

Kola was ten years old. Both she and her seven-year-old brother Baka had survived the slaver attack, but had been orphaned in the process. Now, as Dagash shouted orders and his men hurried to obey, the little girl knew what to do. It was pointless to resist, and punishments could be painful, so she ordered Baka to stand and take his place in line.

"I won't!" the boy said rebelliously. "I'm hungry . . . and tired."

"We all are," Kola replied patiently. "Now do as I say, or one of the men will hit you."

"So what?" Baka demanded sullenly. "I've been hit before. They're just going to sell us."

"That's true," the little girl acknowledged calmly. "But we will live. More importantly, *you* will live. And so long as you live, all of our ancestors live."

Having no written records to rely on, each Dinka child was required to memorize his or her entire lineage at a very early age. It often went back for hundreds of years. Because to remember one's ancestors was to keep them alive.

And since females took their husbands' names, and Baka was the last male in their immediate family, the weight of the entire ancestral line rested on his narrow shoulders. A heavy responsibility indeed. Having been reminded of his place in the world, Baka stood.

"I'm sorry," he said contritely. "You're right."

The two children held hands as they made their way over to where the lead Land Cruiser was waiting, and took their places in line. The 4×4's engine rumbled, and its parking lights served as beacons as the children trekked across the desert.

Somewhere, out beyond the curtain of darkness, millions of people slept.

FOURTEEN

ABÉCHÉ, CHAD

Agent 47 was exhausted by the time the Mog pulled into Abéché, so much so that he skipped dinner and went straight to bed, which consisted of a narrow section of concrete located adjacent to a thin mattress on a latticework of creaky springs. The rock-solid floor seemed to move at first, as if he were still in the truck, but the sensation vanished as sleep pulled him down.

And that's where 47 was—dreaming about a game that had no rules—when Gazeau touched his shoulder.

"Wake up Alex. We need to get out of here." If the fact that his client had chosen to sleep on the hard floor rather than in the bed struck the Libyan as strange, he gave no sign of it.

Agent 47 squinted at the dial of his watch.

"Give me a break . . . it's two in the morning."

"That's right," Gazeau agreed, "which is why this is the perfect time to leave! Remember the helicopter? The one parked next to the police station in Mongo? It put down ten minutes ago. And guess who went out to meet it . . . Mr. Citroën."

The assassin swore, threw the blanket off, and stood. An old Citroën had been following them ever since Mongo. Gazeau saw light glint off one of the stainless steel pistols that Taylor habitually carried, and realized that the weapon had probably been pointing at him moments earlier.

"How do you know this stuff?" the assassin inquired.

"Numo followed Mr. Citroën to the airstrip," the Libyan answered simply. "But that's not the worst of it . . . Al-Sharr was on board the helicopter. I think it's safe to assume that Mr. Citroën works for him."

The agent's pants were draped over the back of a rickety chair. He hurried to pull them on.

"Al-Sharr? The cop?"

"One and the same."

"We can't outrun a chopper," Agent 47 observed, as his shaving kit went into a suitcase.

"No," Gazeau agreed, "but the helicopter isn't armed. Sure, they can hose us down with an AK-47, but that's all."

The assassin smiled thinly. "Isn't that enough?"

"It could be a tad uncomfortable," Gazeau admitted wryly. "But we can shoot back! Choppers are delicate machines. I doubt the pilot will linger."

"But what about the authorities? Won't Al-Sharr call for help?"

"Possibly," Gazeau allowed calmly, as he led his client out through the hotel's grubby back door. "But I doubt it. Remember, this may be Chad, but bribes are still illegal. The fat man can't let his superiors know what he's up to."

Agent 47 hoped the Libyan was correct, but still had

plenty of misgivings as he took his place in the back-seat, and Numo guided the Unimog out into the cold Saharan night. It was about a hundred miles to Oum-Chalouba. Where, if The Agency was correct, Al-Fulani had already checked into a hotel and was probably enjoying a good night's sleep. Would the fat policeman give chase? And would the Moroccan stay in Oum-Chalouba long enough for the assassin to catch up?

There was only one way to find out.

It would have been dangerous to drive very fast, since many traps lay beneath the shifting sands, so hours were spent driving through the tunnel created by the truck's headlights while waiting for the Eurocopter EC 135 to roar overhead. But nothing happened, and thanks to their early-morning departure—likely coupled with Al-Sharr's apparent unwillingness to pursue them during the hours of darkness—47, Gazeau, and Numo were able to make good progress. When the sun rose they were on a flat *piste,* or track, traveling at about 30 mph, as they followed the road toward a clutch of basalt towers that were the only things worth looking at.

Distances could be and often were deceptive, which meant that even though the rocky spires appeared to be relatively close, they were actually many miles away.

The better part of half an hour passed before the outcroppings grew appreciably larger, and the track swung out to the west of them. That was when something appeared in the sky, circled behind the rock columns, and emerged to race straight at them. The EC 135 was no more than fifty feet off the deck and growing larger with each passing second.

"There it is!" Gazeau said grimly. "It looks like the fat bastard finally rolled out of bed."

Agent 47 tried to watch as the helicopter passed over them, but the cab's roof blocked his view. His mind went to the weapons stashed in the back, but he knew that neither one of the long guns would be very effective against the chopper.

Then, having turned back, the Eurocopter pulled up next to the left side of the truck and sped along, not 60 feet away from the driver's-side window. Dust blew backward and boiled into the air. *Sous-Prefet* Al-Sharr was clearly visible beyond the Plexiglas, and gestured for Gazeau to stop. The Libyan offered a rude gesture by way of a reply, which caused the chopper to pull ahead and enter a wide turn.

"Uh-oh," Gazeau said. "How much do you want to bet Al-Sharr brought one of his cops along?"

Agent 47 never had an opportunity to reply as the helicopter passed along the truck's right side and a man opened fire with an AK-47. It took practice to fire an automatic weapon from a moving platform, especially when shooting at a speeding target. And it soon became apparent that the policeman knew what he was doing.

The assassin heard a series of *pings* as half a dozen 7.62 mm slugs hit the Mog. Then the EC 135 was gone, giving the gunner time to slam a fresh thirty-round magazine into the weapon's receiver, and prepare for the next pass. Agent 47 was thrown against his shoulder restraint as Gazeau hit the brakes.

"What the hell are you doing?" he demanded. "They'll shoot the hell out of us!"

"No they won't," the Libyan replied. "They *expect* us to stop."

Agent 47 heard a familiar clacking sound and turned to discover that Numo had assembled an AK-47 of his own. The Libyan grinned as the Mog skidded to a halt. First the rifle . . . now this. It seemed that Gazeau kept a small arsenal aboard his truck. Which, given the way things were unfolding, was a pretty good idea.

The chopper's dual Pratt & Whitney PW 206B2 turbine engines howled wildly as the pilot put the ship into a wide turn, blew sand across the now-stationary truck, and hovered just off the *piste*. The helicopter had an *Avionique Nouvelle* cockpit, and the large glass canopy allowed Al-Sharr to see the truck in front of him, but it also meant that the occupants could see him as well. That, plus the fact that the aircraft's nose-in position made it impossible for the AK-47-wielding corporal to make use of his weapon. It was a fatal error.

However, just as the *Sous-Prefet* was about to say something over the chopper's PA system, Numo jumped down from the Unimog and fired a three-round burst. Thanks to the fact that the aircraft was square in his sights, two of Numo's slugs struck their intended target. A hole appeared just over Al-Sharr's head, the pilot panicked, and that led to a second mistake.

Rather than back away and protect his engines, the chopper jockey turned to starboard. That gave Numo the opportunity he'd been waiting for—a clear shot at the port engine. The AK-47 rattled as the Libyan emptied his clip into the exposed turbine. It coughed, burped smoke, and the chopper started to spool down.

The EC 135 rocked as the pilot shut off the fuel supply to the port engine and goosed its twin. The nose dropped, the remaining turbine screamed, and the aircraft began to move away. But Agent 47 had exited the Mog by that time, drawn both of his Silverballers, and was striding toward the helicopter, firing as he went. Empty shell casings arced away from the assassin and a tight grouping of holes appeared around the chopper jockey's head as he slumped forward.

The man that Gazeau knew as Alex Taylor quickly ran out of ammo, but by then there was a fresh clip in the AK-47, and Numo was still firing when the Eurocopter hit the ground. The remaining engine screamed as the aircraft did a nose-over, the main rotor shattered, and pieces of blade scythed through the air.

The long-slide went back into its holster. The act of slipping a fresh magazine into the shorter weapon was as natural as breathing, but there was no need. The fat man was still alive, struggling to free himself by then, but it was too late, and 47 caught one last glimpse of the policeman's desperate face as the 135 blew. There were three explosions in all, and even though he was about seventy-five yards away, it was still necessary to go facedown in the sand as a wall of heat rolled past and pieces of flaming debris fell all around.

Finally, once the explosions were over, the assassin stood. Gazeau appeared at his side.

"It will take days for the government to sort this out . . . assuming they ever do. Still, there's bound to be a whole bunch of gendarmes running about. So it would be a good idea to get in and out of Oum-Chalouba as quickly as we can."

Agent 47 nodded.

"That works for me. Let's get out of here."

Oum-Chalouba, Chad

The town of Oum-Chalouba had the one thing that no desert traveler can do without and that was water. Evidence of it could be seen in groves of lush date palms, private gardens that could be glimpsed through partially opened gates, and a tiled fountain located in the public square.

Unfortunately the fountain was dry at the moment, and had been for the better part of two years, ever since its sixty-year-old pump had broken down. A new one was on order, or so the *maire* (mayor) claimed, but none of the local residents expected to see water flowing into the big bowl anytime soon.

The city's architecture included a lonely Catholic church, three mosques, a French Colonial administration building, and a poorly maintained military base. There were also three truly fine nineteenth-century houses, dozens of flat-roofed structures of the sort seen throughout the Middle East, and a sprawling metal-roofed *souk* that had been in business for more than a thousand years.

And that was where Al-Fulani and his entourage were, as shop owners hawked their wares, loud music blared from ubiquitous radios, and a silversmith hammered ornate patterns into a large platter. The air around them was hot and heavy with the odors of spices, broiled goat meat, and tanned leather.

People claimed that one could buy anything in the *souk,* and based on what Marla had seen, they were correct. In addition to food, clothing, and household goods the *Puissance Treize* agent had seen shops filled with military uniforms, used auto parts, artificial limbs, exotic animals, hashish, and all manner of weapons. Which was to say, something for everyone.

But the *souk* had another category of merchandise for sale. Something that had once been trafficked in the main square, as hard-eyed Tuaregs stood all around and camel caravans plodded through town. That was human flesh, which was what Al-Fulani had traveled all the way from Fez to buy. Children, specifically, who could be put to work in his so-called "orphanage," where they would service wealthy pedophiles until they were too old to be considered young.

At that point the slaves would be resold. Such was the market that the Moroccan and his bodyguards sought—but only after pausing to inspect all manner of merchandise, chatting up the shop owners, and buying a variety of trinkets. It was a process Al-Fulani clearly enjoyed.

Marla had a different perspective, since she saw the labyrinthine market as the perfect place for an ambush. Yet it was a concern Al-Fulani was unwilling to take seriously.

"I have faith in you, my dear," the businessman said, when reminded of the dangers. "Besides, who would come after me *here*?"

So what could have been a ten-minute walk through the *souk* was transformed into an hour-long shopping expedition that eventually delivered the group into the shattered remains of what had once been a small palace. Artillery shells had destroyed the structure's dome during the war with Libya in the early '80s. Having been artificially opened to the azure sky, the mostly intact walls embraced an arena in which a myriad of animals were bought and sold each day. The smell of

their feces was so strong that Marla found it necessary
to breathe through her mouth as she followed Al-Fulani
into the circular enclosure.

Women were a seldom-seen sight in the arena, and
men turned to stare as the Moroccan and his entourage
entered. Three of the onlookers were dressed in *kef-
fiyeh,* and ankle-length black *thawb*s, slit open at the
sides so the wearers could access their guns. And,
thanks to the sunglasses and goatee he was wearing,
Agent 47 felt confident that he wouldn't be recognized.

Finding the house that Al-Fulani was staying in had
been easy, thanks to Numo's scouting skills, and everyone in the *souk* seemed to be aware of why the Moroccan had come to town. So, rather than follow the
businessman and almost certainly be spotted, the assassin had chosen to anticipate his movements instead.
And now, as Marla paused to wrap a scarf around her
face, 47 knew he'd been right.

There were other potential buyers as well, some of
whom were known to Al-Fulani and greeted the Moroccan respectfully as he made his way to a section of
seats reserved for wealthy VIPs. Once the businessman
was seated, a tray bearing a tiny cup of very strong coffee and a selection of sweetmeats was summoned, and
Al-Fulani took full advantage of it as he chatted with
the man seated to his right.

Marla stood immediately behind her client, where she
could protect his back as her eyes inventoried the huge
enclosure. Buyers and sellers formed a circle, interrupted by two lanes through which merchandise could
be herded in and out of the open area. But her eyes were

elsewhere, sweeping the cheap seats, looking for any sign of a threat.

Suddenly a force of ten uniformed policemen filed into the arena. A vision of the burning helicopter popped into 47's mind. The assassin swore silently, and was sliding one of his hands into his voluminous *thawb*, when Gazeau nudged his shoulder.

"Look!" the Libyan said. "They're on the take."

And sure enough, rather than put a stop to the slave auction, it soon became apparent that the police were there to protect it. The first thing they did was to secure both entryways, before spreading out to control the entire room. And it was a good thing too, since many of those present were carrying large amounts of cash.

The assassin released his grip on the short-slide, pulled his hand back into the open, and ordered his body to relax. He'd been hoping for an opportunity to snatch Al-Fulani right out from under Marla, but the police presence put paid to that idea, so all he could do was wait.

The slave auction got under way shortly thereafter, as a man who was wearing a linen skull cap and dressed in an immaculate white suit appeared. He addressed the crowd in French and, judging from the matter-of-fact cadences involved, it was a speech he had delivered many times before. The essence of it was that the market was in no way responsible for the mental, emotional, or physical health of the human beings who were about to be bought and sold. All transactions would be conducted in euros, all merchandise would be collected immediately after the auction, and all sales were final.

With that preamble out of the way, the first batch of

slaves was herded into the room. They were exclusively male and, judging from appearances, all from the same geographical area. The Sudan probably, or the Central African Republic, where there was very little enforcement in place to protect them. A rough-looking, white South African purchased the entire lot, to work in an illegal diamond mine perhaps, or to harvest crops on some remote farm.

The next group of slaves was female, all of whom had been stripped naked before being forced out into the open, and there were multiple bidders. There was no way to know for sure, but it seemed likely that the more comely women were destined for the sex trade in any of a dozen possible countries, while the rest would be incorporated into wealthy households where they would live lives of forced servitude.

But Al-Fulani had no interest in them. It wasn't until all of the women had been accounted for that Mahamat Dagash led his band of emaciated children out into the arena. Then the Moroccan put his coffee cup down, and began to examine the slaves through a small pair of binoculars.

Kola and her brother Baka were frightened by the crowd, and clung to each other until Dagash forced them apart.

There was a flurry of activity as the auction resumed, and Al-Fulani found himself competing with a dark-skinned man from Nigeria. When the process was over, the Moroccan was well pleased with the eighteen children who would accompany him to Fez.

Kola burst into tears as Baka was taken from her and forced to join those the man had purchased.

"Remember my name!" the little girl shouted desperately as they took him away. "As I will remember yours!"

Baka tried to respond, but staggered as a backhanded blow struck him across the mouth, and a man armed with a whip shouted orders the youngster couldn't understand.

"We'll follow Al-Fulani's slaves," Agent 47 said. "Then, once he links up with them, we'll make our move."

Gazeau nodded agreement, but deep down he knew it wouldn't be that easy, because nothing in North Africa ever was.

The auction was over, and as the crowd began to break up, Marla caught a glimpse of a man who at first looked familiar. But then, having taken a second look, the *Puissance Treize* agent realized she was wrong. Not only was the man wearing the wraparound sunglasses dressed in a *thawb*, he was clearly in the company of a couple of Arabs, and Agent 47 was known to work alone.

Then the moment was over, the arena began to clear, and life ground on.

Northwest of Oum-Chalouba

A full day had passed since the auction in Oum-Chalouba, and things were not going well. Having watched Al-Fulani's four-vehicle convoy depart the city, and having followed them out into the desert, Agent 47 and his companions had been about to close with the Moroccan when a truck loaded with police roared past them. A few miles later, having topped a plateau, the assassin was able to look to the northwest, and that was when he saw five columns of dust, all in close proximity to one another, indicating that Al-Fulani had a police escort. Which, when combined with Marla and her bodyguards, would be impossible to overcome—certainly out in the open.

So, frustrating though it was, all they could do was follow the Moroccan and wait for something to break his way.

Hour after tedious hour passed, until the red-orange sun hung low in the western sky, and the town of Faya appeared ahead. According to the map, it was bigger than Oum-Chalouba, and boasted its own airport, so Agent 47 was surprised when the distant columns of dust veered to the right and headed due north.

"What the hell is he up to?" the assassin muttered as the Mog bucked its way over a series of bumps, and Gazeau battled the big steering wheel.

"There's no way to know for sure," the Libyan said grimly. "But it's my guess that the *Sous-Prefet* in Faya is a lot less accommodating than the one in Oum-Chalouba, and perhaps takes a dim view of slavery. That would force Al-Fulani to use the only other airfield around—and that's the strip at Quadi Doum."

Agent 47 frowned. "Quadi Doum?"

"Yeah," the other man replied. "Back in the '80s, when Muammar Gaddafi was trying to take over northern Chad, he built a military base about twenty miles north of here. But it was overrun."

"So the airfield is still operational."

"The metal runway is still there," Gazeau replied darkly. "But first you have to find your way in through the minefield that surrounds the base."

"And Al-Fulani can do that?"

"Lots of people can do that," the Libyan responded. "Including me. My father showed me the way. But it's extremely dangerous."

"We don't have a choice," Agent 47 replied grimly. "Besides, if we can reach Al-Fulani before his plane lands, he won't have any place to run. This may be the opportunity I've been waiting for."

"I was afraid you'd say something like that," Gazeau replied dryly. "That means we'll have to transit the minefield tonight, so we'll be in position come morning."

"Sounds like fun," 47 said as he stared out through the filthy windshield. "I can hardly wait."

It had been necessary to pull over and wait for the fall of darkness, lest the column of dust that the Mog generated give the pursuers away. While vehicles were to be expected on the way to Faya, once Al-Fulani and his convoy left the *piste,* any sign of a tail would make them suspicious. And given the size of the Moroccan's security force, Agent 47 knew he would need the advantage of surprise if he were to win any sort of engagement.

When night arrived, they began the final trek into Quadi Doum. With Numo walking ahead and Gazeau behind the wheel, 47 struggled to focus his sleep-deprived eyes on the GPS receiver that was duct-taped to the top of his left thigh. That left his hands free to deal with the much-creased map and a long list of directions provided by the Libyan. What light there was came from the headlamp Agent 47 wore as he gave instructions over the radio.

"Five, four, three, two, one . . . execute a hard left turn."

Numo, who was equipped with a Motorola Talkabout 200 walkie-talkie, executed a neat turn and walked due west. He had a compass that glowed dimly in the palm of his hand and served to keep him on course. Gazeau waited for the Mog to reach the exact turning point, yanked the wheel to the left, and downshifted. The Mercedes jerked as the clutch was released, picked up a tiny bit of speed, and continued to roll forward.

The assassin, who hadn't been aware that he was holding his breath, let it out slowly.

"Damn, why so many turns?"

"It may not look like it," the Libyan replied, "but we're on a road. When Gaddafi ordered his forces to build the airstrip, they laid mines in precise patterns that allowed anyone who was equipped with a watch and compass to access the base via four two-lane roads. One for each point of the compass. The turns were supposed to keep the bad guys out."

"Did it work?"

"Hell, no. The base was under the command of one Colonel Khalifa Assa Uadi. In spite of the fact that he had 4,000 men, 20 aircraft, and some 200 tanks, the idiot allowed a ragtag force of Chadians to find their way through the minefield, chop holes in the security fence, and infiltrate the base. It fell within a matter of hours."

"You seem to know a lot about the battle."

Gazeau grinned. His teeth gleamed in the light provided by the instrument panel.

"During the years after my father left the French Foreign Legion, he accepted freelance contracts from time to time. He was with the Chadian forces when they entered the base."

"So he mapped the roads?"

The Libyan shook his head.

"There was no need to. One of Uadi's officers sold my father a map for the equivalent of twenty-five dollars U.S. Later, after Libyan forces left, the airstrip was abandoned. Papa always kept a stash of supplies there, and so do I. About two years ago I took his directions and converted them into latitude and longitude, in order to take advantage of the GPS system."

Agent 47 made use of his right hand to trigger the handheld Motorola.

"Stand by. We have another turn coming up."

Numo, whose job it was to look for any mines that might have migrated along with the constantly shifting sands, clicked the transmit button by way of acknowledgment.

The desert was surprisingly cold at night. Still, he seemed oblivious to any physical discomfort, and most likely he was ignoring it to focus on the task at hand.

This was the Sahara, after all, where death lay only meters away.

By the time a long, thin crack appeared along the eastern horizon, and pink light washed the sky, Agent 47 was ready to make his first kill.

The Mog had been left at the bottom of a dry *wadi* and covered with the camo netting that Gazeau always carried. Now, having made it all the way to the air base's perimeter without blowing themselves up, all 47

and his companions had to do was neutralize a combined force of something like eighteen bodyguards and
police officers in order to have a nice, productive chat
with Al-Fulani. It was no small task, but one the operative thought the three of them could accomplish, so
long as they played it smart.

In order to gain every possible advantage, Agent 47
had Gazeau draw three identical maps of the base, and
divide each into sectors. Then, having checked to make
sure their radios were operational, the men low-crawled
into position roughly three hundred feet out from the
perimeter of the base. The assassin estimated that the
old radio mast was approximately one hundred feet
tall. That made it the perfect watchtower—a place from
which a sharp-eyed lookout could monitor activity for
miles around. Had he been the one playing defense, 47
would have stationed one of his very best people up
there.

But would Marla do likewise? It was an important
question, because if she had, then it would be necessary
to kill the lookout in order to maintain the element of
surprise. But it was still too dark to be sure.

He found it frustrating, lying there as the sun continued to rise, knowing full well that valuable time was
slipping away. But Agent 47 forced himself to remain
where he was and gradually, bit by bit, the early morning light began to illuminate the tower. There, about
halfway to the top, a platform could be seen. The image
wobbled as the assassin brought the Walther WA 2000
to bear. It was difficult to hold the weapon steady because of the steep angle, but there was no mistaking the
lookout who was crouched on the tiny triangle of
metal, or the sticklike rifle that was slung across his

back. A safety rope secured the sentry to the tower and he was looking toward the north. The assassin turned to Gazeau.

"There's a lookout all right. But I need something to rest my rifle on. Get up on your hands and knees."

The Libyan made a face, but crawled into position, and felt the gun barrel come to rest on his back. It was a rather undignified pose, and something the sentry was sure to notice if he turned toward the south. And Gazeau knew that he, rather than "Taylor," would be targeted first.

In the meantime, Agent 47 found that even with the improvised gun rest, the elevation was such that the shot would be difficult to make. Yet there wasn't any choice. So the assassin worked a cartridge into the chamber, slid the crosshairs over the lookout's torso, and made a slight adjustment to allow for the westerly breeze. Then, having taken a deep breath and forced it out again, he took all of the slack out of the trigger.

The Walther nudged his shoulder, there was a soft *phut* as the bullet left the barrel, and the man on the tower seemed to sag.

The lookout couldn't fall—given the safety rope—but his binoculars did. Agent 47 held his breath as the glasses plummeted toward the ground, disappeared behind one of the intervening buildings, and presumably smashed themselves into a hundred pieces on the concrete below. Would someone hear?

It seemed all too likely, but twenty seconds, then a minute, then five minutes passed without producing any sign of an alarm. The assassin allowed himself to breathe normally.

Gazeau was back at his side by then and ready for the next step.

"Okay, Pierre, work your way over to the tower. Climb it if you can, eyeball the base, and tell me where they are." The operative turned to his left. "Numo, circle around to the west. Find a good position and get ready to fire on targets of opportunity."

Both men nodded and scuttled away as 47 elbowed his way toward the sand-drifted remains of a much-abused security fence. There were plenty of holes, so he chose the closest.

Once inside he found himself at the edge of what had been a military parade ground. The concrete was cracked in places and partially covered with windblown sand, but still recognizable as what it had been. The problem was that all of the buildings were located on the far side of the hardscape. Agent 47 didn't want to cross that much open ground, but there wasn't any choice unless he wanted to take a long detour, the length of which would pose its own risks.

So the operative got up and began to run.

The Mossberg pump gun bounced against his back, and the weight of the spare ammo slowed the assassin down as he ran toward the three aluminum flagpoles that marked the front of what had once been the facility's administration building. The prefab box was made of corrugated metal, and was riddled with hundreds of bullet holes. There was no way to know whether the shots had been fired by the Chadians as the base was overrun, or by vandals later on.

Three steps led 47 up to shattered double doors that sagged inward. The assassin slipped between them and instantly found himself in a murky reception area. A quick reconnaissance revealed half a dozen offices that lay beyond, one of which was larger than all the rest, and probably had belonged to the commanding officer. Agent 47 could imagine the feckless Colonel Uadi sitting behind his desk, trying to understand what was happening as his command disintegrated around him.

The building had been looted more than once, which meant that anything of value had been taken, but a few symbols of the past remained. Among the items that caught 47's eye was a cloth jacket, still hanging from its hook; a photo of a pretty woman, on the filthy floor; and a plaque celebrating some sort of achievement, still bolted to the wall. None of which mattered to the operative as long as he had the place to himself.

Marla didn't have enough people to secure the entire base, so she would do the next best thing, which was to choose a defensible area within the complex, establish a perimeter, and sit tight until the plane arrived. As the assassin took another look at Gazeau's hand-drawn map, he thought he knew which area she had chosen. The area he would choose, if the decision were up to him.

The likely candidate was what had been the air base's maintenance facility, which consisted of a large prefab building that fronted the main taxiway, but was at least a hundred feet away from the neighboring hangars. That structure would allow Marla to bring the vehicles inside where they couldn't be spotted from the air, keep all of the slaves in one place, and maintain good fields of fire all around.

So, assuming that his assumptions were correct, it would be important to close with the maintenance facility before the opposition tried to make contact with the dead lookout, or the plane came in for a landing. It could be on its way already.

With that in mind the assassin slipped outside, made his way along the front of the building, and vanished into the ruins of Quadi Doum.

It was still cold enough for Marla to see her breath as she sipped hot tea and stared out across the sand-strewn runway toward the quickly rising sun.

The security chief was nervous, which seemed stupid, given the size of the force at her disposal. But even though the *Puissance Treize* agent had sixteen men on hand, six were policemen who weren't about to take orders from a woman. And while the other ten knew better than to defy her, Marla estimated that only seven of them could be counted on in a firefight. The rest were relatives of Al-Fulani's who were a lot better at carrying weapons than actually firing them.

So, counting herself, the Moroccan had roughly eight people who could be relied upon to protect him.

Still, Marla thought, *our lookout will spot trouble long before it arrives and give us plenty of warning*. It was a comforting thought, and having finished her tea, the *Puissance Treize* agent turned to go back inside the building.

A child started to cry, a man barked an order, and the noise stopped.

Had it not been for the broken glass that made a crunching sound as Agent 47's boot came down on it, the policeman might never have learned of his impending demise.

In spite of orders from Al-Fulani's European whore,

he had gone out to take a look around, just in case several generations of looters had missed something of value. Nothing major, he was too realistic to expect that, but an adjustable wrench perhaps. Or a good clasp knife, or—

But that was when he heard a *crunch*, felt the bottom fall out of his stomach, and made a grab for the big revolver that hung on his hip. Unfortunately the fiberwire loop was tightening around his throat by then, which caused him to pluck at the relentless ligature in a vain attempt to loosen it.

The world went black.

The policeman collapsed, and 47 was left to consider his next move. It was tempting to appropriate the dead man's uniform, but that would burn time, and might set him up as a target for Numo. So the assassin towed the body into a shed, and was careful to close the door on it before he continued on his way.

Gray buildings lined both sides of the street. What appeared to be barracks and warehouses were off to the left, with a long line of one-story hangars to his right. The numbers on them were still legible. Everywhere 47 looked he saw partially stripped vehicles, heaps of no longer identifiable machinery, and all manner of garbage. There was very little rust, thanks to the dry climate.

Judging from the graffiti on many of the buildings, not to mention the remains of a recent campfire, the assassin got the impression that there were others who knew how to find their way in through the minefields. But those thoughts were interrupted as a bullet chipped the concrete directly in front of him, the flat *whip-crack* report of a rifle shot echoed between the buildings, and the element of surprise was forever lost.

No sooner had the sound of the shot died away than Marla was on her radio, checking in turn with each of her troops. It took moments to establish the fact the man in the tower was dead, that one of the policemen was missing, and that it had been the second lookout who had had the good fortune to spot the intruder from his rooftop perch, and subsequently opened fire on him.

Unfortunately the bastard missed. But at least he was awake and paying attention. As were all of her men by then.

"Good morning, my dear," Al-Fulani said, as he ambled over to where the *Puissance Treize* agent was standing. He had just gotten up, and having spent the night with two of the children, was still dressed in red silk pajamas. "What's going on?"

"That's what I'm trying to piece together," Marla replied quickly. "Somebody is out there, that much is clear, but who? It might be locals, who want to steal our vehicles, but the fact that they aren't afraid of the police, and the way they killed our lookout, would seem to suggest another possibility."

"Well, I'm sure you'll take care of the matter," the Moroccan said confidently. "All you need to do is keep them at a distance. The plane will be here in three hours at the most."

It was good advice, and Marla took it to heart as she left to begin her rounds. Here was an opportunity to prove what she was capable of, put the Kaberovs of the world in their place, and secure a lasting reputation within the *Puissance Treize*. Then, with Al-Fulani's continued sponsorship, the sky was the limit!

Buoyed by those thoughts Marla started to climb the stairs that led to the building's flat roof.

"They're in the maintenance building," Gazeau said from his perch on the radio tower. It was very exposed up there, some twenty-five feet below where the lookout's body still hung, and the Libyan knew the Moroccan's security forces could see him because bullets were pinging the metal around him.

The transmission served to confirm what Agent 47 already suspected as he continued to work his way in toward what they were calling "section six."

"Good work," the man known as Taylor replied, his voice little more than a terse whisper. "Now get down off that tower before someone shoots you." Gazeau was well ahead of him, and was already descending the metal ladder by the time he heard the transmission, but appreciated the sentiment as a bullet tugged at his sleeve.

He heard the man trying to reach Numo by then, as well.

"Can you hear me?"

"Yes," the Libyan replied. "I can."

"Do you have any sort of shot at the maintenance building?"

Numo stared through his sight. From his perch on the walkway that circled the elevated water tank, he could look down on the building in question and the two— no, make that three—people standing on the roof.

"Yes, I do."

"Then go to work on it," came the instructions. "Bullets will go right through that metal siding. I want you to drive them out into the open. Try not to shoot Al-Fulani however. That's a no-no."

It was an extremely cold-blooded order, because there were children inside the maintenance building, and it was clear that the man named Taylor didn't care. But Numo had children, lots of them, and wasn't about to shoot someone else's.

That didn't apply to the adults on the roof, however, so he said, "Will do," and chose the first person to kill.

Marla could already feel the sun's warm promise as she opened the door and stepped out onto the metal roof. Soon—within an hour or so—the surface would be too hot to stand on. She knew that the man on the tower had been forced down onto the ground. But as she turned to take a quick look around, the *Puissance Treize* agent spotted movement up on the water tower!

"Get down!" she shouted. "There's a man on the—"

But the warning came too late, as the shooter squeezed the trigger and sent a bullet spinning toward his target. The man nearest to Marla was in the process of turning toward her when the bullet slammed into his torso and threw him down. Then, before anyone could react, another rifle shot was heard and a second man fell.

Marla felt as if she were wading through quicksand as she turned back toward the door, and threw herself into the darkness that lay beyond. There was a loud *clang,* followed by a report, as a third bullet flattened itself against steel. That was the moment when she realized the truth.

What had been a sanctuary had been transformed into a trap.

A slender, nearly emaciated corporal was in charge of the surviving policemen. Not only was he angry about having lost one of his men, but the whore's repeated attempts to exert control infuriated him more.

So when the shooting began, he led his men past the cowering children to the building's back door.

Then, knowing how important good leadership can be, he exited first.

Agent 47 was within fifty feet of the maintenance building by that time, and was just about to check the seemingly unguarded back door when it unexpectedly flew open. And, having prepared himself for close-in fighting, he already had the 12-gauge shotgun in his hands.

As the police rushed the assassin, the pump gun made its characteristic *boom-clack,* over and over again, as the weapon jumped, and the double-aught buck tore the men apart. Blood sprayed the concrete, the doorway, and inside the building.

Marla was back down on the main floor by that time, and any thoughts she had of charging through the open door were put to rest when she saw blood come spraying in through the portal. So she and the rest of Al-Fulani's bodyguards opened up on the exit with automatic weapons. That forced the shooter to withdraw—thumbing shells into the shotgun's receiver as he backed away.

It was Agent 47.

Just as the threat faded Marla heard the roar of an engine. The vehicle sounded like a maddened beast as it came across the taxiway, and a Mog crashed into the huge double doors that guarded the interior, slamming them aside. That was followed by the sound of screeching tires, as the driver stood on the brakes, and a cacophony of screams as terrified children ran in every direction.

Marla might have rallied her surviving troops at that point, but a big fender struck the *Puissance Treize* agent a glancing blow and threw her into one of the parked vehicles.

That knocked the security chief unconscious.

Agent 47 was forced to step on the dead corporal's chest in order to enter through the back door.

Four of Al-Fulani's bodyguards had the presence of mind to respond, but both of the Silverballers were out by that time, and 47 fired them in quick succession. The hapless guards were forced to perform a macabre dance as the heavy .45 caliber slugs slammed into them.

Then more shots were heard—only muffled this time—as the remaining bodyguards attempted to escape via a side door, only to be met by bullets from the sharp-eyed Numo.

Satisfied that the situation was under control, 47 took the time required to reload both handguns before going in search of Al-Fulani.

The agent found the Moroccan cowering in a storage room, where he was shaking like a leaf and had recently shit his lovely silk pajamas.

"Good morning," the assassin said politely, as the terrified businessman stared up at him. "My name is Taylor, and I have some questions to ask you."

There weren't any historians present to record the moment, but the airfield at Quadi Doum had fallen for the second time, and vultures were circling above.

FIFTEEN

Diana had flown to Rome for a three-day vacation and was asleep in her suite at the St. Regis Grand when the men in black came to get her.

The door was double-locked, of course, yet that was a minimal obstacle to the men who gathered outside her door. They picked the lock with ease, positioned themselves with weapons drawn, and prepared to enter.

But when the lead assailant turned the doorknob and put his shoulder to the wood, the only reaction was the strident *beep, beep, beep,* generated by the wedge-shaped miniature alarm Diana had pushed in under the door.

It took less than ten seconds to shove a long, thin pry bar in under the barrier and dislodge the wedge. Nonetheless, Diana was already firing by the time the door slammed open.

The first agent through the door took a 9 mm round right between the eyes and went down as if pole-axed from above. The man immediately behind him was more fortunate in that he was wearing body armor, and took two bullets to the chest without sustaining serious injury.

But as the impact took the second operative down Mr. Nu fired a Taser X26, which shot two probes at Diana. Both struck their target and delivered a shock powerful enough to bring her still-twitching body down.

"Get everyone into the bedroom," Nu ordered tersely. "I'll take care of the hotel's security people." There was a mad scramble as Diana was laid out on her rumpled bed, the dead agent was dumped into her bathtub, and the man who had taken two 9 mm blows to the chest was led over to an easy chair that occupied one corner of the ornate bedroom.

By that time Mr. Nu had shed his suit coat, removed his tie, and mussed his hair. With the improvised disguise in place he stepped out into the hall and was waiting there when two of the hotel's plainclothes security people stepped off the elevator.

"I heard three loud firecrackers go off," Nu complained belligerently. "Do you have children staying on this floor? My wife and I expect some peace and quiet for the kind of money we're paying. Especially at the St. Regis."

Both security people quickly turned apologetic and promised to conduct a complete investigation. They even went so far as to knock on neighboring doors so that other cranky guests could abuse them. Then, having been unable to pinpoint the exact nature or the origin of the firecracker-like noises, the two were forced to withdraw.

Mr. Nu reentered Diana's suite and returned to her bedroom. Like most of the heterosexual men who had

HITMAN: ENEMY WITHIN   223

met her, the executive had often wondered what Diana would look like without any clothes on. And now he knew. The fact that her wrists and ankles were secured to the bedposts made the tableau all the more interesting.

Though still recovering from the effects of being tasered, the controller was clearly conscious and, judging from the look in her eyes, extremely angry. Her full—and apparently natural—breasts were somewhat flattened thanks to her supine position. Not her nipples though, which were pink and fully erect.

From there Nu allowed his eyes to travel down along the flat plane of her stomach to the intersection between her legs. Most of her pubic hair had been removed, and based on the small triangle of white skin he saw there, it was clear that the controller had a preference for thongs. Diana's hips were a bit narrow for a woman, or so it seemed to Nu, but her shapely legs more than made up for what he saw as a shortcoming.

"Are you finished yet?" the controller inquired contemptuously. "Perhaps you'd like a cigarette."

Mr. Nu smiled thinly as he sat next to her on the bed.

"My dear, dear, Diana. You sound so very brave! But as you know better than most, it's hard to talk tough once the cutting begins. We'll use the surgical cautery, of course. That was one of your innovations, as I recall. And a good one, too! Because the cautery seals the blood vessels off even as it slices through them. That prevents blood loss, and prolongs the subject's life. And then there's the rather distinctive burning odor, which adds yet another dimension to the process.

"Take this nipple, for example," Nu said, as he took the nub between a thumb and forefinger. "You would be able to watch us cut it off, feel the excruciating pain, and smell your burning flesh all at the same time! Who knows? Maybe we could pop the little morsel into your mouth so you could taste it, too. Or," the executive added thoughtfully, "you could simply tell me the truth."

"About *what*?" Diana demanded. "And get your hands off me."

"About your relationship with the *Puissance Treize*," Nu answered gently, as he continued to squeeze, harder now.

Diana winced.

"I don't have a relationship with the *Puissance Treize*."

"Ah, but I think you do," the executive corrected her. "How else can you explain the one million dollars that was deposited into your checking account four days ago, the two-million-dollar New York condominium deeded over to you three days ago, and the three million dollars' worth of United States Treasury bonds that appeared in your portfolio the day before yesterday? We pay you well, *very* well, but how can you account for an extra six million in less than a year? Especially from a *Puissance Treize* front company?"

Mr. Nu had squeezed all of the blood out of the nipple by that time, and try as she might, Diana couldn't conceal the pain. Her face was drawn as she spoke through gritted teeth.

"It's a trick. Can't you see that? The *Puissance Treize* is trying to protect the real traitor. So he or she can continue to sell us out! And besides, if I were the person you're looking for, do you think I would be so stupid as to take payments from a front company? Don't insult me that way."

Nu released the nipple and put his hand on her stomach. The controller's skin was soft and warm. His index finger drew circles around her navel.

"Six million is a lot to spend on a red herring."

"Not if the business you're trying to hijack grosses over a billion a year," Diana countered tightly.

"There is that," the executive allowed smoothly. "Which is why you're still alive. The Chairman has something of a soft spot for you, and rather than destroy something so beautiful, perhaps without cause, he wants to wait until all of the facts are in. Agent 47 said he was close to catching up with Al-Fulani the last time he phoned in a report. So, who knows? Maybe our enterprising friend will come up with the real traitor.

"But if he doesn't, your immediate future will be somewhat painful."

The comment didn't call for a response, and the controller kept her mouth shut as Nu stood and turned toward the nearest agent; a skinny man who found it difficult to take his eyes off Diana's naked body.

"Get something to cover her," the executive instructed. "Then pack her things, take care of checkout, and get her to the airport. The Chairman wants her back aboard the *Danjou* by tonight." He turned back to Diana.

"The rest will be up to Agent 47."

Aristotle Thorakis was at his home in Sintra, Portugal, when the phone rang. It was just after two in the morning, but he was still up, going over the company's quarterly financial reports, when Mr. Nu came on the line. The shipping magnate was careful to hide the glee he felt as the executive told him about Diana's detention, and the very real possibility that the controller had been the source of the devastating leaks.

It wasn't until the phone was safely on the hook that he felt it was safe to utter a celebratory "Yes!" and pump his right fist up and down.

He wanted to call Pierre Douay at that point, and thank the Frenchman for protecting him, but knew better than to do so. There was a very good chance that The Agency was still monitoring his phone calls. So, having no one to share the good news with, Thorakis was forced to celebrate alone.

The Scotch was expensive, smooth, and very good.

SIXTEEN

QUADI DOUM, CHAD

It was warm on the roof, very warm, by the time Al-Fulani was assisted up the stairs and out onto the hot metal surface. Two bodies lay where they had fallen, and the air around them was thick with flies, as the Moroccan was led over to one of the camp chairs originally brought along for his comfort. The businessman was still dressed in his red silk pajamas, but they were badly soiled, and offered little protection from the scorching heat.

Once Al-Fulani was seated, Numo secured him to the chair with several feet of duct tape, which made a scritching sound as it came off the roll.

"That looks good," Agent 47 said approvingly. "Now for the umbrella."

The mention of an umbrella caused the Moroccan's spirits to rise, but they subsequently fell when the blue-and-white-striped sunscreen was set up a full fifteen feet away, and six of the older children were invited to sit in the shade. The Dinkas were equipped with bottles of spring water, too—all taken from Al-Fulani's private larder. The girl, Kola, who had been raped the night before, couldn't stop sobbing.

They sat there for a while, Al-Fulani, the assassin, and the children, and the silence was maddening. The heat seeped into his every pore, but he withstood it, and refused to give in. Finally his captor stood, and walked over to the group of slaves.

"Here," the assassin said without emotion, as he issued each child a knife. "Keep these handy."

Al-Fulani's face paled as he saw the knives, understood their purpose, and quickly lost his resolve. Before long, he began to blubber.

"Please!" he said piteously. "I implore you! Don't let them cut me."

"Don't worry, I won't," 47 lied reassuringly. "As long as you answer my questions, I promise that you will come to no harm.

"There are two things I want to know," the assassin added intently as he returned to his seat on an upturned bucket. "First, what is the name of the organization that is attacking The Agency?"

"I can't tell you that," the Moroccan insisted. "They would kill me! Surely you can understand that."

"I do understand that," Agent 47 responded soothingly. "The problem is that I don't care. You," the assassin said, as he turned toward the little girl with big brown eyes. "What's your name?"

"Kola," the Dinka answered shyly, as she attempted to wipe the tears away.

"Well, Kola," the operative said. "Come over here and bring your knife. The truth is hidden somewhere inside this man—and your job is to cut it out. Don't kill him though. Not until we have what we need. Here, I'll help you get started."

The little girl's expression showed that she remembered what had been done to her the night before, knew what that meant within the context of her Dinka culture, and hate filled her eyes. She stood, and was halfway to the chair when Al-Fulani began to rock back and forth.

"No!" he screeched. "Don't let the little bitch touch me! I'll tell you what you want to know."

Agent 47 held up his hand and Kola stopped, but she stood there glaring at the Moroccan.

"All right," the assassin said, "enlighten me. Which one of The Agency's competitors are we dealing with?"

"The *Puissance Treize*!" Al-Fulani answered eagerly. "I swear it!"

"Now we're getting somewhere," the assassin said approvingly. "That's consistent with what we already know. So tell me something I don't know. Who did they turn?"

"His name is Aristotle Thorakis," the businessman said.

The operative frowned. "The Greek shipping magnate?"

"Yes!" Al-Fulani replied. "He sits on the board . . . and he owns a number of shipping lines. Big ones. But there were problems with his holdings. Lots of problems, until the *Puissance Treize* loaned him 500 million euros."

"In return for information about The Agency's operations," 47 said, his voice thick with disgust. "But how can I be sure that you're telling me the truth? How do I know you're not setting him up as a patsy?"

"I swear it before Allah," Al-Fulani said sanctimoniously.

Agent 47 nodded. There was no way to be absolutely sure, of course, but the accusation had the ring of truth to it. So the agent turned to face the children.

"Okay, boys and girls, he belongs to you. You can set the bastard free, if you want—or slice him into a hundred pieces. Whichever you prefer."

At that point he motioned to Numo, and they headed for the stairs.

"*Nooooo!*" Al-Fulani protested. "You gave me your word!" But the two men were soon lost to sight.

The Moroccan began to scream. It lasted for a long time.

The plane was half an hour late.

It was little more than a dot at first, but gradually grew larger, and eventually turned into a war-weary C-27/G222 Spartan that, judging from its camouflage paint job and blacked-out markings, had once been the property of Italy's air force. The twin-engined turbo-prop circled Quadi Doum twice as if the pilot were looking for signs of danger.

The lookout's body had been replaced by a white towel that flapped in the breeze, and functioned as a wind sock. All three of the bodies had been removed from the maintenance building's roof, Al-Fulani's vehicles had been driven out onto the taxiway, and the children were instructed to wave as the transport roared over them.

Finally, satisfied that things were as they should be, the pilot turned back toward the north.

His name was Bob Preston. He was wearing a faded New York Yankees baseball cap over military-short black hair, and sported a stylish pair of Ray-Ban sunglasses. The ex–air force officer's brown skin had proven to be an asset in Africa, as was his ability to speak French, Arabic, and a trade language called Lingala. But even with those advantages, running a one-plane transport service was a financial challenge.

Which was why Preston had been forced to supplement his regular income with jobs he and the copilot Evan Franks referred to as "specials." Meaning the sort of low-altitude, terrain-hugging flights that were required in order to deliver—or retrieve—shipments of weapons or other cargo to airstrips that barely deserved the title, often under trying circumstances, with people shooting at them.

But this trip looked like a piece of cake as Preston put the starboard wing down and turned into the wind. According to information available on the Internet, the original airstrip was nearly 10,000 feet long, which was a whole lot more than the Spartan would require, since the plane was designed to take off and land on short 1,500-foot runways.

No, the problem—if any—would stem from the condition of the strip. Many years had passed since maintenance had been performed on the metal mesh the Libyans had laid down. Which meant a lot of sand had been blown over the top of it, and that raised the very real possibility that the C-27's nose gear would hit a drift, bringing the plane to a calamitous halt.

Still, that was why they paid him the big bucks. And it was the chance Preston would have to take if he wanted to collect the rest of the $10,000 that Al-Fulani had promised to pay. Plus, there were the orphans to consider.

Mercenary though he was, the pilot had a soft spot in his heart for children. And despite his other, more questionable dealings, Mr. Al-Fulani still took the time to remove refugee children from truly horrible situations, and place them in his orphanage in Fez. Where, based on what the Moroccan had told him, they were well cared for.

So the key was to land in the shortest distance possible, thereby reducing the odds of hitting deep sand.

The gear went down with a palpable *thump*, the ground came up fast, and Franks began to pray out loud—a practice Preston found objectionable back during the early days of their relationship. He had since come to not only accept it, but take a certain amount of comfort from it. They were alive, in spite of the many forces that had conspired to kill them. He figured that meant help was coming from somewhere.

In any case, the prayer worked. Or perhaps it was Preston's skill that brought the plane in for a perfect landing in spite of the sand that billowed up around them. The engines roared in protest as the props went into reverse, the hull rattled as if it were about to come apart, and the C-27 screeched to a shuddering stop. Then, happy to have kept his livelihood in one piece, Preston guided the plane over toward the point where his passengers were waiting.

Agent 47 stood, briefcase in hand, as the transport taxied up to a point about a hundred feet away and came to a stop. The engines made a loud whining sound as they wound down, a door opened just aft of the cockpit on the port side of the fuselage, and a set of fold-down steps appeared.

The assassin took that as his cue to approach the plane. Numo was right behind him. The cargo plane had been chartered by Al-Fulani, which might present a problem. But thanks to the briefcase full of money that 47 had recovered from the businessman's Land Rover, there was a reasonably good chance that the person in charge would be willing to switch employers.

If not, they would be forced to cooperate, or, if absolutely necessary, the assassin could make an attempt to fly the C-27 himself. Although he hadn't logged any hours on a Spartan, and really didn't want to push his luck.

He had tried to contact The Agency to tell them what he had learned, but something was interfering with his transmission. Gazeau explained that it was a problem most travelers experienced in this part of the desert, but regardless of the reason, it lent new urgency to their trip back to civilization.

So the operative had a smile on his face as he approached the stairs and boarded the plane.

"Hello!" he said engagingly, as he arrived on the flight deck. "My name's Taylor—and this is Numo. There's been a change of plans. I hope that's okay."

Preston frowned. There was something different about the man who was standing in front of him. Something dangerous. And whenever he heard the words "change of plans" come out of a client's mouth, trouble usually followed. Still, it's often better to go with the flow, so the pilot would wait and see.

"Glad to meet you," the pilot responded warily. "My name is Preston. Bob Preston. And the man who's sitting in the cockpit, when he should be outside inspecting the landing gear, is my copilot, Evan Franks."

"Nice to meet you," Franks said, as he pushed by. He had reddish hair, lots of freckles, and a farm-boy grin. "Don't worry—his bark is worse than his bite."

Agent 47 smiled as the copilot exited the ship.

"What sort of changes did you have in mind?" Preston inquired suspiciously. "And where is Mr. Fulani?"

"He was . . . delayed," 47 responded noncommittally, as he eyed the Browning 9 mm that dangled under the pilot's left arm, "and won't be able to join us. But I need transportation to Sicily, which, if I'm not mistaken, is well within the range of your plane."

"Yeah, but that wasn't part of the deal," Preston objected sourly. "We were hired to fly to Fez. Six up front—with six on delivery." That was two-thousand more than Al-Fulani had agreed to, but Preston saw no harm in amping the amount, just in case the man named Taylor was good for it.

"So we owe you six," the assassin said agreeably, as he turned to place the briefcase on a fold-down table. The latches made serial clicking sounds as they were released. "Here's six large," he said, as he turned to offer the pilot a sheaf of currency. "And if you'll fly me to Sicily, I'll pay you six more on top of it. Agreed?"

Preston accepted the money, thumbed the stack to make sure there weren't any blanks in the middle, and tucked the wad away.

"What about the children?" the pilot wanted to know. "Surely you don't plan to leave them here?"

In all truth, the question of what would become of the children hadn't even crossed 47's mind. But seeing the look of concern on Preston's face, the operative was quick to respond.

"No, of course not," the assassin replied glibly. "That's the whole point of going to Sicily. There's an orphanage that's ready to take them."

Preston smiled. He had very white teeth.

"All right then!" the American said enthusiastically. "What are we waiting for? Let's load the kids and get the hell out of here! Chances are my lazy copilot forgot to file a flight plan. So it would be best if we weren't caught on the ground."

With his transportation in place, Agent 47 left Gazeau and Numo to herd the children onto the plane while he went to check on Marla. Having been knocked unconscious during the battle with Al-Fulani's security team, the *Puissance Treize* agent had been duct-taped into a sleeping bag, tied hand and foot.

But when the agent went to visit her, Marla was gone.

Judging from the way the restraints had been cut, it appeared that Marla was carrying a blade of some sort—one that had been small enough and so well hidden that they had missed it in their initial, cursory search. Once she came to, it would have been relatively easy for the woman to feign unconsciousness, wait for the rest of them to leave, and cut herself free.

Now, armed with any of the weapons that had been left lying about, Marla was hiding in the ruins. The assassin could go out and hunt her down, of course. But to what end? He had what he'd been sent to get—and there wasn't any price on her head. So it made sense to let her go.

That didn't mean Marla would be as understanding, however. So rather than risk a long-range rifle shot,

Agent 47 loaded his luggage into Al-Fulani's Land Rover and drove it out to the plane. Even though he parked the four-wheeler in a spot that would shield the bottom of the fold-down stairs, he would be exposed as he stepped onto the flight deck, but only briefly.

Even though 47 knew Gazeau and Numo would loot Al-Fulani's vehicles prior to submitting a final bill to The Agency, he gave each man five thousand dollars anyway. Both as a bonus, and because he might have need of them in the future.

"Take care of yourself," Gazeau said, as the two shook hands.

"Watch your back," 47 responded. "Especially on the way out. Marla's on the loose. And she's armed."

"Thanks for the warning," the Libyan said, as he hooked a pair of aviator-style sunglasses over his ears. "Maybe I can buy her off with the Land Rover. Unless you object, that is."

"No," 47 replied, "That's entirely up to you."

Then, with a wave to Numo, the assassin mounted the stairs.

No rifle shots were heard, but Gazeau saw a glint of reflected light coming from the direction of the water tower, as if someone were eyeing the airstrip through a pair of binoculars. With that possibility in mind, he went around to open the driver's-side door, removed the keys from the Land Rover's ignition, and held them up where they were plain to see.

Then, having given the woman plenty of time to look, he slid the key ring down onto the vehicle's antenna.

The C-27 had taxied away by then, leaving a minia-ture dust storm in its wake, as it made the turn onto the runway. The General Electric T64-P4D engines roared as its pilot advanced both throttles, the transport jerked forward, and quickly gained speed.

The plane took to the air a few seconds later.

Near Noto, Sicily

The airstrip dated back to the days of World War II, when German planes had used it as a place to refuel before taking off for North Africa. And later, when things began to go poorly for Rommel, a squadron of fighters had been stationed there so they could attack allied shipping in the Mediterranean.

But those days were long over, and the field was primarily dedicated to civilian aviation, plus the occasional emergency landing by commercial jets.

As the sun was beginning to set, a lonely figure stood in front of the tiny terminal building and stared toward the south. Though not Agent 47's friend in the conventional sense of the word, Father Vittorio was his spiritual adviser, to the extent that the assassin needed one. The operative believed he was headed for hell, and given all 47 had done, that was certainly possible.

But God never gives up, nor can I, the priest told himself. *Because there is a kernel of goodness buried deep within 47's soul, even if he isn't aware of it.*

And there was evidence to support the priest's hypothesis. The assassin had once taken shelter at Vittorio's church, where he worked as the gardener in an attempt to put his violent life behind him. But men with 47's skills were hard to come by, and it wasn't long before the past caught up with the assassin, forcing him to take up arms once again. Those had been bloody days, in a land already soaked with blood, and it was something of a miracle that both Vittorio and his former gardener were still alive.

A cold breeze came up, as if somehow summoned by the priest's dark thoughts, and tugged at his cloak as the plane appeared in the south. Its running lights were on, and it was gradually losing altitude.

The phone call had come like a bolt out of the blue. Vittorio knew who it was the moment he heard 47's voice. The agent was on a plane loaded with orphans, headed for Sicily, and in need of someone to care for the youngsters. Why was a hired killer flying north with a planeload of children? There was no way to know.

And it really didn't matter. The orphans were in need of help, and Father Vittorio would do his best to provide it. No simple matter, given all of the legalities involved, but the local customs agent was a member of Vittorio's parish. The Holy See could be counted on to help, and the Lord would take care of the rest.

There was a brief screech of tires as the airplane put down, the engines roared, and it wasn't long before the twin-engined transport turned off the runway and onto the taxiway in front of the terminal. It stopped a few minutes later, and the big props continued to turn for a few revolutions before finally coming to a halt.

A door opened, stairs were lowered, and Agent 47 appeared. The assassin was wearing his usual black suit, white shirt, and red tie. When he was halfway down the stairs, he turned to accept two briefcases, then two suitcases. Three of the objects were left next to the plane as he crossed the tarmac.

Vittorio noticed that 47's skin was darker than usual, as if he'd been spending a great deal of time in the sun, and wondered how long the agent had been in Africa.

"It's good to see you, my son," the priest said, as the two men embraced.

"And you, Father," Agent 47 replied. "Thank you for agreeing to help."

"Such is the Lord's work," Vittorio said, as he eyed the plane. The children were being unloaded by then, and the scrawny youngsters made for a pitiful sight as another man, who looked to be the pilot, led them toward the terminal. "What can you tell me about the little ones?" the cleric inquired. "What happened to their families?"

"Their parents were killed by slavers. They were on their way to a whorehouse in Fez when something happened to the man who owned them," 47 replied.

Vittorio crossed himself. He could well imagine what the "something" was.

"But unlike most orphans, they come with an endowment," 47 added, as he presented Al-Fulani's briefcase to the clergyman.

The priest released the latches, took a peek inside, and closed the lid.

"That looks like a lot of money, my son."

"It is," 47 agreed. "And it's tax free."

The conversation was interrupted as the pilot arrived with the children in tow. The man was about to introduce himself when the orphans rushed Father Vittorio and quickly surrounded him.

"My name's Preston," the pilot said, as he extended his hand. "The children went to a mission school, before the priest was murdered and all of the villagers were forced to flee. So they know what a clerical collar means."

The copilot joined the group at that point. He had a briefcase tucked under one arm and was toting the two suitcases. "I don't know what you have in these things," he complained to 47, "but they're damned heavy!"

"That makes them harder to steal," 47 said lightly as he accepted the briefcase. The situation appeared to make the agent uncomfortable, and he seemed eager not to linger.

Before the operative could make his escape, one girl detached herself from the rest of the children and came to stand directly in front of him. Her big brown eyes were solemn, and her voice was clear as she spoke.

"Thank you, Mr. Taylor. All of us will remember your name."

That was probably the highest honor the Dinka children knew how to bestow. But as Father Vittorio looked at 47, he saw genuine consternation on the assassin's face. He suspected that it had never been the man's intention to help the children, and he wasn't sure how to respond.

The agent just nodded awkwardly, and mumbled, "You're welcome," as he slung the briefcase over a shoulder and took a grip on both of the suitcases.

There was a long moment of silence as three men and a little girl watched 47 walk away. Finally, having given a shake of his head, Father Vittorio spoke.

"The ways of God are mysterious, my friends . . . very mysterious indeed."

ROME, ITALY

It was early the next morning by the time Agent 47 arrived in Rome, took the train in from the airport, and checked into a nice but low-key hotel not far from the Spanish Steps. Then it was time to take a shower, brush his teeth, and grab some sleep.

Before he had left for Rome, he had tried again to contact Diana, and an unfamiliar voice had responded, claiming to be her replacement. That had been so out of the ordinary that 47 had decided not to trust his important information to a stranger, and had cut the connection immediately.

It was now light outside, but the heavy drapes served to keep most of the dawn sunshine out, and some of the traffic noise, as well. The carpet was equipped with a good pad, which meant the assassin was more comfortable than usual, and had little difficulty falling asleep.

Strangely—from 47's perspective at least—it was raining when he awoke. Dark clouds obscured the sun, and raindrops pattered against his window as he carried out his morning routines. Except that it was midafternoon by then, which meant it was going to be very difficult to find a decent breakfast, especially in a country where the first meal of the day normally consisted of coffee and a roll. A meal so nonexistent that they might as well not have bothered, insofar as 47 was concerned.

The solution was to eat at a hotel that not only catered to Americans, but boasted its own restaurant, because such an establishment was likely to offer eggs, pancakes, and bacon. Finding one involved a three-block walk without benefit of an umbrella, so 47 was soaking wet by the time he was shown into an over-decorated dining room and escorted to a table. The good news was that the restaurant did, indeed, serve American-style breakfasts.

The bad news was that they were serving lunch. Yet as always, money worked wonders, and having slipped a fifty-dollar bill to the waiter, the assassin was soon dining on a breakfast of waffles, bacon, and sausage, with hot coffee to wash it down.

With a full stomach, and a newly purchased umbrella to protect his head, the assassin made his way back to his hotel. His room had been cleaned, and his luggage was secure, so it was time to get back to work.

The first order of business was to call in again and try to speak with Diana, who, he hoped, would be back on duty. Since she hadn't heard from the agent in days, she could be counted on to chew him out, especially since he had hung up on her "replacement."

But having activated the satellite phone and entered the appropriate code, Agent 47 again found himself talking to a stranger. Not unheard of, but rare, since Diana was something of a workaholic, so he didn't cut the connection this time.

Equally unusual, however, was the fact that the man who answered the phone immediately routed the call to Mr. Nu, who 47 had last seen in Yakima. There was a thirty-second wait, but once the executive came on, he was clearly anxious to take the call.

"Agent 47? Is that you? We've been trying to reach you for days."

"I was kind of busy," the assassin replied honestly. "Where's Diana?"

The executive knew how attached field agents could

become to their controllers and was ready for the question.

"We need to talk, 47. Face-to-face. Where are you?"

"In Rome," the assassin answered cautiously.

"Okay, Rome it is," the executive replied. "I can be there in time for a late dinner. We'll eat, I'll bring you up to date on Diana, and you can tell me about Africa. How did it go, by the way? Were you able to catch up with Al-Fulani?"

The question hung between them as the assassin considered his options. He could—and probably should—tell Mr. Nu what he had learned, but something felt wrong. Something having to do with Diana.

So rather than answer the question, the agent chose to end the conversation.

"I'm sorry," he said, "but there's someone at the door. Let's catch up tonight. Where should we meet?"

Nu sensed the agent's hesitancy, but thought it best to let the matter slide, confident that he would learn whatever there was to know later in the day. So instead, he gave the name of his favorite restaurant.

"I'll see you at nine," he said, and he waited for 47 to be the one who broke the circuit.

He opened another channel, and a quick conversation with a technician in the *Danjou*'s control room was sufficient to confirm that, based on the tracker built into 47's phone, the agent really was in Rome. It wasn't that the executive didn't trust the assassin. But still . . .

Diana had been above suspicion until recently and now nothing seemed certain. Suspicion was like a communicable disease, and once contracted, it was almost impossible to beat.

"Call the airport," Nu said. "Tell our pilot to file a flight plan for Rome. I'll be there in thirty minutes."

Now that he thought about it, maybe he didn't trust the assassin. In fact, maybe he didn't trust anyone.

It was still raining, and Agent 47 had been watching the restaurant for more than an hour when a cab pulled up and Mr. Nu got out. The assassin had no reason to expect a trap, but it always paid to be careful, so he waited for a full five minutes to see if anyone else showed up. He scanned the nearby buildings, as well, but saw nothing that appeared to be suspicious. Finally, satisfied that the restaurant was reasonably safe, he stepped out into a cold drizzle.

Five minutes later he was seated across a linen-covered table from his superior. A small oil-fed lamp had been placed at the center of the surface and it lit the executive's face from below.

"All of the food here is excellent," Nu said, as he gestured toward a waiting menu, "but I'm especially fond of the chicken risotto. The chef uses the Carnaroli grain, which holds its shape better than the Arborio, yet absorbs the stock extremely well. Or, you might like the *Pasta Rustico,* which generally appeals to those with hearty appetites."

In the end 47 ordered the pasta dish, which turned out to be delicious and went perfectly with the house red. Once they had eaten the main course, Nu got down to business.

"You inquired about Diana," the executive said somberly, "and I put you off. That's because it looks as though she's the person we've been looking for."

Agent 47 opened his mouth to protest, but Nu raised a hand.

"The two of you have a close working relationship. I know that. But hear me out."

So 47 listened as the executive laid out the evidence against Diana, and their dessert arrived.

"So, that's it," Mr. Nu concluded gloomily. "It would appear that Diana sold us out—except that she claims the payments are part of an elaborate trick. An effort to direct attention away from the true culprit. Personally, I hope she's correct—but it doesn't look likely. Not unless you have information to the contrary."

Agent 47 met the other man's eyes. "Yes, I believe I do, although I need more proof. According to Al-Fulani the man we're looking for is Aristotle Thorakis. Al-Fulani claimed that Thorakis is—or was—in serious financial trouble. Such deep trouble that it was necessary to accept a loan from the *Puissance Treize* to remain in business. And they've been draining him dry ever since."

Nu frowned. "Are you sure? We knew he was having problems, but when our accountants went over his finances, he came up clean. All the money he borrowed seemed to come from legitimate sources."

"Tell the bean counters to take another look," Agent 47 suggested dryly. "It's my guess that those 'legitimate sources' are actually fronts. Or firms that are beholden to the *Puissance Treize* in some way."

"What you say makes sense," Nu acknowledged. "But even you admit that we lack proof. What if the bean counters don't find anything?"

"Then hopefully *I* will," 47 responded. "I plan to track Thorakis down and see what I can learn. But don't tell the board. If Thorakis gets wind of what we're doing, he'll take additional steps to cover his tracks or run."

"Understood," the executive said. "But until such time as we can prove that Thorakis is guilty, Diane will remain under lock and key. And there's a lot of pressure to punish her now."

"From whom?" 47 wanted to know. "From Thorakis?"

"Yes," Nu confirmed. "But from others as well. They want blood."

"I need time," 47 responded.

"How much?"

"Two weeks."

"Okay," the executive said reluctantly. "That's a lot, but I'll do my best. It won't be easy, though."

"No," Agent 47 agreed soberly. "It won't be easy."

When Agent 47 awoke the next morning he could feel the clock ticking.

Not for himself, but for Diana, which was strange, because he barely knew her. And how could it be otherwise? Given the fact that most of their relationship consisted of five-minute phone conversations.

But with the exception of extremely rare face-to-face meetings like the one with Nu, Diana was his only genuine link with The Agency. And his only hope for help when a mission went awry. So that made the controller important to 47's survival, which, all things considered, made her very important indeed.

Such were the assassin's thoughts as he downed a quick breakfast at the American hotel, and went back to his room to conduct some online research. The sort of thing The Agency normally took care of for him, but he would need to handle himself, lest he reveal his interest in Aristotle Thorakis.

The first and most pressing problem was where to find the shipping magnate. The Greek was very well known, so having entered the name "Aristotle Thorakis" into a popular search engine, the agent came up with 1,918,000 hits.

Most of them had to do with the shipping tycoon's business dealings. And it was then—while sampling some of the stories about the way Aristotle had improved the family-owned company—that 47 came across an article regarding one of the Greek's competitors. A Mexican businessman named José Alvarez, who had just been starting to take business away from a Thorakis-owned cruise line when he had the misfortune to drown in his own swimming pool. It was a terrible accident. Or that's what the stories claimed.

The assassin already knew about the incident, because he'd been there that night. Instead of using scuba gear, which would produce bubbles, 47 had been equipped with a military-style rebreather, and was already submerged at the deep end of the pool when Alvarez dove in. Pulling the entrepreneur under had been relatively easy. Keeping him down had been a little more difficult.

By continually refining his search terms, 47 was able to find dozens of newspaper and magazine articles about Thorakis, his family, and the lifestyle they enjoyed. And after skimming a number of those stories, the assassin came to the conclusion that when not attending a business meeting in London, New York, Hong Kong, or some other center of international finance, the shipping magnate spent most of his time on the family estate near Kalomata, Greece, at his high-rise condo in Athens, aboard the sleek superyacht *Perseus,* or in a relatively modest mansion located in Sintra, Portugal.

Which, the operative soon learned from the tabloids, was rumored to be the house where the businessman kept his Ethiopian mistress. A relationship his wife was said to be aware of, but chose to ignore.

Having determined the places where Thorakis was most likely to be found, the assassin's next step was to zero in on the shipping magnate's current location. It had begun to seem hopeless, until the agent discovered that there were weekly papers that made it their business to keep track of Hollywood starlets, spoiled aristocrats, and yes, wealthy businessmen like Thorakis. Especially when they were being naughty, which according to the very latest edition of *La Dolce Vita,* the Greek definitely was.

According to the breathless text that accompanied a much-magnified shot of the shipping magnate nibbling on a woman's bare foot, Thorakis was currently lying low in Sintra with his mistress. And judging from the six suitcases that had been unloaded from his limo, the businessman was planning to stay for a while.

A quick phone call to a small paper in Sintra was sufficient to confirm the Greek's presence.

But rather than travel to Sintra, and improvise some sort of cover subsequent to his arrival, 47 wanted to do it the right way. Which was to construct an alternate identity before he boarded a plane. It was the sort of thing Diana normally took care of for him, yet now, having been forced to do his own research, the operative already knew the unsavory sort of person he wanted to impersonate.

As a member of the freewheeling, hypercompetitive, and often unethical band of photographers frequently referred to as the *paparazzi*, he could hang around the Thorakis mansion at all hours of the day and night, carry a variety of cameras, and openly follow the Greek wherever he went. All without eliciting any suspicion.

Of course first, before assuming his new identity, Agent 47 knew it would be necessary to change his appearance. Not just a little bit, but a lot, because Thorakis knew very well what he looked like, and if he really was a turncoat, the *Puissance Treize* would want to protect him.

So the assassin made some phone calls, took down an address, and set the alarms on his luggage.

Agent 47 had learned a lot about makeup and theatrical appliances over the years. So much so that when he entered the *Portello Dell Fase* he was able to successfully pass himself off as a British actor who had unexpectedly been called upon to play Shakespeare's Falstaff. There was much bustling about as the proprietress, a onetime stage actress herself, went in search of the perfect strap-on foam belly. An appliance that, when combined with a half-halo of black hair and some cheek inserts, would transform her customer into the shameless, lying tub of lard that was Falstaff.

The woman was equipped with costumes as well, and though of the opinion that 47 was too tall to play Falstaff, she said that she was willing to make the necessary alterations anyway.

Agent 47 demurred, however, insisting that the theater

company would provide his costume, so he was able to exit gracefully after spending what seemed like an exorbitant amount of money in the shop.

With those purchases made it was time to visit a men's clothing store, where the assassin insisted on looking after himself, and eventually left with a wardrobe that the cashier knew was too large for him.

Satisfied with his new look, and confident that it would fool just about anyone, 47 went back to the hotel, where he returned to his room. And it was there that Tazio Scaparelli was born. The *paparazzo* was a homely man, with a bald pate surrounded by unruly black hair, fat cheeks, a mole on his upper lip, and a substantial gut that not only hung out over his belt, but threatened to split his cheap sports shirt wide open. A pair of baggy pants and some thick-soled shoes completed the outfit.

He wasn't going to take the Silverballers, the Walther, or the shotgun into Portugal. Nor did he want to take his regular clothes, since Scaparelli couldn't wear them. So the assassin only took what he needed, packed all of it into his briefcase, and left the hotel via an emergency exit.

Ten minutes later the agent stepped up to a pay phone, dialed a long series of digits, and waited for the inevitable answer. When it came he cut the controller off. "This is 47. Please send someone to get my luggage. Oh, and one other thing, tell whoever you send to leave the locks alone. Otherwise something could go *boom!*"

The controller started to respond—but the conversation was over.

SEVENTEEN

PARIS, FRANCE

Conditions inside the *Prison de la Santé* in the XIVe *arrondissement* of Paris could only be described as a living hell. The cells were filthy, the noise was deafening, drug use was rampant, communicable diseases took a constant toll, rapes were a common occurrence, and the only way to escape was to commit suicide. Which inmates frequently did.

All of which made *Santé* a very dangerous place to be for any person other than Louis Legard, who as Managing Director of the *Puissance Treize*, had the benefit of bodyguards, specially prepared food, and a host of other privileges that most inmates could only dream of.

Still, privileged or not, the last place Legard wanted to be was in *Santé*. So as one of the Frenchman's muscular bodyguards cleared a path for the crime boss, who had been forced to use crutches since the most recent attempt on his life, Legard was anything but happy. In spite of more than two million euros spent on lawyers, bribes, and appeals, he had yet to find a way out of the festering hole that the French government had put him in.

Not for murder, which he deserved, but for tax evasion. *An offense so pedestrian as to be ridiculous.*

Prisoners and guards seemed to simply melt away as the *Puissance Treize* chief and his entourage turned into a main corridor and made their way toward the security checkpoint where Legard would be searched prior to being released into the visitor center that lay beyond. The screening process was something not even Legard could avoid, although the normally arrogant guards were careful to preserve the prisoner's sense of dignity, knowing what could happen to them if they didn't.

In fact, it had been less than a year since a new staff member had referred to Legard as an *estropié repugnant*. The guard, his wife, and both of their children had been mysteriously murdered three days later. No one had been arrested for the crime as yet, but the message was clear, and Legard had been treated with the utmost delicacy ever since.

Having been cleared through the security checkpoint, he was left to lurch across an open area to the row of narrow cubicles where prisoners could talk to visitors through sheets of cloudy Plexiglas. Consistent with the prepaid bribes that he had received, the guard responsible for regulating the flow of inmates took care to slot Legard into a booth between two empties; a seemingly trivial favor, but one that would serve to protect the man's privacy—something that was very important to him.

Pierre Douay had come to dread his visits with Legard. Both because of the unpleasant surroundings and the Managing Director's ceaseless demands for a new trial, better medical care, and more fresh fruit. As Legard entered the cubicle on the other side of the Plexiglas and laid the crutches on the floor, Douay dipped a hand into a coat pocket and activated a scrambler that resembled a popular brand of MP3 player.

The Managing Director had always been a small man, but had lost quite a bit of weight since the failed assassination attempt, and was about the size of an average teenaged boy. He had thick white hair, a face that could only be described as gaunt, and lips so thin his mouth resembled a horizontal slash. A chromed metal grille was mounted in the Plexiglas, but given how loud the background sound was, both men were forced to lean in close in order to hear each other without being overheard by others.

"Good morning, sir," Douay began politely. "How are you?"

"How the hell do you *think* I am?" Legard demanded sourly. "I feel like shit! When are you going to get me out of this stinking cesspool?"

"Soon," Douay promised soothingly. "Very soon."

"That's what you said last time," the older man complained bitterly. "Yet I'm still here."

"These things take time," Douay replied. "The wheels of government grind slowly. But the lawyers tell me that in four months, six at the most, our request for an appeal will be granted. Once we know which judge and prosecutor have been assigned to the case, we'll bring them around. But until that time, we simply don't know who to target."

Everything Douay said was true, and Legard knew it, but the crime boss was rightfully suspicious.

"So you say, Pierre . . . so you say. But I'm no fool! The longer I remain locked up in prison—the longer you remain in charge of the *Puissance Treize*."

Douay had been on the receiving end of that accusation many times before, and his answer was ready.

"But I'm not in charge, sir. *You* are. All I do is pass your instructions along to the partners. And, because you have sources of information other than myself, you know that I continue to serve you well."

"The profits are good," Legard admitted grudgingly. "But what about the Sinon Project? How is that going?"

Sinon was the ancient Greek spy who, if the legends were correct, was the person who convinced the Trojans to open the gates and allow the wooden horse to enter Troy.

"It's going well," Douay answered honestly. "By planting large amounts of money on one of The Agency's most trusted employees, we were able to divert attention away from the real traitor. And he continues to provide us with a continual flow of useful information. Some of which must be ignored, if we are to preserve the source."

"I understand that," Legard grated as he stared through the Plexiglas. "But remember this: It's my intent to crush The Agency. Not just nibble it to death! And one of the best ways to accomplish this is to destroy their most effective operatives. You missed Agent 47 the first time. Don't make the same mistake again."

Whether it was true or not, Legard expressed the belief that the mysterious Agent 47 had fired the 7.62×51 mm bullet that was responsible for his useless leg. This was one reason why a trap had been laid for the operative during the earliest phase of Project Sinon. But every attempt to eliminate 47 had failed, and the assassin was still on the loose.

"Yes, sir," Douay said humbly. "If we see an opportunity to kill him, we will."

Blood rose to suffuse Legard's otherwise pallid face, his eyes seemed to glow as if lit from within, and spittle flew from his lips as he spoke.

"*Make* an opportunity, goddamn you! Or I'll put *you* on crutches—or worse—and see how you like it!"

This time the crime boss's voice had been loud enough to turn heads, and Douay was conscious of the fact that people were staring at him as he lifted a fruit basket up off the floor.

"I brought some apples, sir. Plus bananas and grapes. I'll pass them to the guards on my way out."

"I'm sorry," Legard said contritely, and sighed as he looked away. "I'm an old man, and I say foolish things. I know you'll do your best."

"It's very difficult in here," Douay said sympathetically. "I realize that—and I'm sorry."

The visit came to an end shortly after that. Douay gave the basket of fruit to one of the guards, followed a young woman and her little girl out onto the busy street, and paused to reacclimate himself. That was when he took a deep breath, gave thanks for everything he had, and all he was going to have.

Because it would be a cold day in hell when Louis Legard left *Santé* prison and felt warm sunshine on his ugly face.

EIGHTEEN

LISBON, PORTUGAL

The Portela airport had been opened in October of 1942 at the height of World War II. Because it was used by both the Germans and the British, the airfield had been the nexus of all sorts of espionage. And as Agent 47 entered the large, rather institutional terminal building, it was as if some of that history still lingered in the air.

A large group of tourists had just come off a British Airways flight from London. Many were cranky, having just learned that their luggage was back in Heathrow, and wouldn't arrive until the following day. The newly created *paparazzo* Tazio Scaparelli had no such difficulties, however, as the photographer went to retrieve his cheap vinyl suitcase, and hauled the bag out toward the front of the terminal. Thanks to the fact that he was traveling from one member of the European union to another, he wasn't required to show a passport. A change for the better, insofar as lawbreakers such as himself were concerned.

As the operative walked, his Nikon D2x digital camera had a tendency to bounce off his potbelly. Rather than walk around with a new camera, which might give him away, 47 had been careful to buy one that had already seen plenty of hard use, and showed it. Consistent with the Scaparelli persona, the Nikon was hanging at the ready, should some unsuspecting starlet cross his path. A little thing, it was true, but important, especially to the knowledgeable eye.

As the assassin made his way through the terminal, he could feel dozens of eyes slide across him as a multitude of policemen, con artists, spies, drug dealers, thieves, gun runners, and other players compared his countenance to the ones they were looking for, then moved on. If any of the onlookers were employed by the *Puissance Treize,* none took notice of the fat man.

The terminal building had been remodeled more than once over the years, and the current iteration consisted of a gently curved façade made out of glass, flanked by two rectangular columns. A row of tall, spindly evergreens stood guard between the main building and the parking lot. There were plenty of taxis, and having flagged one of them down, 47 was careful to negotiate the fee in advance. Just as he fancied Scaparelli would do.

The town of Sintra was located eighteen miles northwest of Lisbon. The first part of the drive took the cab through Lisbon's not very distinguished suburbs, but once clear of the urban blight 47 found himself in one of the most beautiful places in Portugal, if not the world. An area known for its cool summer air and lush vegetation, it was so pleasant that Portuguese kings and aristocrats once spent their summers there.

Later, as word of Sintra's beauty continued to spread,

a steady stream of travelers visited the area. And they were still coming. Agent 47 knew that many tourists use Sintra as a base from which to explore the coast, while others take in local attractions like the *Palacio Nacional de Sintra* (Sintra Palace), the Regional Museum, and the Moorish Castle.

But for people like Aristotle Thorakis, who could afford a three-hundred-year-old home situated on a half acre of very valuable real estate, the town was a quiet retreat. A place to escape the media that prowled the streets of London, Paris, and Rome. Or that's what the glitterati were hoping for, although it was becoming increasingly difficult to escape the long lenses of men like Tazio Scaparelli.

For his own quarters, Agent 47 had chosen the Hotel Central, which had been *the* place to stay back in the early 1900s, but had long since been overtaken by generations of newer establishments. Yet as the operative paid his fare, and towed his shabby bag into the dated lobby, some of the hotel's original charm could still be seen in the richly polished wood, Portuguese tiles, and sturdy furniture that surrounded him.

All of which served to confirm that the Central was the sort of slightly seedy hostelry where a man on a limited expense account would choose to stay. Not to mention the fact that it was located across from the Sintra Palace, which put the hotel right at the center of all the tourist activity, and not far from the sort of restaurants that a man like Thorakis was likely to frequent.

As it turned out, Agent 47's small, somewhat threadbare room was on the second floor, facing a rather noisy square. But that was okay with the assassin, since he didn't plan to spend much time in it, and rarely had trouble falling asleep regardless of the din.

Consistent with the part he was playing, Agent 47 made no attempt to secure his belongings. With the exception of the seemingly innocuous fiber-wire garrote, and what appeared to be an insulin kit, all of the assassin's weapons were back in Rome. The whole idea was to let people search his luggage if they chose—knowing full well that everything they found would support his cover rather than blow it.

Even the password-protected laptop and the satellite phone were consistent with the requirements of Scaparelli's profession.

Pleased with the way things had gone so far, and with plenty of daylight left, the operative took the Nikon and went down into the street. As he followed a gently curving street toward the area where most of the mansions were located, he noticed that the houses along the way had red-tiled roofs, all manner of wrought iron balconies, and generally looked sturdy rather than graceful. Peaked roofs were common, as were lots of evenly spaced windows and narrow passageways that ran between the buildings.

But as the street took him down into what felt like a canyon, the architecture became increasingly diverse, and in many cases more elegant. A significant number of the homes built in this area over the last hundred years had been inspired by the architecture their owners were already familiar with or the rampant romanticism of the late eighteenth century. And the house Thorakis had chosen for his mistress fell into the latter category. It was three stories tall, and capped by all manner of interlocking pitched roofs. The walls were made of well-fitted gray stone, pierced here and there by windows that seemed too small for a building of that size, and were adorned with sculptural panels clearly imported from Germany or Bavaria.

Consistent with both its size and importance, the house was set well back from the street, surrounded by deciduous trees that were hundreds of years old, and separated from its neighbors by a largely ornamental stone wall. Some rather obvious surveillance cameras could be seen here and there, which when combined with at least two uniformed security guards, would be sufficient to keep the Scaparellis of the world out.

Conscious of the need to both establish his cover, and capture photographs of the mansion, 47 was careful to remove the lens cap before he brought the Nikon up and began to snap pictures. The long lens couldn't reach through the curtained windows into the rooms beyond, but the assassin was able to obtain valuable close-ups of what appeared to be a card reader mounted next to the front door, both of the security guards, and the German shepherd that followed the men around.

The operative had captured thirty-four exposures by the time a stranger appeared at his elbow. The newcomer was American, judging from his accent, and no more than five foot six. His clothes were black, as if that might make him look slimmer, and the soles of his shoes were at least an inch-and-a-half thick. He was armed with two cameras, one for long shots and the other for close-ups. Bright inquisitive eyes peered out from under thick eyebrows—and a two-day growth of black stubble covered his cheeks.

"The Greek ain't home," the little man said laconically. "He went to Lisbon. He'll probably be back for dinner, though. But you never know when Miss Desta will make an appearance."

"Thanks," 47 said cautiously, as he lowered the camera. This was the situation he feared most. A one-on-one conversation with a genuine member of the *paparazzi*, in which he might give himself away. "I'm Tazio Scaparelli. I just flew in from Rome."

"My name's Tony Fazio," the other photographer said. "My family's from Italy—but that was a long time ago. I grew up in New Jersey. Who are you shooting for?"

Agent 47 had been waiting for that question, and had his answer ready. "I'm a freelancer. How 'bout you?"

"*Star Track* sent me," Fazio replied. "They want pictures of Thorakis humping his mistress. Shot from three feet away, if possible."

Agent 47 laughed. "Only *three* feet? You get the easy assignments."

The conversation lasted for another five minutes or so—and the operative had some valuable nuggets by the time he turned away. First, the master bedroom was best photographed from the hillside behind the house, the upper slopes of which were on public property. Second, the Greek's Ethiopian mistress had once been a model, and was far from camera shy. Third, the couple ate out at least three times a week, often at the same French restaurant.

It wasn't clear which, if any, of those pieces of information would prove to be important, but 47 was more than satisfied with the results of his preliminary outing as he made his way back to the hotel. The next couple of hours were spent transferring the pictures he had taken to the laptop, going over them one by one, and learning as much as he could about the Greek's security precautions.

And it was during that process that 47 began to entertain new doubts. Not about his ability to penetrate the security cordon, and get close enough to kill Thorakis, but about the wisdom of doing so without more proof. The penalty for mistakenly assassinating a board member would be severe indeed.

So, what to do? The answer—or so it seemed to Agent 47—was to make all the necessary preparations, but stop just short of killing Thorakis. Then, at the very last moment, he would call Nu and tell him to leak a lie, and wait to see what occurred.

If the shipping magnate was the mole, he would immediately contact the *Puissance Treize* and ask for help. Thereby signaling his guilt.

The plan was somewhat convoluted, but necessarily so, given the situation. More reconnaissance would be necessary, but thanks to the information he had gleaned earlier in the day, he felt reasonably sure that he would eventually find a way to enter the mansion.

The killing itself—should it become necessary—couldn't be done overtly. A homicide investigation might lead back to his employers. And it might alert the *Puissance Treize* that The Agency was onto them. Something best left until the reprisals were over, and the enemy was burying its dead.

That suggested an "accident" of some sort. The kind everyone would accept. But *how*?

That was a problem the assassin would have to work out on his own.

* * *

The *Bon Appétit* was everything 47 expected it to be, which was to say a Portuguese imitation of a French restaurant, complete with Eiffel Tower wallpaper, candlelit tables, and an imperious staff. According to the information provided by Fazio, Thorakis and his mistress typically ate dinner at 8:00, so Agent 47 arrived at 7:30. The Nikon was concealed in a shopping bag.

Having been scrutinized by the maître d', and clearly been found wanting, the man with the bald pate and protruding paunch was shown to a tiny table located right next to the kitchen. Which, ironically enough, was the sort of spot Agent 47 often chose for himself so he could escape out the back should the necessity arise.

Indeed, it was a terrible table, since the heavily laden waiters had a tendency to brush it as they came and went, not to mention all the noise that emanated from the kitchen itself. However, 47 could hear snatches of conversation every once in a while, some of which were quite entertaining. The maître d' was known as *o porco* (the pig), somebody named Joao was HIV-positive, and a person referred to as "the goddamned dishwasher" had quit without warning.

Meanwhile, in between bits of culinary gossip, Agent 47 was served a hot *hors d'oeuvre,* yellow pepper soup, and a hearty *boeuf Bourguignon,* which left the assassin too full for dessert.

At neighboring tables tourists from all over the world talked to one another about the castles they'd seen, what they were planning to do during their visit, and a variety of personal matters, all of which seemed to center around money, sex, and power. What 47 thought of as the "unholy trinity," since those issues were at the heart of every murder he was hired to carry out.

But while such contemplations were interesting, his true reason for eating at the *Bon Appétit* was nowhere to be seen. So 47 paid the bill, took his camera, and left the establishment.

Once outside, the assassin retraced his steps from earlier in the day, except that this time he went uphill when the street split, rather than follow it down as he had before. It was dark by now, but the soft night air, the spill of light from the old-fashioned street lamps, and the buttery glow that emanated from the surrounding windows combined to create a surreal sense of peace and quiet.

It wasn't long before he arrived at a point directly above and behind the stone house. Others were out and about as well, so it was necessary for him to bend over awkwardly, and retie a shoelace while a German couple walked past. Then, once the tourists were a good fifty feet down the street, it was time to swing a leg up over the iron railing and lower himself into the inky blackness beyond.

The hillside was steep, and 47 very nearly lost his balance as his street shoes sent a small avalanche of dirt and gravel down the slope, but he was able to prevent what could have been a disastrous fall by grabbing on to a sturdy branch.

Most of the mansion's lights were on, but there was a good deal of foliage in the way, so the agent knew it would be necessary to work his way farther downhill before there would be any possibility of seeing in. And that was unfortunate, because while it had been merely annoying up on the street, the potbelly was a real encumbrance on the hillside, and made it difficult for him to move.

Nevertheless, he got a better grip on the shopping bag, chose his footholds with care, and gradually worked his way down until he was standing on top of an ancient retaining wall. It was some fifteen feet higher than the stone wall that surrounded the property, and but a single glance was sufficient to confirm that he could see into at least some of the windows, including what appeared to be a well-lit master bedroom.

He lowered the shopping bag to the ground, fumbled for the Nikon, and was in the process of removing the lens cap when the German shepherd began to bark. The assassin froze as a security guard passed through the pool of illumination generated by a spotlight mounted under the eaves. The man said something unintelligible to the animal, which came over to collect a pat on the head before following the human around a corner.

The agent waited a full ten seconds before bringing the camera up and turning it on. He could see that there was someone in the bedroom, and once he brought the image into focus, everything came clear. A beautiful black woman was seated in front of a mirror, brushing her hair, and staring at her own reflection. The Nikon made its characteristic *click-whir* as Agent 47 began to take pictures. Not so much of her as of the room—reconnaissance that could be of value later on.

And he was still at it when he heard a rock rattle down the slope, and went for a Silverballer.

Except that his pistols were back in Rome.

That meant that his best defense would be to react the way Scaparelli would, which was with an aggressive attitude, and a certain amount of bluster.

"Who's there?" he demanded with a hiss. "I have mace!"

"Save it for someone else," Fazio said *sotto voce,* as he skidded into the shadow 47 currently occupied. "I never should have told you about the back-shot. So, is she naked?"

"No," 47 said lightly. "But one can hope!"

"One sure can," the American replied, as he brought a camera up to his eye. "Wait a minute. Who do we have here? *Thorakis,* that's who! Okay, boys and girls, give me the money shot."

Satisfied that he wasn't about to be attacked by a counterassassin, Agent 47 turned back toward the house, and discovered that the *paparazzo* was correct. Thorakis had entered the bedroom, and judging from the towel that was wrapped around his waist, he was fresh from a shower. His broad shoulders were thick with curly black hair. The woman said something as the shipping magnate bent over to kiss her.

"Here we go!" Fazio enthused, as his camera clicked away. "Screw the bitch! Take her standing up!"

But as newsworthy as such an act might have been, it wasn't going to happen. The window was open to let the night air enter the room, which meant both men could hear the phone ring. Fazio swore as Thorakis went to answer it, and his mistress left the room a few moments later.

The two lurkers waited, hoping for something more, but other than a few brief sightings, nothing particularly exciting happened. And once the upstairs lights went out, it was obviously time to adjourn.

"Looks like it's time for a nightcap," Fazio said glumly. "Want to join me?"

Agent 47 had absolutely no desire for a drink, but knew Scaparelli would accept the offer, which meant *he* had to as well. So the assassin followed the American through the trees, up the steep hillside, and onto the street above. From there it was a short walk to a bar where Fazio was greeted by his first name.

After a round of beers and a game of darts, 47 was able to excuse himself and return to the hotel. Once in his room he pushed the dresser in front of the door, made a place for himself on the floor, and promptly fell asleep.

There were dreams, however. Strange dreams that centered around a house that contained many rooms, a very elusive woman, and a clock that continued to tick even after the assassin fired six bullets into it.

Even though the back door was propped open, and a floor-mounted fan was positioned just inside, the kitchen's interior was hot and steamy. Conditions Agent 47 was still in the process of getting used to, even though he'd been the *Bon Appétit*'s dishwasher for more than six hours by then. A job he had obtained by the simple expedient of showing up and asking for it. Not as Scaparelli, foam belly and all, but as a British drifter looking for a day's pay on his way to the French Riviera.

Originally the ploy had seemed like a good idea, since it would put him inside the restaurant where Thorakis preferred to eat, but now he wasn't so sure. What if the Greek failed to show? He would be trapped in this disgusting place, all those hours of hard work would be wasted, the better part of another day would have passed, and he would be no closer to his objective.

It seemed foolish to quit at that point, however, since the dinner crowd was filtering in, and the pace had started to quicken. The waiters shouted orders, the chefs swore at each other, and the fan roared as snatches of music came over the greasy boom box that rested on a shelf. Taken together, the noise, heat, and cooking odors made for a hellish environment.

Thankfully part of his job involved leaving the chaos of the kitchen for the relative calm of the dining room, where it was his job to retrieve plastic bins filled with dirty dishes. And even though it seemed as if time had slowed to a crawl, the room continued to fill.

And the moment the assassin had been hoping for finally arrived.

He had just left the kitchen to pick up the latest load of dishes when there was a commotion near the front entrance, and 47 turned to watch Thorakis and his entourage enter the restaurant. They were followed by a series of bright flashes as Fazio and a second member of the *paparazzi* tried to follow the party in, and the maître d' forced them back. There was a sudden buzz of conversation as everyone turned to watch the newly arrived guests make their way back to the tables that had been reserved for them.

Most of those who were present had no idea who the couple were, but a few recognized them, and word began to spread. There was a rumble of approval as Thorakis held a chair for his mistress—followed by more conversation as the businessman's two bodyguards were shown to an adjoining table. They looked tough, and judging from the way they handled themselves, they knew what they were doing.

Still another reason to come at Thorakis sideways, rather than head-on.

But there was a fifth member of the entourage, a sleek

man with slicked-back hair, who was making his way back toward the kitchen door. That struck 47 as interesting, so he carried his bin full of dishes back into the kitchen, and placed them next to the sink. It was easy to listen in because the sleek man had already entered into a shouting match with the senior chef.

"Mr. Thorakis eats here all the time!" the cook proclaimed indignantly. "So I am well aware of his allergy—and I can assure you that *nothing* harmful will be served to him. Perhaps you should get a *real* job, assuming you are qualified to cook a meal, which I doubt."

"Are you *insane*?" the sleek man demanded, as he waved a piece of paper under the other man's nose. "Look at this menu! What's the third special from the top? *Monga*, which is a recipe from French Guinea. And what is the primary ingredient of *Monga*? Two pounds of roasted peanut butter, plus two tablespoons of peanut oil, which is enough to kill Mr. Thorakis a thousand times over!"

"But only if we were to serve it to him," the chef countered angrily, "which we won't!"

"Not intentionally, no," the sleek man agreed. "But who knows how many of your cooking implements and surfaces have been contaminated? The choice is simple. You can prepare my client's food under *my* supervision, or the entire party will leave, and never come back."

That was a potent threat, since Thorakis was known as a big spender, and a draw for other customers, as well. So the chef knew how the restaurant's owner would respond—and was forced to back off.

Agent 47 was ordered to clean a work area under the sleek man's supervision—even as the necessary cooking utensils were scrubbed and dipped in boiling water. Then—and only then—was the restaurant's head chef allowed to prepare the chicken breasts stuffed with goat cheese that Thorakis doted on.

Three additional hours passed before Agent 47 washed the last dish, collected his pay, and departed the restaurant. It had been a long, hard day, but a profitable one. One part of the puzzle had been filled in. Thorakis had a weakness, a potentially fatal weakness, and all 47 needed to do was find a way to take advantage of it.

It was late afternoon, and the air was still warm as the domestic made her way down the street and stopped at the corner. There wasn't all that much traffic, but Maria was careful to look both ways before she crossed to the other side. She was tired, *very* tired, as were all the staff whenever Mr. Thorakis was in residence.

Miss Desta could be trying, especially when she spent too much time looking at herself in the mirror, but the Ethiopian model had been born into poverty, and knew what it was like to serve others. That made her more understanding.

Not Mr. Thorakis, though . . .

The Greek was often irritable, especially when his business was doing poorly, which seemed to be all of the time these days. That was when he threw things, like the Gucci loafer that had hit her earlier that day, and the magazine the day before. Such acts were almost always followed by a twenty-euro bill a few hours later. But like most of the staff members, Maria would have preferred an apology.

She could quit, of course, but to do what? Lacking the sort of good looks that would attract a man, or the skills that businesses were looking for, Maria knew her only other choice would be to work in one of Sintra's hotels. The sort of job that would not only pay less, but force her to endure a year-round grind as an endless procession of tourists came and went. Even though things were difficult at the moment, Thorakis typically spent most of his time elsewhere, which made for relatively easy days when he was gone.

Such were the maid's thoughts as a man carrying a complicated-looking camera stepped out to bar the way.

"Hello!" he said cheerfully. "May I speak to you for a moment?"

Maria had heard about men who did horrible things to young women, but this man, with his big potbelly, looked harmless enough, and there were plenty of tourists in the vicinity, so she paused.

"You want to speak with *me*?" she responded. "Why?"

"Because you're an important member of the Thorakis household, that's why," the man responded. "And I work for *Le Monde*. It's a newspaper. We're doing a profile on Mr. Thorakis, and would like to learn more about his home life."

Maria was intrigued. No one ever asked her opinion on anything—not even her parents—and here was a man who thought she was "important."

"What would you like to know?" she inquired cautiously. "Will it get me in trouble?"

"Trivial things for the most part," the fat man said reassuringly. "Quality of life things. Like what time does Mr. Thorakis go to bed? When does he eat? That sort of stuff. And don't worry—I won't use your name. Plus, if you join me for a cup of coffee at that café over there, I'll pay you one hundred euros for your time."

Maria glanced at the establishment in question and back at the man again. Coffee was safe, the café was safe, and a hundred euros was a lot of money. Plus, what was there to go home to? Her mother's nagging? And her father's endless demands?

"Okay," she said slyly, "but I want fifty euros up front."

The man smiled. "You're a very smart young woman. Let's adjourn to the café, where I can give you the first half of the payment without anyone taking notice."

Maria liked that idea, because Sintra was a small town, and she didn't want to be seen accepting cash from a foreigner, especially not out here on a main street. Even a whisper of scandal would cause Maria's father to whip her with his belt. Because in his view, his daughter's virginity was the only asset she had.

So the two of them went to the café, where the man slipped fifty euros to the maid under the table, and ordered coffee for both of them. The conversation lasted for more than an hour, because the reporter from *Le Monde* was not only fascinated by the most mundane details of Maria's job, but by the people she worked with, as well as their interpersonal relationships.

Therefore she was exhausted by the time the interview finally came to a close—and the fellow passed another fifty-euro note under the table.

"Thank you, Maria," he said sincerely. "You've been very helpful. Now remember, I won't mention your name in the article—and you must remain silent, as well. Otherwise you could lose your job."

Maria nodded, came to her feet, and glanced at her watch. It was dinnertime! And Maria wasn't there to help. Her mother would be furious.

Still, the interview had been worth it, and the maid felt happy as she hurried away.

Having determined the internal layout of the house, along with the habits of those who lived there, 47 was that much closer to being ready. But one problem remained, and that was how to enter the mansion, and do so at the correct time. Which, based on information provided by Maria, would be during the day. The most difficult time of all.

The assassin drained the last of his coffee, left the café, and waddled up the street.

The assassin was worried—and had good reason to be, he knew—as the minutes and hours continued to tick away. More than half the time allotted to him by Mr. Nu had already come off the clock, and there was still a lot of work left to do. Finding a way to enter the mansion during the day was proving to be difficult. No, impossible, since none of the schemes he had considered proved feasible.

Take the "magazine" man, for example. His name was Pedro, and based on the research that the assassin had carried out, he was a retired carpenter who pulled in a few euros a day by driving his beat-up sedan into Lisbon at four in the morning, buying newspapers and magazines that wouldn't arrive in Sintra until late that afternoon, then delivering them to the mansion so Thorakis could scan them while he ate his breakfast. That raised the possibility that 47 could bribe the man, pose as his son, and come along for the ride. Then, once the guards were used to seeing the new face, the rest would be easy. Except that Pedro never spent more than five minutes in the house, which meant his fake son wouldn't be allowed to either, which left the assassin back at the starting point.

A couple of other possibilities were eliminated in the same fashion. That left the operative with growing frustration, and he was beginning to wonder if his whole plan was going down the drain.

Finally, he decided that the simple approach would be the best. Once most of Sintra's citizens were asleep, he would enter the mansion during the hours of darkness, hide until daylight, and carry out the assassination. Then, rather than flee, he would return to his hiding place and remain there until the ensuing ruckus was over.

Assuming the plan was successful, the Greek's death would look like an accident, which meant no one would come looking for him. Once nightfall returned, Agent 47 would sneak out of the house again, and slip over the wall.

From what the assassin had observed, Thorakis's security had been allowed to lapse somewhat. Perhaps due to the cost and the business setbacks Maria had mentioned. According to her, the number of guards was one-third what it had once been, and the Greek had stopped monitoring the cameras twenty-four-seven. Perhaps he hoped their very presence would fool an intruder into thinking the place was secure.

He needed to find a way to neutralize the damned dog, though. Not kill it, because that would put the security guards on high alert, but incapacitate the animal for a while—long enough for him to get in and out.

The answer was the sedative that 47 had stolen from a local veterinarian's office along with a variety of things meant to cover what the assassin really wanted. And, because the vet doubled as the local animal control officer, the assassin had been able to steal a dart gun as well.

Thus equipped, it was time for a dry run. This was one of the most important assignments of his career, and he wasn't about to leave anything to chance.

Having left the Scaparelli outfit back at the hotel, Agent 47 eased his way down the hillside behind the house and bellied up to the stone wall. It was late, so most of the lights were off, and with the exception of the dog and two security guards, the entire household was clearly in bed.

The German shepherd was allowed to roam free, so it wasn't long before the dog rounded a corner and paused to sample the night air. Agent 47 heard the animal growl deep in its throat, knew a bark would follow, and took careful aim. The air pistol could fire only one hypodermic dart at a time—which meant that the first shot would have to be dead-on. It was a lot to ask at night, especially since he was using an unfamiliar weapon.

The bark was already starting to form itself in the German shepherd's throat when 47 squeezed the trigger. There was a soft *phut* as the dart flew straight and true, followed by a startled yelp as the needle entered flesh and delivered a 5:1 combination of ketamine and xylazine into the dog's circulatory system. The animal took three staggering steps, wobbled as it tried to remain upright, and collapsed. Which was perfect.

But had anyone heard?

Agent 47 hesitated for a moment, blood pounding in his ears, before vaulting over the wall. The guards would find the dog—that was a given—but how soon? The challenge was to recover the dart and enter the house before the animal was discovered.

One of many things the operative had learned from Maria was that the security cameras went unmonitored during the day, on the theory that there was no need for electronic surveillance as long as the guards were patrolling the grounds. Was the same true at night? Agent 47 would find out soon enough as he raced across the yard to the point where the semiconscious dog lay, plucked the yellow-feather dart out of the animal's side, and slipped it into a pocket. This small detail was crucial. With nothing else to go on, the guards would conclude that the animal was sick, and hopefully focus on him rather than search for an intruder.

Moments later a male voice was heard calling for the German shepherd and it became steadily louder. The assassin felt something heavy land in the pit of his stomach as he made for the back door. Would there be sufficient time to pick the lock? No, 47 was pretty sure that there wouldn't be, as he put his hand on the doorknob and twisted.

The knob turned, the door opened, and he was inside!

What about the alarm? Surely Thorakis would have one. But no, the house was as quiet as a tomb, with only the ticking of a grandfather clock to break the otherwise perfect silence. This suggested that the person who was in charge of security was entirely too reliant on the human factor.

Worried lest he make noise, or track telltale dirt through what Maria claimed was a spotlessly clean house, 47 removed his shoes, tied the shoelaces together so he could hang them around his neck, and ghosted from room to room.

After a short time, confident that he knew the layout by heart, he followed the dimly lit back stairs all the way up to the unfinished attic, where—according to Maria—the senior housekeeper had occasional trysts with the shipping magnate's chef, who was something of a ladies' man.

Having attained his goal, Agent 47 shrugged his way out of the day pack, reloaded the air pistol, and zipped the weapon away. Maybe, if he had gauged the dosage correctly, he would be able to escape without having to sedate the dog again. Especially if the guards took the animal to a vet and left it there overnight. In the meantime there was plenty of food and water in the pack along with an MP3 player to see him through the boring hours ahead.

Moving with extreme caution, he made his way over to a jumble of boxes, and crawled behind several of them. The floor was hard, but he was used to that, and found a spot that was both comfortable and defensible.

Meanwhile, one floor below, the man Agent 47 was planning to kill was wide awake and staring at the ceiling.

Even though things were going well for him, and he had every reason to be happy, it felt as if ice-cold fingers were clutching his intestines.

Why?

There was no way to know—and the hours seemed to crawl by.

PATRAS, GREECE

Sunlight sparkled on the surface of the bay, and a powerful speedboat carved a long white line through the blue water as it towed a bikini-clad teenager past the *Jean Danjou*'s lofty stern. The young woman waved, and although Mr. Nu waved back, Diana didn't.

Which wasn't too surprising, given the controller's official status as a prisoner, and the chrome bracelet that encircled one of her shapely ankles. The leg iron was connected to a stanchion by a six-foot length of stainless steel chain intended to keep the woman from diving off the ship and swimming ashore. A long pull, but a feat that Diana thought she was probably capable of.

However, the bracelet and chain were really a kindness, a way to let Diana up on the deck, rather than keep her confined in the brig below. More than that, a sign that Mr. Nu was willing to give her the benefit of the doubt, even if many of The Agency's board members were already convinced of her guilt and eager to see her punished.

But Diana found it difficult to sit at the linen-covered table and soak up the Mediterranean sun knowing that the last days of her life might be ticking away. Even though Agent 47 claimed to have knowledge of who the real turncoat was, the assassin was in Sintra, Portugal, and hadn't been heard from since his meeting with Nu.

Was that because he had followed the wrong lead?

Because he was dead?

There was no way to know. So as Diana surveyed the harbor and took a sip of chilled wine, death was very much on her mind. The controller wanted to live, but knew that she, like every other member of the human race, was one day going to die.

The only question was: When?

A uniformed crew member approached the table. He was dressed in a short-sleeved white shirt, matching shorts, and deck shoes. As with all of the other crew members he was careful to ignore the ankle bracelet and chain.

"There's a phone call for you, sir," the crew member said respectfully. "Should we put it through?"

Everyone was aware that Nu coveted the hour between five and six. It was when he liked to sit on the stern and enjoy an uninterrupted cocktail. So, given the fact that the people in the control room had seen fit to send a messenger, the call was probably important. Mr. Nu sighed. "Who is it?"

"Agent 47, sir," the crewman answered.

Diana felt her heart leap, and saw her companion's eyebrows rise.

"Patch him through," Nu instructed. "I'll take the call."

"They already have," the messenger said expressionlessly. "He's on line two."

The phone was already on the table. All the executive had to do was to push the appropriate button. Diana was grateful he put the call on speaker.

"Agent 47?" Nu inquired. "I must say, it's about time."

The assassin kept his voice low, which led Diana to

believe that he was in a position that could be compromised.

"Sorry, sir, but I've been busy."

Nu glanced at Diana.

"Don't keep me in suspense, 47. What, if anything, have you been able to learn?"

"I still believe Thorakis is the man that we're looking for . . . but I haven't been able to find proof. That's where you come in."

Nu frowned. "I don't understand."

"Here's what I want you to do," 47 explained. "Tell all of the board members—including Thorakis—that I know who the traitor is, and that I'm on my way to kill that individual. But don't identify anyone by name. And find an opportunity to let the name 'Hotel Central' slip out. It's an establishment that Thorakis is bound to recognize.

"If our man is innocent, he won't do anything at all. But I'm betting that he'll phone his contact within the *Puissance Treize* and beg for help. When that help comes, I'll be waiting. And *that* will constitute the proof we need."

"And then?" Mr. Nu wanted to know.

"And then Mr. Thorakis is going to have an accident," the assassin responded flatly.

The sun was on the edge of the horizon by then, and Diana felt a sudden chill. She lacked a sweater, so she wrapped her arms around her torso instead.

"I like it," the executive replied coldly. "I like it very much. But be careful. Assuming things go the way you expect them to, the people the *Puissance Treize* send will be very, very good. Do you need help?"

"Thanks," 47 replied. "But no thanks."

"All right then," Nu said. "Keep me informed."

"I will," the assassin assured him. "And I have a message for Diana. . . . "

The executive looked from the phone to the controller and back again.

"Yes? What is it?"

"Tell her she owes me."

Diana was about to reply when she heard a *click*, followed by a dial tone.

She deserved to die for some of things she had done. By most people's standards anyway. But maybe, just maybe, a guardian angel was about to save her.

If so, he would be a dark angel, sent from a place other than heaven.

NINETEEN

A large banner had been strung between two of the weather-beaten columns that were evenly spaced along the front of the sun-splashed terrace. It read HAPPY BIRTHDAY NICOLE, in big blue letters. Colorful groupings of balloons bobbed here and there, a long narrow table occupied the center of the space, where dirty plates and the half-eaten remains of a very expensive birthday cake could still be seen.

Children squealed with excitement as they chased each other back and forth, completely unaware of the dark deeds that had been carried out within the castle during the last five hundred years, or the blood money required to purchase and maintain the fortress now. And even though some of the adults who were seated around well-set tables knew about such things, they too were lost in the moment.

Pierre Douay's daughter, Nicole, had just turned seven, the children were enjoying themselves, and it was a lovely day.

Such was the scene when the phone in Douay's

pocket began to vibrate. The Frenchman didn't want to answer it, but that particular number was known to less than thirty people, every one of whom was extremely important in one way or another. So Douay swore silently, went inside in order to get away from the noise, and eyed the incoming number.

The call was from Aristotle Thorakis, a man the executive had come to detest, but was still in a position to provide the *Puissance Treize* with valuable information. Which was the only reason Douay thumbed the device on.

It was like opening a floodgate.

"Pierre?" Thorakis demanded emotionally. "It's a disaster, I tell you. An unmitigated disaster! A man named Agent 47 captured one of your people, a Moroccan I think, and found out about *me!*

"Agent 47 reported in and he's on his way to *kill* me! I need protection, Pierre. *Lots* of protection—and I need it *now.*"

Douay had always been able to remain calm, even when those all about him were losing their nerve, and began his analysis by cross-checking the known facts.

Al-Fulani was missing, and had been for more than a week, which seemed to lend credence to the story. Couple that with the failed attempt on Agent 47's life, and that individual's reputation for tenaciousness, and there was the very real possibility that the Greek was correct.

But why protect him? Especially given how annoying the shipping magnate had become.

The answer was glaringly obvious. Thorakis was into the *Puissance Treize* for 500 million euros. A significant sum that might go unrecovered if the Greek was killed.

And what then? the executive wondered. Who would the partners blame? That, too, was glaringly obvious.

Besides which, there still might be a great deal of valuable information to extract from the annoying man's brain before they decided whether or not to kill him.

"Stay where you are," Douay ordered. "I'll send a team. A good team. They'll kill 47. Then, with him out of the way, we'll pull you out of Sintra. The Agency will be angry, but we'll cut a deal with them."

"Really?" Thorakis inquired hopefully. "You can do that?"

"Of course I can," Douay replied confidently. "Don't worry about it. Just stay where you are and wait for my people to arrive."

The shipping magnate was grateful, almost too grateful, and the Frenchman felt a sense of disgust as the Greek told him where the assassin would be staying. Then the line went dead.

The next part was easy, as a two-person hunter-killer team was taken off an assignment in Prague and redirected to Sintra.

Once that chore was out of the way, Douay had to face something more difficult. He needed to activate the alternate identities that had been established for his wife and children, years before. Once that was accomplished he would send them to the retreat in French Polynesia and prepare for the reprisals that were sure to follow. Even if the *Puissance Treize* were able to eliminate 47 and protect Thorakis, The Agency would come looking for someone to kill. And Pierre Douay's name would appear near the top of the list. While Legard, ironically enough, would be relatively safe in prison!

It felt as though the sunshine had lost all of its warmth as the Frenchman stepped out onto the terrace. The laughter sounded discordant, and the smiles looked false.

That was the moment when Douay realized how exposed the terrace was, how easy it would be for someone to shoot Nicole from a thousand yards away, and he called to his guests.

The party was over.

TWENTY

Having successfully escaped from the Greek's mansion during the hours of darkness, Agent 47 had returned to the hotel and was sitting in the lobby when the *Puissance Treize* hunter-killer team checked in. It was no accident that he'd been waiting for them. They were dressed like tourists, but the assassin knew them the same way that one animal knows another. They were towing their own luggage, so no one could tamper with their belongings, notice how heavy the suitcases were, or accidentally misplace them.

The man was about six-two, well built, and had fair skin. His hair was blond, too short to grab hold of, and worn in a flattop. He was dressed in a dark blue sport shirt that was one size too big so it would hang over the bulge high on his right hip.

And as Mr. Flattop took care of the check-in formalities, his female companion was facing the lobby, rather than the counter. That was the key to the hunter-killer concept. One person, the woman most likely, functioned as the hunter. Her job was to spot the prey, bring him in close if that were possible, and provide security while the killer took the target out.

Like her partner, the hunter was blond, with athletically short hair and the long lean body of a tennis player. Her clothing was very chic, except for the fanny pack she wore draped across her lower abdomen. The perfect place to keep a semiauto and some spare magazines. She had very blue eyes, and when they came to rest on the man with the big paunch, he was already snapping pictures of her.

It was just the sort of thing Tazio Scaparelli would do if he saw a pretty woman and didn't know who she was. Who could possibly keep track of all the starlets, models, and aristocrats who were roaming Europe? The safest thing to do was take pictures, and establish their value later. Agent 47 could tell that the hunter didn't like having her picture taken, but there wasn't much she could do about it, and her eyes drifted away as the camera was lowered.

So Al-Fulani was right, Agent 47 mused. *Thorakis is guilty—and Diana is innocent. Mr. Nu will be pleased, and all things considered, so am I.*

With the basic assessment out of the way, the assassin took his armchair analysis to the next level. The hunter and the killer were professional partners, but were they lovers as well? If they were, then Mr. Flattop would feel protective toward her. Something 47 might use against him, and one of the reasons why the assassin preferred to work alone.

As the couple received their keys and turned to follow a bellman toward one of the Central's ancient elevators, the operative came to the conclusion that the answer to his question was a definite "yes." The two were lovers.

His observation wasn't based on anything obvious, like a wedding ring, but on more subtle factors. Like the failure to maintain enough space between their bodies, the familiar manner in which they touched each other, and the way Mr. Flattop allowed his partner to board the elevator first.

All of which meant that by the time the elevator doors closed on the couple, 47 had already decided how to kill them. Their strength stemmed from the hunter-killer concept and closeness of their relationship. So the first thing to do was divide and conquer.

But how?

The logical thing to do was eliminate the hunter first, because she would be easier to kill, and because her death would make Mr. Flattop angry. And it was 47's intention to use the other man's grief and rage against him.

The man known as Tazio Scaparelli fought his way up out of the armchair and waddled away. The war was about to begin—and it was time to prepare.

The woman's name was Tova Holm, and it was her job to find the target so Hans Pruter could kill him. And thanks to the fact that The Agency assassin was already registered at the hotel, the task would be that much easier. Once they figured out who the man was.

The first step would be to gain access to the Central's guest list by bribing one of the clerks, flirting with one of them, or hacking into the hotel's computer system. An often tiresome process that Holm wanted to avoid if possible.

Having donned a skimpy tennis outfit, the shapely blonde went down to the front desk and approached a clerk, who clearly couldn't take his eyes off her. Having smiled beguilingly, she launched into a story about having spotted an old friend as she entered the elevator, and wanting to contact her. The problem being that she had forgotten the woman's married name. She would remember the name, however, if she could take a look at the guest list.

The clerk knew it was wrong, but wanted to please the pretty young woman, and agreed to provide the blonde with a printout, as long as she wouldn't tell anyone. So ten minutes later, Holm and Pruter were sitting in their room, going over the registry, and highlighting the names they considered to be most promising.

"He's an expert where disguises are concerned," Pruter reminded her. "But there are certain things one can't hide. Height being the most obvious."

While Pruter remained in the room, so he could clean his weapons, Holm took the list and went to work. The obvious place to start was with the maids, all of whom were poorly paid and eager to make a few extra euros. It wasn't long before the guest list had been reduced to three men. Alexandru Cosma, a Romanian who had arrived earlier that morning. Tazio Scaparelli, the Italian photographer who had taken her picture in the lobby, and George Fuller, an American tourist.

So far, so good . . .

But which one of them was Agent 47? In order to answer that question, and "surprise her brother," Holm managed to "rent" a master key from a maid who was about to go on a lunch break. That, combined with the uniform she had "borrowed," would allow her to enter all three rooms. Not to make the kill, but to eliminate the false positives and identify the target. At that point

Pruter would join the hunt, they would stalk the enemy assassin together, and take him out.

Just as they had thirty-two times before.

Given his appearance, and the fact that he'd been staying at the hotel for more than a week by then, Tazio Scaparelli seemed like a poor bet. That being the case, Holm chose to examine the Italian's room first. She approached the door the way any maid would, rapped three times, and shouted, "Housekeeping!"

Then, having heard no response, the *Puissance Treize* agent slipped the master key into the door and let herself in. Once inside, she had to check Scaparelli's belongings to see if the corpulent *paparazzo* was the person he seemed to be. A delicate task, since it was necessary to search the room without disturbing anything. It soon became apparent that the Italian was a fat, somewhat slovenly diabetic, who was about to run out of clean underwear.

Satisfied that Scaparelli had been eliminated from the list, Holm set out to check on the recently arrived Romanian. His room was on the third floor. The routine was the same: Three loud knocks followed by a loud, "Housekeeping!"

Having received no response, the counterassassin entered the room and pulled the door closed behind her. A suitcase was resting on the bed, and Holm went over to inspect it. And that's where she was, leaning over to look inside the open bag, when Agent 47 stepped out from behind the heavy floor-length curtains.

The *Puissance Treize* agent heard the unexpected *swish* of fabric, and was reaching for her pistol when the assassin fired the air gun. Holm felt the dart bite her neck, paused to pluck the object out, and was busy examining the projectile when she felt a burning sensation. That was followed by a sharp pain in her chest, a moment of vertigo as her heart stopped, and a long fall into darkness.

A series of flashes strobed the room as the man named Alexandru Cosma, Agent 47, *and* Tazio Scaparelli took a series of pictures.

Then it was time to retrieve the dart, Holm's *Fabrique Nationale* Forty-Nine, and two extra clips of .40 caliber ammunition. The FN constituted a much heavier piece than 47 had expected to acquire, and made for a welcome addition to his modest arsenal.

With those chores accomplished, the operative let himself out. The DO NOT DISTURB sign would keep the hotel's staff at bay until the next day. At that point they would find a dead guest, who was not only dressed as one of their maids, but lying in the wrong room. A room registered to Mr. Cosma, who was nowhere to be found. It was a mystery that would keep the local authorities busy for months to come.

The hunter was dead. . . .

The killer was waiting.

Holm had been gone for hours and Pruter was beginning to worry about her, when a bellman knocked on the door. Or was he a bellman?

The German positioned himself next to the door with the Glock at the ready. "Ja?"

"I have a package for you, sir," the teenager said politely.

The killer peered through the keyhole, confirmed that the bellhop was holding a manila envelope in his hand, and opened the door a crack. The package slid in, a five-euro note went out, and the transaction was complete.

There was a positive *click* as the door swung closed. Pruter was a cautious man. That was one of the reasons why he was still alive. So rather than open the envelope right away he took a moment to examine it. The block lettering on the front said, TO HANS PRUTER. But there was no return address.

The killer felt ice water trickle into his bloodstream as he held the envelope up to the light. Could it contain a bomb? Or a dose of anthrax? Anything was possible— but he didn't think so. Some dark rectangles could be seen through the paper, and when he rotated the container they slid from side to side.

The knife generated a soft *click* as the blade locked into place. Rather than open the top of the envelope Pruter was careful to slit one of the sides to avoid any triggering mechanisms hidden inside.

But the effort was wasted. The only items inside the container were a series of photographs that spilled out onto the floor: Pictures of Holm lying on a rug staring sightlessly into the camera.

The German's knees made a solid *thump* as they hit the carpet. The killer's hand shook as he began to sort through the photos that 47 had been able to print at a do-it-yourself kiosk in the local drugstore. They were of Holm, dressed in a maid's uniform, lying dead on a rug that was identical to the one beneath him. Meaning that her body was somewhere inside the hotel.

The inarticulate bellow of rage and pain was followed by a long series of sobs that wracked his body, and tears flowed down his cheeks. Then Pruter saw that a picture postcard lay among the photos. It showed a panoramic view of gray, vegetation-clad battlements. The caption read, *Costelo dos Mouros*.

It was an obvious invitation—and one that Pruter planned to accept.

The Castle of the Moors had been constructed in the eighth or ninth century. The sprawling structure was situated on two neighboring mountain peaks, and offered magnificent views of both Sintra and the countryside beyond. Which meant that on the day when Dom Alfonso Henriques and his army arrived to liberate the area in 1147, the Moors must have been able to see the nobleman coming.

Later, during the Romantic period, repairs had been made. But there was little sign of that now as the sun started to dip below the western horizon, and the tourists began the long walk down to the city below.

Yet Pruter remained behind. Once the sun set and darkness settled over the battlements, Agent 47 would come. And, while nothing could ever compensate the German for Holm's death, killing the assassin would make him feel slightly better. Not to mention the fact that it was his job to do so—and as a killer, he had a reputation to protect.

The main problem was that the castle not only covered a large area, but was built along the top of a steep hillside, and followed the contours of the land. As a result there were dozens of paths that led up and down, and hundreds of stone steps, all bordered by a jumble of ruins. So the first thing he had to do was familiarize himself with the complex, find the best spot to hide, and let 47 come to him.

Then, with the aid of the night-vision gear stowed in

his pack, Hans would put the other assassin down for good.

The German went to work.

The satellite phone produced a series of soft *beeps*. The assassin's eyes popped open and he activated the phone. The voice that came over the headset was insistent.

"Wake up, Agent 47. . . . It's time to go to work."

It was dark inside the cavelike recess, but by craning his neck, he could catch a glimpse of city lights below. He fumbled the penlight, but aimed it away from the entrance.

"Diana? Is that *you*?"

"Of course it's me," the controller replied sweetly. "Who else would give up a perfectly good dinner to keep an eye on someone like you? Are you sure you want to go through with this? It seems like an iffy plan to me."

"No," 47 replied honestly. "I'm not sure. But it's too late to bail out. The target should be in the ruins by now. Or am I wrong?"

"Oh, he's there, all right," Diana confirmed, as she eyed the monitor in front of her. The spooky-looking thermal images were being provided by one of three state-of-the-art surveillance satellites that The Agency owned. Just one of the reasons why it took so much money to keep the murder-for-hire organization up and running.

The *Puissance Treize* killer was represented by a stationary green blob. Smaller heat signatures, all of which belonged to various animals, left occasional streaks on the screen.

"He arrived an hour and sixteen minutes after you did."

Having been forced to leave his weapons in Rome so he could play the part of Tazio Scaparelli, Agent 47 felt woefully underequipped. But the nearest armory was in Madrid, so there wasn't enough time to acquire more firepower.

Having no desire to battle the *Puissance Treize* agent in Scaparelli drag, the assassin was wearing a new set of clothes, all of which were black. He had armed himself with the woman's FN Forty-Nine, the DOVO razor, and the garrote. He was also carrying the air gun, plus three darts, which he planned to use on the German shepherd later that night. Assuming everything went well, that is—which was far from certain.

Meanwhile it seemed safe to assume that the opposition would be armed with a pistol, some sort of submachine gun, and a sniper's rifle. Not to mention night-vision goggles. Of course, The Agency's satellite—plus Diana's ability to keep him advised of the German's movements—would help to compensate for that.

"So, what did he choose?" 47 wanted to know. "The highest tower—or the rock pile above the ruins?"

"The rock pile," the controller answered clinically.

"That's what I would choose," the operative said thoughtfully. "You can see just about everything from the tower, but there's no way out, and our friend will want an escape route."

"He isn't your friend," Diana said sternly. "Are you ready to move?"

There were hundreds of nooks and crannies in the ruins. The space 47 had chosen was vaguely rectangular in shape, barely high enough to stand in, and equipped with a dirt floor.

"I will be soon," the agent said, as he aimed a stream of urine into a corner. A moment later, he said, "Okay, here I go. Keep me informed."

"I will," Diana promised him. "Be careful out there—and don't forget to zip it up."

The sun had set hours earlier, and it had turned cold. But the *Puissance Treize* assassin had anticipated that problem, and was dressed appropriately. And he could still see, thanks to the ambient light and the night-vision goggles he wore. The device worked better when he didn't look directly at the lights of Sintra. So the German did the best he could to avoid that, while continually scanning the area around him.

It was a monotonous task that caused him to miss Holm even more. With her at his side, there had been no need to worry about the possibility that someone would sneak up on him from behind. But Holm was dead, and he was about to do battle with her killer.

Or was he? There was no sign of the assassin so far. Was the other man scared? Or had the postcard been a ruse? A trick intended to sideline the opposition while the enemy operative made an attack on Thorakis?

Suddenly that seemed all too possible, and Pruter was considering a strategic withdrawal when he saw an image appear downslope from him. It was there for a fraction of a second, then gone, as if someone were working his way uphill using the ruins as cover. Pruter removed the goggles, picked up the German Blaser 93 LRS2 rifle, and looked through its night-vision scope.

The target had disappeared, but the counter-assassin was a patient man, and was willing to wait.

Agent 47 paused, eyed the open stretch of walkway that lay ahead, and hoped that the *Puissance Treize* agent was busy sipping hot cocoa. Then, knowing he couldn't put the task off forever, the assassin launched himself out into the open. There was a loud *spang* as a 7.62 mm bullet bounced off a paver, and disappeared into the night.

Not only was the German paying attention—he was a good shot!

Agent 47 heard another slug *ping* off the crenellated wall to his right as he took cover behind some stone blocks. It was dark all around him, and it would have been easy to lose his way, except for one thing: Having visited the ruins prior to sending the photos to Pruter, the operative had not only carried out a general reconnaissance, but surreptitiously sprayed night-glow paint along some of the paths. So all he had to do was follow the blobs to one of two wires. Which, like the paint, batteries, and a few other odds and ends, had been purchased at the local hardware store.

"He's still in the same place," Diana put in helpfully. "And I don't see anyone else in the area."

Thus reassured, Agent 47 continued to follow the glowing green dots to the point where the number one remote was hidden. His movements resulted in a flurry of silenced shots, one of which came so close that rock chips sprayed the side of his face as he scurried along the path.

Then he was there, rolling in under the protection of a stone wall, as bullets continued to *ping, whine,* and *spang* all around him. The expenditure of that much ammo seemed nonsensical at first, until 47 realized what his opponent was up to, and the potential danger involved. The *Puissance Treize* agent was hoping to bounce a slug into him, just like a bank shot in a game of pool. And even if that strategy failed, the fusillade was bound to exact a psychological toll.

So Agent 47 forced himself to concentrate as his fingers probed the crevices to either side of a glowing dot. Once he had located the hidden switch it was time to pull the .40 caliber pistol, and pray.

Even as the thought crossed his mind, he realized the Supreme Being was very unlikely to take sides in a battle between hired killers, so he decided he would have to rely on skill, and an element of luck.

With that, the assassin pressed the button, an electrical charge ran up the wire, and delivered a spark to the container of petrol hidden among the rocks. The results were even more spectacular than what 47 had hoped for. There was a dull *thump,* followed by a sudden gout of flame that shot upward to light the surrounding area with a ghastly glow. Though completely untouched by the fire, his opponent was lit from behind as he stood to get a better look at the surrounding area.

Agent 47 was on his feet by then, with the FN clutched in both hands, firing uphill. A series of sharp reports were heard, the pistol jumped, and empty casings arced through the air. Pruter staggered as a slug hit him in the chest, but he must have been wearing body armor, since he brought the HK MP-5N submachine gun up into firing position. And thanks to 47's muzzle flashes, the *Puissance Treize* agent had a point to aim at as he fired a long ten-round burst.

"He's coming toward you!" Diana warned.

"No shit," 47 responded as he was forced to duck, and dump the empty clip. The second one slid in smoothly, the FN's action pushed another bullet into the chamber, and the pistol was ready to fire again. If the German bastard ever stopped shooting, that is!

The opportunity he needed came a few seconds later when the submachine gun ran dry and Pruter was forced to reload. That was when 47 popped up, saw the blocky form outlined against the quickly fading flames, and was careful to aim low. The heavy slugs cut the German's legs out from under him. He staggered, fought to keep his balance, and fell. The body tumbled downhill, bounced into the air, and there was a sickening *thump* as it landed.

"Forty-seven?" Diana inquired. "Are you okay?"

"So far," the assassin replied cautiously. "Hold on."

The operative kept the FN pointed at the body as he approached it, felt for a pulse, and confirmed that Pruter was dead. Not from a bullet, although the German's legs were a bloody mess, but from injuries suffered during the fall.

Not having heard any sirens, 47 took the time necessary to drag the body into a niche, where loose stones could be stacked in front of it. Then it was necessary to get the penlight out, search the area for empty casings, and collect the German's belongings from higher up the hill.

Finally, having pulled the wire for both incendiary devices and thrown everything into the makeshift crypt, it was time to wall Pruter in.

Eventually, after days of sun, some unfortunate tourist would notice the smell. At that point the *Puis-*

sance Treize assassin would be disinterred and linked to the body of the mysterious Tova Holm. There was no way to know what the authorities would make of that, and 47 didn't care.

An hour later, with his opponent's pack on his back, Agent 47 made his way down the hill. The night was relatively young—and the real target was still alive.

By the time 47 arrived at the top of the hillside behind the mansion, it was nearly 3:00 a.m. Late, but not too late, given the task at hand. Which was to dart the German shepherd if necessary, sneak into the house the same way he had before, and wait for morning. But by the time Agent 47 was halfway down the slope it became apparent that everything had changed.

Judging from the bright glow that could be seen through the foliage, every light in the house was on. And once the assassin got closer he realized that six uniformed security guards were roaming the grounds, rather than two. Not only that, but more dogs had been brought in, and it seemed safe to assume that the surveillance cameras were being monitored now, as well.

Agent 47 had been expecting some sort of reaction to the increased threat level, but nothing like what he was looking at, and had no choice but to retreat back up the hill. It took the better part of half an hour to reach the street above, then make his way back to the hotel, where he entered via a side door. From there the assassin went straight to Pruter's room, made use of the German's key to let himself in, and took a quick tour of the German's possessions.

Then, having selected a well-cut gray suit, along with some other odds and ends, 47 went back to Tazio

Scaparelli's room where it was time to take a shower and begin work on plan B. The first step was to call Diana, tell the controller about the change of plan, and request some help.

The second step was to put aside everything he would need for the coming day, and cram the rest into Scaparelli's expandable suitcase. That included the foam belly, the hairpiece, the *paparazzo*'s clothes, Holm's pistol, Pruter's knapsack, and a variety of smaller items. Then, having gone over the room again to make sure he hadn't missed anything, he took a nap.

As always, Agent 47's eyes snapped open at 5:58 a.m. He got up, took Pruter's Glock into the bathroom, and put the DOVO to work. Twenty minutes later he was shaved, dressed, and ready for the new day.

Pruter's suit was a little too large, but otherwise satisfactory, even if it was gray rather than black.

The room had been paid for in advance, so there was no need to check out. Agent 47 carried Scaparelli's heavily laden suitcase and Pruter's black leather briefcase down the fire escape and out through the door he had used the night before. Someone was bound to discover the woman's body before long—and the assassin wanted to be clear of the hotel when they did.

Rather than dump the suitcase near the hotel where the police might find it, the operative towed the bag to the *Bon Appétit*. The restaurant wasn't open for business yet, but the Dumpster was, and given how much the big metal box reeked, there was very little chance that anyone would want to climb inside it. The suitcase went in, the lid closed with a *clang*, and the task was complete.

From there it was a short walk to a busy bakery, where the assassin had a long, leisurely breakfast. Though not up to his standards, it was a lot better than nothing. Then, at precisely 10:30 a.m., he entered a cab. By no means was he too lazy to walk, but the person he was about to become would arrive by taxi, and such details were important. If the cabdriver thought the short trip was strange, he gave no sign of it as the operative handed over a five and told him to keep the change.

Three members of the *paparazzi* were present as 47 got out of the cab, including Tony Fazio, and all of them watched intently as the man with the black briefcase exited the car and approached the front gate. The additional security was plain to see, and the activity within indicated that Thorakis might be getting ready to leave Sintra. Though this was not world-shaking news, it would be worth a few shots, and provide the *paparazzi* with something to feed their voracious editors.

As Agent 47 arrived in front of the gate, a uniformed security officer was there to greet him.

"Yes?" the man said suspiciously. "What do you want?"

The operative noticed that the security officer's right hand had already come to rest on the butt of a huge revolver.

"My name is Gerrard," 47 lied. "I believe you're expecting me."

As it happened, the security guard had been told to expect a Mr. Gerrard, so the hand came off the pistol, and the assassin was allowed to pass through the gate. From there the security officer escorted the agent to the front door, where a man in a blue blazer and khaki trousers was waiting. He had hard eyes, a no-nonsense manner, and appeared to be in his early forties. Ex-military perhaps? Yes, 47 thought so.

The entryway was half-blocked by an oak table. Beyond that the operative could see the ornate flight of stairs that led up to the second floor, along with the entry to the dining room on the left, and the door to an old-fashioned sitting room on the right. He knew from previous experience that the hall, which paralleled the stairs, led back to the kitchen.

"Good morning, sir," the man with the hard eyes said. "Are you armed?"

"Yes, I am," the assassin replied, as he placed the briefcase on the table. "I'm carrying a Glock, a razor, and a garrote."

If the ex-paratrooper was surprised, he gave no sign of it.

"And in the briefcase?"

"A satellite phone, a laptop, and some other odds and ends."

"Thank you," the man said matter-of-factly. "Please remove all of your weapons and place them on the table. Once that process is complete, I'm going to search you. Or you can leave the property, if you prefer. The choice is up to you."

"I have no objection to being searched," 47 said, as he placed each weapon on the table in front of him. "In fact, I would like to commend you on your professionalism."

The man nodded politely, but clearly didn't care what the visitor thought, as he came around to run his hands over 47's body. That was the point he came across the atomizer.

"What's this?" the man wanted to know, as he held the bottle up for inspection.

"Sunblock," the agent answered expressionlessly. "I have a tendency to burn."

The ex-paratrooper nodded, spritzed a bit of the liquid on his wrist, sniffed and—apparently satisfied—put the atomizer back where he had found it.

"Okay," the man with the hard eyes said. "You can retrieve your briefcase and weapons on the way out. Please step under the light."

A stand-mounted spot had been set up in the hallway. Agent 47 could feel the heat from the lamp as he took his place beneath it. The man opened a folder, withdrew a sheet of paper, and held it up for a side-by-side comparison. The fax was modeled on a similar document The Agency had recovered during a raid on a *Puissance Treize* safe house in Moscow three days earlier. The first paragraph, which had been authored by Diana, was the equivalent of an introduction.

"Mr. François Gerrard will arrive prior to 12:00 p.m., and should be given full access to the premises so that he can make plans for a Class III extraction. Please grant him your full cooperation."

And, because both the photo and the description of Gerrard matched the man standing in front of him, the former soldier began to relax.

"Could I have your identity code please?"

"It's BXY-892," Agent 47 replied.

The code was correct, so the security officer slid the fax back into its folder, and rang a bell.

The woman who responded was none other than a

harried looking Maria. With the departure imminent, Thorakis had probably been very difficult that morning—and 47 imagined that the last thing she needed was a visitor to take care of. And because the man in front of her looked very different from the photographer Tazio Scaparelli, she never appeared to make the connection.

Fortunately for Maria, the man in the gray suit had no need of her services, and having said as much, he began to prowl the premises after she took her leave.

Agent 47 eyed his watch. Based on the information he had obtained from Maria earlier, he knew that the kitchen staff were required to prepare a green salad for Miss Desta each morning, and leave it outside the master bedroom at precisely 11:30. With rare exceptions, it was the ex-model's practice to remain incommunicado until 1:00 p.m., when she was ready to greet the world.

Assuming the salad rule was still in force, the assassin had five minutes to get upstairs and position himself in the vicinity of the master bedroom. With that in mind, he produced a small notebook, made some meaningless notes in it, and returned to the main hallway. From there he climbed the stairs and was standing on the landing above when a girl appeared at the other end of the hall. Having made use of the back stairs himself, Agent 47 knew they led up from the kitchen, which was consistent with the tray the youngster held in her hands.

The operative saw a teapot, a matching cup, and a plate with a silver dome over it. The teenager placed the offering on a table, paused to make sure the tray was square with the edge of the table, and turned back toward the stairs.

Agent 47 took a quick look around to make sure no

one was visible, hurried down the hall, and lifted the domed lid. Then, still holding the cover aloft, he aimed the atomizer at the perfectly tossed salad. The bottle made a gentle wheezing sound as peanut oil misted the air and drifted down to coat the greens below.

Having replaced the lid, the operative turned back toward the front of the house. He was halfway down the front stairs, on his way to retrieve his belongings, when he heard the door open and Miss Desta emerge to get her salad.

The assassin was more than a mile away when Aristotle Thorakis took Miss Desta in his arms, nuzzled her hair, and began to kiss her.

A few minutes later, as they were just starting to make love, the Greek's throat started to constrict. His face turned red, it was no longer possible for him to breathe, and he struggled to speak.

But Thorakis couldn't get the necessary words out. He made gasping noises, clawed at his throat, and began to thrash about.

Miss Desta, frightened, rolled out of bed and ran to the intercom. Unfortunately the former model didn't know enough Portuguese to effectively communicate with the staff in the kitchen. Valuable time was lost while half a dozen members of the shipping magnate's domestic staff rushed upstairs to see why Miss Desta was screaming hysterically.

The chef was among them, and even though he couldn't imagine how such a thing could have happened, he recognized the symptoms for what they were. Fortunately an injector preloaded with epinephrine was sitting on top of the dresser next to the businessman's wallet.

Maria watched in open-mouthed horror as the chef removed the locking cap from the EpiPen and rammed the exposed needle into his employer's meaty thigh. There was an audible *click* as the spring-loaded device delivered the correct dose of medication into muscle.

But unfortunately for Aristotle Thorakis, his mistress, his family, and the *Puissance Treize,* the shipping magnate was already dead.

Fazio and his peers were present to witness the moment when the medics arrived, after which the famous businessman's body was removed from the house.

As for the proximate cause of the Greek's death, that was clear, although no one could figure out how a small amount of peanut oil had found its way onto Miss Desta's salad, in spite of all the precautions taken in the kitchen.

At the exact moment when CPR was suspended, and then while Thorakis was being loaded onto a stretcher, Agent 47 was standing on the ramparts of Pena Palace, a fairy tale–like keep that sat atop a peak not far from the remains of the Moorish castle where Hans Pruter's body was beginning to rot.

The sun was out, the air was clean, and a hawk could be seen circling in the distance.

The killer was at rest.